MANSION for MURDER

When *Mavis Seidlitz*, a seductive and saucy private eye, takes on the dangerous job of impersonating the wife of the tall, dark and handsome heir to a multi-million dollar fortune, she sets herself up as the tempting target in a mansion of potential murderers.

Chances are five to one she'll never live to collect her fancy fee because these five people will divide the fortune if she dies:

A crafty psychiatrist and his red-haired wife

A smooth-talking lawyer who knows all about the black arts

A brother who speaks through a wooden dummy

A brunette housekeeper who plays with masks and chains in the cellar.

All of them want money . . . and each of them is capable of killing for cash.

Written by *Carter Brown*, author of the bestselling AL WHEELER mysteries, this fast-paced thriller introduces *Mavis Seidlitz*, a luscious private eye who deals a fast curve when it comes to love or murder.

Other SIGNET Thrillers by *Carter Brown*

THE BODY
  Al Wheeler, colorful new detective, unearths a call girl racket and murder lurking behind the facade of a swank funeral home. (#1527—25¢)

THE BLONDE
  Detective Wheeler plunges into a case involving Hollywood nymphomaniacs, blackmail, and — of course — murder. (#1565—25¢)

THE MISTRESS
  A girl—lovely but dead—turns up on the County Sheriff's doorstep, and Al Wheeler tangles with a gambling syndicate as he tracks down her killer. (#1594—25¢)

THE CORPSE
  A torrid tale of blondes, brunettes, blackmailers, and murder—and Wheeler, the unorthodox cop who takes all of them in his stride. (#1606—25¢)

THE LOVER
  Investigating a phony religious cult, Al Wheeler uncovers blackmail and an extortion ring. (#1620—25¢)

THE VICTIM
  A hit-and-run accident leads Al Wheeler on the path of a diabolical skip-tracing outfit. (#1633—25¢)

CARTER BROWN

The LOVING and the DEAD

"The next best thing to a man is a murder, but what I really like is a man who's murder!"
—Mavis Seidlitz

A SIGNET BOOK

Published by
THE NEW AMERICAN LIBRARY OF WORLD LITERATURE, INC.
in association with *Horwitz Publications Inc.*

© Copyright 1959 by Horwitz Publications Inc. Pty. Ltd.
Sydney, Australia

Reproduction in part or in whole in any language expressly forbidden in any part of the world without the written consent of Horwitz Publications Inc. Pty. Ltd.

First Printing, April, 1959

SIGNET BOOKS are published by
The New American Library of World Literature, Inc.
501 Madison Avenue, New York 22, New York

printed in the united states of america

CHAPTER ONE

He was the bachelor girl's dream come true. The one you always get around three A.M. when a glass of hot milk just isn't the answer. I took one look at him and sighed deeply. Luckily I was wearing a strapless bra, so nothing gave—except me, I guess.

The guy was tall, dark, and handsome. There was a look about him as if he'd been through a lot of grief in his time. I guessed he'd given a lot of grief in his young life, too. I'd bet there'd be an assortment of blondes, brunettes and redheads who'd give testimony to that.

"This *is* the office of Rio Investigations?" he asked in a deep voice. He gave me that up-down-off-with-the-clothes-and-tape-the-vital-statistics look, but from him I didn't mind.

"It sure is," I said huskily. I didn't even have to close my eyes to see us in a situation my mother calls compromising, but I call fun. "I'm Mavis Seidlitz," I told him. "I'm the half of Rio Investigations that doesn't get its name stenciled on the door."

"Huh?" he said blankly.

"I'm Johnny Rio's partner," I explained carefully. "I just do the secretarial work around here for kicks." I sneered down at my typewriter, just to prove I wasn't kidding. "That is," I added quickly, "in between clients."

"Oh?" he said. He didn't sound really interested. "My name is Ebhart."

"Ebhart what?" I asked him. I guess I felt kind of disappointed, because it would be hard to get romantic about a guy called Eb. Maybe I could change my name to Flo, which is a joke.

"Donald Ebhart!" he snarled at me. That snarl was a

5

bad habit I'd change later on. I like my guys' bad habits to be interesting.

"I see, Mr. Ebhart," I said and gave him my special smile. The sexy one I practiced in front of the mirror, where I drop the lower lip half an inch and pout it just a little. I think it's sexy even if Johnny Rio does say it makes me look like I've lost my marbles. I think when he says that, he's lost his marbles, or something.

"I have an appointment to see Mr. Rio," Ebhart said and he snarled again. "Will you tell him I'm here, or are you too busy being a partner?"

"So, all right," I said coldly. "You aren't the only client we have, you know!"

"I didn't know," he said. "And I don't care. If I don't get in to see Rio within the next twenty seconds, you'll have one client less. That I do know!"

I just shrugged my shoulders, which made him forget to snarl, and picked up the phone. I told Johnny that a Mr. Ebhart was here to see him.

"Send him in," Johnny said quickly. "You haven't talked to him yet, have you, Mavis? No, you couldn't have—he's still there. Just send him in. You remember which is my office, don't you?"

"Why, sure," I said. "We only have one office, don't we?"

"That's good, Mavis," he said encouragingly. "Your memory is improving."

I put the phone down and told Mr. Ebhart that Johnny would see him right away. "Thank you," he said. "For what, I'm not sure, but thank you anyway." Then he walked into Johnny's office and closed the door behind him.

Sometimes I figure Johnny must think I'm dumb or something, but that's stupid. Would I be a partner in Rio Investigations if I was dumb? Would I have taken a cut in salary to become a partner if I didn't have ambitions?

By the time I had all that figured out, the phone rang. I picked it up and said: "Rio Investigations," in my crisp we're-open-for-business voice, but I was wasting my time.

"I know," Johnny said. "This is the internal hookup, remember?"

"That's what the doctor said when he took out my appendix," I told him, but he didn't even laugh. Neither did I when it happened. I mean, the scar is permanent and it's in a most awkward place. That doctor didn't do a good job and I told him so. He couldn't kid me. If the operation was O.K., how come he was still calling on me six months later? He used to sit there, just looking at that scar and I could tell he was worried, the way he kept breathing hard all the time.

"Come in here, will you, Mavis?" Johnny shouted in my ear. "For the third time! Have you been struck dumb or something, I hope?"

"I was just thinking," I said coldly.

"Cheez!" he said. "A masochist yet!" Then he slammed down the phone, before I could even tell him I was a hundred per cent American.

So I walked into his office and Johnny looked at me and smiled. Mr. Ebhart smiled at me too, so maybe I'd done something clever I didn't know about yet.

"Sit down, Mavis," Johnny said gently, and I guessed he must be sickening for something. The only time he gets sentimental is when he's sick, or when I bring up the question of my salary.

So I sat down and I guess I must have crossed my legs kind of carelessly because Mr. Ebhart got a suddenly intent look in his eyes while he made my knees a point of focal departure. I pulled down my skirt—not too much, but enough—and he relaxed again.

"Mavis," Johnny said, "this is Mr. Ebhart. I think you've met."

"We certainly did," I agreed and smiled at Mr. Ebhart.

"Mr. Ebhart is now our client," Johnny went on, so I hitched my skirt up again a little. A paying customer is entitled to some sort of service around the office.

"I think maybe you'd better tell Mavis the story," Johnny told Mr. Ebhart. "I could get fouled up along the way." Then he closed his eyes and buried his head in his hands. Johnny *was* sickening for something.

"It's like this, Miss Seidlitz," Mr. Ebhart said in his nice deep voice that kind of kinked my spine. "My problem is one of inheritance." He kept his eyes lowered while he spoke and I figured he was bashful until I remembered about the skirt and adjusted it again. I wanted for him to be able to concentrate on his problem.

"My father was Randolph Ebhart," he went on. "You may remember him?"

"I meet so many talent scouts up and down the Sunset Strip," I told him. "But none of them are really in pictures. You know what it's like in Hollywood. If your father really worked for a studio, I'd remember him O.K."

"Mavis," Johnny said in a strangled voice. "Randolph Ebhart was the oil tycoon. His estate was worth ten million dollars—after taxes!"

"Oh," I said faintly.

Mr. Ebhart smiled at me encouragingly. "It's all right, Mavis. It's my father's estate that has complicated things. I'm the eldest son, you see. I have a sister and a half-brother by my father's second marriage, and they are both younger than I. My old man died five years back, and he left his estate in trust. I have thirty thousand a year income, the other two have ten."

"That sounds a lot to me," I said. "What do you do with all that money?"

"Just listen, Mavis," Johnny said. "Shut up and listen!"

"Well, you don't have to be rude to me just because I'm your partner," I told him. "You never used to be rude to me when I was just a secretary."

"Secretaries are hard to get," he snarled. "Listen!"

Mr. Ebhart smiled again. "Like I said, my old man was a strange character in a lot of ways. And he didn't approve of me. So he made a lot of conditions in his will. When I reach my thirtieth birthday, the estate is divided between the three of us, except for some three hundred thousand to charities. My sister and half-brother get a million dollars each, I get the rest of the estate— but only under certain conditions."

He lit himself a cigarette. "I must be married. My wife and myself must spend the last three days prior to my birthday at 'Toledo.' That's his old house: my mother came from Spain, and he named the house after the district where she was born."

"Well," I said, "that doesn't sound too hard. You shouldn't have any trouble. I'd marry you myself just for the thirty thousand you're getting right now."

"Thank you," he said frigidly. "As it happens, I am already married, Miss Seidlitz."

I should have known when I first saw him. Nearly all the good-looking guys get snapped up fast. Not that I really want to get married, not yet, anyway. I mean, being faithful all your life to the one guy isn't my idea of a ball. I guess it's O.K. for dogs, but what does it get them, even? Into a doghouse, that's all.

"Maybe I should tell Mavis the rest of it?" Johnny said, looking at Mr. Ebhart, who nodded for him to go ahead. "This is the point, Mavis," Johnny said to me slowly. "This is why Mr. Ebhart has come to us. His present wife is his third wife. He was first married four years ago. His first wife died in an automobile accident six months after they were married. He married again a year later. His second wife died eight months later. She fell over the edge of a cliff. . . ."

Johnny lit himself another cigarette. "In both cases, a coroner's court found the deaths to be accidental. But both girls died alone: there was no one with them, no eyewitnesses."

"I'm terribly sorry," I said to Mr. Ebhart. "I had no idea. . . ."

"How could you have known?" he said, his face somber.

"If Mr. Ebhart is not married at the time of his thirtieth birthday," Johnny went on, "his inheritance is equally divided between his sister and half-brother. He gets only the thirty thousand a year income for the rest of his life."

"But as he's married again," I said, "he doesn't have a problem."

"Supposing his first two wives didn't die an accidental death, Mavis," Johnny said quietly. "Supposing they were murdered by someone clever enough to make both deaths look accidental?"

I had a sudden cold feeling right way down my spine. "Who would murder them?" I asked weakly.

"Around seven and a half million dollars is a terrific motive for murder," Johnny said. "When Mr. Ebhart spends those three days in his father's old house, he has to have his third wife with him. His sister and his half-brother will be there also. They are the two people with strong motive for murder. If they could get rid of Mr. Ebhart's wife just before his birthday, they'd share his major portion of the estate."

"Then don't take your wife up there, Mr. Ebhart!" I said cleverly.

"I have no choice," he said. "It's a condition of the will, you remember?"

"I get it!" I said. "You want us to act as bodyguards for your wife while she's there?"

Johnny and Mr. Ebhart looked at each other for a long moment, then Johnny said, "Well, not exactly, Mavis."

"You see," Mr. Ebhart said, "we have one advantage. None of the people who will be there have ever met my wife."

"I don't see how that helps," I said. "Because they'll meet her once you both get to the house, won't they?"

They both looked at each other again for what seemed to me a long time. "What's the matter with you two?" I asked them. "Is my slip showing, or something?"

Johnny smiled at me, and suddenly I felt nervous. "Mr. Ebhart has just given us a check," he said. "A retainer of two thousand dollars."

"Cash it, Johnny," I said hopefully. "I'd like to count it in one-dollar bills!"

"You see," Johnny went on very slowly, "like Mr. Ebhart said, none of the other people who will be at the house have met his wife. They don't know what she looks like. He could take any girl up there and say she was his wife, and they wouldn't know the difference."

"And it wouldn't even matter if she got murdered

then," I said eagerly. "Because Mr. Ebhart would still be married and not a real widower at all!"

"I wouldn't worry about that side of it, Mavis," Johnny said quickly. "That's not likely to happen. It would just be a precaution, that's all."

"I've got it!" I snapped my fingers. "Why don't you do just that? Get some dumb blonde to take the place of Mr. Ebhart's real wife!" I smiled triumphantly at them. "How about that?"

"It's a wonderful idea," Johnny said. "We've already thought of it."

"You have?" I felt a little bit sorry they'd thought of it first. "How about the girl? Have you figured out somebody for the part?"

"We sure have," Johnny nodded.

"Well," I said, "don't keep me in suspense! Who?"

"You," Johnny said.

Strapless bra or not—right then something snapped!

CHAPTER | TWO

Clare Ebhart was just a kid with her blonde hair tied in a pony tail, wearing a shirt and a pair of toreador pants. Her big blue eyes had a haunted look in them as she smiled at me. "Let me get you a drink, Miss Seidlitz," she said as soon as I got into the apartment. "What will you have?"

"A gimlet, thanks," I told her, "and please call me Mavis."

"Sure," she said and started to make the drinks. "My name is Clare—I guess Don already told you that?"

"Yes, he did," I agreed. "I've got to get used to calling him Don."

She smiled. "It would sound kind of strange, wouldn't it, calling your own husband 'Mr. Ebhart'?" She gave me the drink and sat down on the couch beside me, her gin and tonic in her hand. "I should be jealous," she said. "You going away with my husband for three days as his wife! You're much too gorgeous a blonde not to make me feel nervous about it. But I'm not jealous really, Mavis. I think you're absolutely wonderful to do it. It gives me the screaming mimis just to think about it."

"Thanks," I said modestly. "It's nothing really. I'm just doing my job, that's all." That's what they always say on television, and who am I to break a habit?

"I'll be so glad when it's all over," Clare said. "You will be careful, Mavis, won't you? If anything happened to you I'd die—I really would!"

"That would make two of us," I said, and finished my drink quickly before I spilled it over the carpet.

"It was nice of you to come and see me," she went on. "I appreciate it a lot, Mavis."

The more she talked, the more like a wake it sounded. If it hadn't been for that check for two thousand dollars, and Johnny telling me I was the only girl who could do it . . . "Thanks," I said again.

"Can I get you another drink?" she asked.

"No, thanks," I said. "This detective business is like necking—a girl needs to keep a cool head or suddenly it's too late to worry."

She laughed overbrightly. "I hope you remember to tell that to Don."

"Don't you worry, honey," I said. "Our relationship will be strictly business." I crossed my fingers when I said that because I hoped it was true, but you never can tell about things like that, and three days is an awful long time when you come to think of it in days—and nights.

"You'll have to be patient with Don," Clare went on thoughtfully. "He hates going back to that house, I know; he was very unhappy there as a child. And he gets awful moody sometimes—won't even speak to you for hours, then he gets all remorseful and he couldn't be nicer. I guess he's never quite forgotten what happened to . . ." Her voice trailed away to nothing.

"Sure," I said, and patted her hand gently. "I know, honey. It won't worry me if he gets moody—I'll understand."

I figured that was the right thing to say, but from the look on Clare's face, it wasn't at all.

"I suppose," she said slowly, "that they'll think it kind of odd? The two of you having separate rooms, I mean?"

"Well, we can always fix that," I said brightly, then I saw the look on her face again. "I mean," I added quickly, "we can always tell them I can't stand crowds."

"Uh?" she said blankly.

"Is there anything else I should know?" I asked her.

"I don't think so," she said. "I've never met any of them, so you don't have to worry about recognizing people. Don doesn't like either Wanda or Carl."

"Who are they?"

"I'm sorry," she said. "Wanda is his sister, and Carl is his half-brother. Wanda's married to a man called Payton—Gregory Payton. He's a doctor, or something."

"How about Carl?"

"Carl isn't married," Clare said. "Not as far as I know, anyway."

"That's good," I said.

She looked at me for a moment, then she laughed. "Gosh! Wouldn't that be funny—I mean, if you and Carl fell for each other. Think of the family scandal that would cause! Don's wife having an affair with his half-brother!"

"I hadn't thought of that," I admitted. And I certainly hadn't. It looked like I was going to have a dull seventy-two hours—I mean, what with being married to a guy I wasn't married to, and all the other guys around thinking I was. Just like some of those letters you read in Aunt Abbie's Column, which are always signed "Worried."

"Are you sure you won't have another drink, Mavis?" Clare asked.

"No, thanks," I told her. "I guess I should be going. It was nice meeting you, Clare."

She got up and walked with me to the door. "It was

nice meeting you, Mavis," she said. "When it's all over, you must come and have dinner with us one night."

"Thanks," I said, and I figured she was crazy if she meant it, but I took another look and saw she didn't mean it.

From the Ebharts' apartment I took a cab back to the office. Johnny was there, waiting for me with a big smile on his face. "How's everything, Mavis?" he said heartily. "Meet the little woman, and all?"

"I certainly did," I told him, "and the way she's talking, I'm wife number three tied to the rails already, with the express thundering down the line!"

"Ha, ha!" Johnny laughed a forced sort of laugh. "That's my Mavis—always kidding!"

"I'm not your Mavis, and I'm not kidding," I told him firmly. "Not that I wouldn't consider a proposition regarding the first part. This thing worries me, Johnny— I'm scared!"

"No need to worry," he said firmly. "I'm moving up to Santa Barbara as soon as you leave."

"You heel!" I said. "I'm going to risk being murdered or something even worse, and you're going on vacation! You're the kind of guy who makes a girl walk home after she's said 'Yes!'"

"Mavis," Johnny said wearily, "do you know where this Ebhart home, Toledo, is?"

"Spain?" I queried. "Don't try and change the subject!"

"It's six miles below Santa Barbara, right on the coast," he said. "I'll be almost within whistling distance."

"Oh," I said, and felt a little better.

"I wouldn't take a chance on letting anything happen to my partner," he said seriously. "You know that!"

"What about the time I was trapped in a lion's cage?" I said coldly. "I don't remember you getting me out."

"I was busy," he said.

"And that time in Mexico," I said, "when somebody pushed me into the bull ring with that enormous bull! You weren't around then, either."

"We're a partnership," he said. "You know that,

Mavis. You're the action side of the partnership and I'm the thinker."

"You're getting close," I told him, "but thinker isn't exactly the word."

He lit himself a cigarette and scowled at me. "Anyway," he said, "Ebhart is picking you up at your place tomorrow morning and you'll drive up there. I've already booked into a motel for the next three days. I'll write the address and phone number down for you. You contact me as soon as you're settled in, and let me know what's cooking."

"It'll probably be me," I said.

"That's what I like about you, Mavis," he chuckled. "Always kidding."

"Johnny Rio," I said, "you'd dance at my funeral! Don't you have any feelings toward me at all?"

"Sure I do," he said, "but they're mainly homicidal. You don't have a thing to worry about. You'll have Ebhart around the whole time. You haven't forgotten what that Marine sergeant taught you?"

"Which one?" I asked him. "Oh, you mean that unarmed combat? I sure haven't." I shook my head firmly. "There hasn't been one get away from me yet."

"One what?"

"Man," I said. "You get awful dumb at times, Johnny."

"I guess it's infectious," he muttered. "Look at it this way, Mavis. Ebhart paid us our biggest retainer ever, and he's paying us another two thousand when the job's finished. All you have to do for your half is take a vacation below Santa Barbara. You should live so long!"

"That's what I wanted to talk to you about," I told him firmly. "Now if you could——"

He patted my shoulder, then hustled me toward the door. "You'd better get on home and start packing, honey," he said. "We wouldn't want to keep a client waiting in the morning, would we?"

"Johnny," I said, "I——"

"Any time you want me up there," he said cheerfully, "just whistle."

"Any time I want you, Johnny Rio, I'll scream!" I said coldly. "And don't think my scream won't carry six miles!"

"That's my Mavis," he said, and patted me again, but not on the shoulder this time. Then somehow he managed to stop patting and close the door at the same time, leaving me outside.

So I went back to my apartment and started packing. I was all through by eight that night, and I figured a good night's sleep might be a help. I had a kind of nervous feeling right under my appendix scar, and I figured what I needed was a tranquilizer, so I switched on the television and got one of those old horror movies, *Second Cousin to Frankenstein* or something. My nerves were so bad by the time I did get to bed that if there'd been a man under it I would have been scared!

By nine the next morning I was ready and waiting for Don Ebhart to pick me up. I'd put my hair into a pony tail and wore the sweater that's two sizes too small, so he wouldn't feel lonely. The other sweaters are only one size too small.

I always remember what that advertising executive told me. "Mavis," he said, "packaging and display are vital when you're selling a product, but never overemphasize one feature at the expense of the rest. A quality product speaks for itself." That's what the man said, and I figured he was right, even if he was interested in only one feature whenever we had a date.

At the dot of nine-thirty, Don Ebhart arrived. I opened the door to him, and he looked at me for a while without saying anything.

"I'm all ready," I told him.

"I'm not," he said. "I'm going to have to get used to you. Mavis, you look terrific!"

"Thanks," I said. "You look pretty good yourself."

"You all packed?" he asked.

"There they are!" I said proudly.

He counted them a couple of times. "Three suitcases, a trunk and two hatboxes," he said hoarsely. "Don't you figure on ever coming back?"

"I thought you'd want me to look nice," I said. "After all, I am your wife, aren't I?"

That seemed to cheer him up for some reason. "Sure," he said. "How could I ever forget that! O.K., we'll get them down to the car."

So half an hour later we were on the highway, heading toward Santa Barbara. Don had a brand-new Corvette, and it was a nice morning with the sun shining and everything. It was starting out like the vacation Johnny Rio said it was going to be.

"We'd better get a couple of things straight before we get there," Don said. "None of them even know my wife's name is Clare, so I guess it'll be easier to keep on calling you Mavis and save confusion."

"It's my name, too," I agreed with him.

"That's why I thought it the best thing to call you," he said in a dull sort of voice. "I don't know if they'll all be there by the time we arrive, but Edwina will be around for sure."

"Edwina?" I asked him. "You don't have two wives already, not counting me?"

"She's the housekeeper," he said tersely. "About thirty-five. She was with my father for the last two years before he died. Under the terms of his will she stays on at the house until I collect the inheritance."

"That means she's going to be out of a job soon?" I said.

"One more reason for her not liking me," he said. "Or you, either. We'll need to watch Edwina. Fabian Dark is sure to be there, too."

"He sounds like something out of a comic strip," I said.

"He doesn't look like it," Don said grimly. "He's the family lawyer and a nasty piece of work at the same time. Put him and a dark night together, and it'll be the dark night that runs screaming first!"

Somehow the morning didn't seem quite so bright after that. We stopped for lunch in Santa Barbara at one of those imitation mission places, and I had a steak, because I figured what with Don on the one hand and all those creeps he'd been talking about on the other, a girl needed to keep her strength up.

Then we drove back down the coast and I was busy looking at the sea, which was a beautiful blue and all the same color, too, when Don stopped the car and said: "There it is."

The house was on the ocean side of the road. It must have been a long way back—maybe half a mile—but it still looked big even at that distance. With the sun streaming down on it, putting a gleam on those white walls and graceful arches every place, it looked real pretty.

"Gee!" I said breathlessly, "it looks beautiful, Don— kind of Spanish."

"Toledo," he said.

"Sure!" I snapped my fingers. "I'd almost forgotten its name."

"It's an authentic replica of the home in Spain where my mother was born," Don said tonelessly. "Much bigger, of course. My father went to a great deal of trouble to get it right. From outside, it looks exactly the same."

I felt a lump in my throat: "Your father must have loved your mother very much," I said softly.

"My mother was very unhappy in Spain," he went on as if he hadn't heard what I said. "She only lived for one thing—to leave the country and never go back. Her parents had been very cruel to her when she was young. She hated everything Spanish, but most of all she hated anything that reminded her of her youth there. So my father built her this house and made her live in it."

"But . . ." I said weakly.

Don turned and looked at me, a vague smile on his face. "It was his idea of a joke," he said.

CHAPTER THREE

I used to think thirty-five was old until I met Edwina. She was tall, with black hair and flashing eyes, and she wore a black silk dress with a white collar. That black silk was much too tight all the way down from her neck to her knees. Anybody with eyesight—any sort of eyesight—got the message. I clung tight to Don's arm like an ever-loving wife who's a little bit scared by the big new house and new people. It wasn't hard to act scared, because I was.

Somehow the house wasn't bright at all once you got inside. There was a closed courtyard, Spanish style, I guess, and inside the rooms were very big with very high ceilings. There were heavy drapes over all the windows and it felt the way a house does the morning after the funeral when the wake has left.

"Edwina," Don said. "I'd like you to meet my wife, Mavis."

Edwina looked straight through me like I wasn't wearing a slip—and how did she know in that dim light? "How do you do, Mrs. Ebhart," she said, in a voice that had its own built-in sneer.

"Hi," I said faintly.

"I have given you your parents' old suite," she said to Don. "I thought you would like that."

Don glared at her for a moment. "That was very thoughtful of you," he said icily.

"You know your way," Edwina said. "I'll have the man bring your baggage up right away."

"You've hired some servants?" Don asked her.

She nodded briefly. "Three—cook, maid and handyman. They are adequate."

"Any of the others here yet?"

"Mr. Dark arrived yesterday," she told him. "I expect your sister and her husband sometime this evening. I don't know when your brother will be here."

"Half-brother," Don growled.

"Of course," she said. That built-in sneer curved her lips. "How foolish of me to forget."

Don looked at me. "I'll show you the way, Mavis, so you don't get lost."

"Thanks," I said. I smiled doubtfully at Edwina. "I guess I'll be seeing you again."

"I shall be here," she said. "Always. I am a part of this house, and its memories." But she was looking at Don while she spoke. He took my arm and hustled me out of the room so fast that I was running by the time we reached the hallway.

"Take it easy!" I told him. "So we're officially married, but that doesn't have to make it a honeymoon, does it?"

"Sorry," he growled, and slowed down a little, "but that woman always makes me mad. She only came here after the old man divorced his second wife. The way she acts, you'd think she'd been his wife." He laughed suddenly. "I guess she was, at that. But she didn't have a ring on her finger to go with it. Maybe that's what's been eating her the last five years!"

We finally got to the suite, and it looked like one whole floor of the Waldorf to me. There was a living room with a tennis court in the middle, or space for one, anyhow. Then there were two enormous bedrooms, each with its own bathroom and dressing room attached.

"Well," Don grinned at me, "that's one problem resolved. Clare will be glad to know about this: now she'll be able to sleep nights."

Five minutes later a sour-faced character staggered in with my trunk. He dropped it in the middle of the living-room carpet, looked at me murderously, then walked out. He was back again ten minutes later with the rest of my baggage and dropped it alongside the trunk. "You want that car up here, too?" he grunted, "or will the garage be O.K.?"

"Just who do you think you're talking to?" I asked him.

"America's most-dressed woman!" he snarled at me, then he walked out again before I could be modest and tell him he was exaggerating, but only a little.

Don came back out of his room and dragged my baggage into the other bedroom for me. "It's four o'clock now," he said. "I guess you'll want to get freshened up a little. Why don't we plan on going down around five and get ourselves a drink?"

"Sure," I told him, "sounds fine to me."

"See you," he said, and went out, closing the door behind him like a gentleman, if not a husband.

I took a shower, then got dressed. I put on the new formal, which is black with thin shoulder straps and cut low enough to prove a girl isn't kidding about what's her own and what isn't. It has a tight crepe flounce from midthigh to just below the knee, and it's kind of cute. The designer says it's a nostalgic silhouette of the twenties, but he didn't kid me. It makes the boys nostalgic all right, but not for the twenties.

I walked out into the living room and Don was there waiting for me. His eyes widened as he looked me up and down, and that gleam came into his eyes. "Don't get any ideas," I told him quickly, "even if I am your wife."

"Mavis," he said softly, "it's going to be a long three days."

We got back to the main part of the house, through the enormous living room and into a sunroom adjoining. The sunroom had a bar, and there was a man leaning against it, a drink in his hand. He was short and a little plump. He was beautifully dressed in an almost lavender-colored suit, and his curly hair had receded a little, leaving him a high-domed forehead. He smiled at me, showing nice even teeth, and when we got close enough I could smell the faint perfume.

He held out one nicely manicured hand toward me. "You are Don's wife, of course," he said. "How nice to meet you. He's been most unfair, hiding you from us."

"This is Fabian Dark, Mavis," Don said curtly, "the family lawyer."

I shook hands with the lawyer and I'd figured his hand

would be limp, but it wasn't. His grasp was very firm, but his hand was cold. I had to stop myself from shivering.

"How dull you make me sound, Don," Fabian Dark said in a reproachful sort of voice. "Please! I'm not one of those musty nineteenth-century characters with a celluloid collar and string tie."

He smiled at me. "Don's taste is better than I thought, Mavis. Our enforced stay here looks definitely brighter already: fraught with promise, one might say. Let me make you a drink."

"I'll have a gimlet, thanks, Mr. Dark," I told him.

"Fabian," he corrected me. "I am definitely not old enough to be your father, for which I'm thankful. How about you, Don?"

"Scotch," Don said. "Any of the others arrived yet?"

Fabian started making the drinks. "Not yet," he said. "A pleasure we can still contemplate. You haven't met your sister Wanda's husband, have you?"

"No," Don told him.

"Gregory Payton," Fabian said smiling. "A psychiatrist. I suspect Wanda found it cheaper to marry him and share his couch, rather than pay fifty dollars a half-hour for the privilege of lying on it."

"Very funny!" Don said sourly.

I giggled—I couldn't help it. "I thought it was kind of clever," I said. "Don't be an old grouch, Don."

"I can see we shall get along together," Fabian said to me. "A sense of humor was never one of Don's strong points."

"If you two are going to have a screaming fit at Fabian's funny remarks," Don said, "I'm going to get some fresh air!"

"Wait a minute, Don," I said, "I——" But I was talking to myself after the first four words. Don was out of the room with the door closed behind him.

Fabian looked at me with a peculiar expression in his eyes which I guessed was sympathy. "He'll get over it," he told me in a soft voice. "You must be used to Don's moods by now; the others are the same—an Ebhart trait that Randolph seems to have successfully passed down to all three of his children."

He handed me my drink and I said thank you. Then he just looked at me, and I started to feel nervous. I mean, I'm used to guys looking at me, and believe me, I'd start worrying if they didn't. But the way he looked at me was different somehow. I wasn't sure I liked it.

"You've met Edwina?" he asked.

"The housekeeper?" I nodded. "Sure, we met when we got here."

"How did she strike you?"

"She didn't get that far," I told him, "but I think she would have liked to."

He laughed for some reason. "We shall get along fine, Mavis," he said. "That sense of humor." I couldn't think of an answer to that, so I drank some of the gimlet. "Edwina is still what they used to call a handsome woman," he said, "and a very frustrated one. For the last five years she has lived here with nothing but her memories, and a brooding sense of injustice. You know Randolph's will stipulated she should remain here as housekeeper until Don came into his inheritance?"

"Sure," I nodded. "Don told me."

"Then she gets a paltry two thousand dollars," Fabian said. "She has been the mistress of this house for the last seven years, and she is repaid with a gardener's legacy." His shoulders twitched as he laughed silently. "We have something in common, you know, Mavis, with Randolph Ebhart. He had a delicious sense of humor!"

"I guess that's why Edwina's laughing all the time," I said, and that made him laugh again.

"Tell me, Mavis," he said, "how has it been—your marriage to Don, I mean?"

"Fine," I said cautiously. "Why shouldn't it be?"

"No reason," he said lightly. "I find him . . . difficult to get along with sometimes. I wondered, that's all. It makes me very happy to hear you say that, Mavis. By the way, I thought your name was Clare?"

"What made you think that?" I asked him, and this time I knew I was nervous.

"You were married in San Diego just over a year ago," he said. "You must remember I'm a lawyer. I obtained a copy of your marriage certificate. I thought it would be easier to do that rather than have to ask Don for it—he's sure to have lost it. And naturally I must have legal proof that Don is married on the day he comes into his inheritance."

"Oh, sure," I said. "My name is Clare really, but I don't like it very much so Don always calls me Mavis."

"I see," he said. "Why Mavis?"

I thought hard for a good reason and wished Don hadn't walked out on me. "It reminds Don of a girl friend he had once," I said desperately.

Fabian raised his bushy eyebrows into that high-domed forehead. "I must say you're a very accommodating wife," he smiled.

"I was never in the hotel business," I said firmly, and the silly goof started laughing again. Maybe he had some private joke he never got tired of.

We had a couple more drinks, which is around my limit—one more and I'd be seeing two Fabian Darks. I didn't want that to happen. I didn't think I could stand two of them laughing at some joke they wouldn't tell me about.

"Well," Fabian glanced at his watch. "If you'll excuse me, Mavis, there are a couple of things I must do before dinner."

"You go right ahead," I told him. Then he bowed, which gave me a kick, because the only other time it's ever happened to me was in a Chinese restaurant, and that wasn't the same somehow.

After he'd gone I walked over to the nearest armchair and sat down in it. I guess maybe it was the drinks and the room being so dark with those drapes pulled across the windows. I must have fallen asleep, because the next thing I knew I was having a nightmare.

A little thing about two feet high sat on the arm of the chair looking at me. He wore a tuxedo and a bright red bow tie, and he never blinked his eyes, not once. He had a crew cut that needed another cut and stood straight up from his head like it was scared of coming in contact with his scalp. His mouth was absolutely square and he had the craziest expression on his face.

"Hiya, doll!" he said suddenly in a high-pitched, high-powered voice. "I'm Prince Charming, come to wake the Sleeping Princess. Don't you kid me it takes only a kiss, either. I'm giving you the full treatment, babe!"

"Go away!" I told the nightmare, but it didn't make any difference: he still sat there, the grin sort of painted on his face.

"Don't give me that innocent maid routine," he said. "How did you get to be a Princess in the first place, huh? What about all those times in the cellar with the Prince, huh? Admit it, babe, you got experience."

"If you don't go away," I told it severely, "I'll wake up, and then where will you be?"

"Right here," he leered at me. "I'd be crazy to walk away from you, sister. You got class—all over."

So I didn't have any choice. I forced myself to wake up. But it didn't work somehow. I had my eyes open O.K., but the nightmare was still there.

Suddenly I was on my feet—I had to be awake. I looked around the room and I saw the empty glasses on the bar. Everything was the same except the room had got a little darker, maybe. I turned my head slowly, and then I had to bite my lower lip to stop from screaming. It was still there, on the arm of the chair.

"No use, babe," it said. "You're stuck with me. I'm maybe a little guy, but I got vitality!"

I guessed it was that sexy look. I'd used it too much lately and Johnny was right. Now I'd really lost my marbles. If I couldn't lose the nightmare, I might as well play ball with it, so I tried to smile and said, "What's your name?"

"Mr. Limbo," he said. "You and me will get along fine, honey. You just got to get used to me, that's all."

"It might take some time," I said in a shaky voice, "maybe a couple of hundred years!"

"What's your name, gorgeous?" he grinned widely at me.

25

"Mavis," I said. "Mavis Sei——" Then I remembered just in time. "Mavis Ebhart."

"You don't mean to tell me my half-brother managed to hook a doll like you!" a deeper voice said in a shocked tone.

I looked around wildly, but I couldn't see anybody. The voice seemed to have come from behind the armchair. I was just nerving myself to take a look, when this guy suddenly appeared in front of me. He *had* been behind the chair.

He wasn't as tall as Don, but maybe his shoulders were wider. He had black hair and a rugged sort of face. He just stood there grinning at me. "If I'd been around at the time, Don would never have stood a chance," he said. "Where dames are concerned, Mavis, I'm lethal."

"Lethal who?" I stuttered.

"I thought you might recognize the family resemblance," he said in a sort of mocking voice. "I thought all we Ebharts wore it on our brows, like the mark of Cain."

"You're Carl?" I said in a quavering voice.

"Sure he's Carl," the nightmare said, and cackled with laughter. "Who did you think he was—Danny Kaye?"

"You shut up!" I told the nightmare. "You've scared me enough already."

"Don't be unkind to Mr. Limbo," Carl said. "If it wasn't for him, we wouldn't have met. He's no dummy."

"Dummy!" I said. "If I hadn't been asleep, I would have figured that one out. You're a ventriloquist, and he's your dummy!"

"You got it wrong again, gorgeous," Mr. Limbo said with that nasty-sounding cackle again. "*I'm* the ventriloquist!"

CHAPTER FOUR

"I think that Carl must be crazy!" I told Don in a whisper, as we walked towards the dining room. "You never told me he was a ventriloquist."

"Who would admit a thing like that?" Don shrugged his shoulders irritably. "How did you meet him, anyway?"

I told him how I'd closed my eyes for a few minutes after Fabian Dark had left the room, and what had happened after I woke up again.

"That's Carl all right," Don snorted. "The perpetual adolescent!"

"He must be very clever," I said. "I mean, being a ventriloquist as well."

Then we reached the dining room. There was a long table all set ready for dinner, with candles burning on it. That's just typical of millionaires—they're mean in small ways. I mean, Don's father built this great big house regardless of expense, then he was too mean to put electricity in the dining room.

Edwina looked up at us from the head of the table, with that deep-freeze still in her eyes. "I have put you beside Wanda, Don," she said, "and your wife is next to Carl."

"And Mr. Limbo," Carl grinned at me. "You mustn't forget Mr. Limbo—he's crazy about Mavis already."

"He's crazy all right," I agreed.

For the first time I noticed there were a couple of new faces at the table. One was a redhead, who looked terrific and also competition. She wore a gown that had cost twice as much as mine and was cut an inch lower in front; how she dared breathe, I couldn't figure out.

"Hello, Don," the redhead said in a low vibrant sort of voice. "You haven't met my husband yet, have you?

And I haven't met your new wife, either. Will you start the introductions, or shall I?"

Don glared at her for a moment, then looked at me. "Mavis, this is my sister Wanda," he said. "I imagine the guy sitting next to her is her husband."

"My name is Gregory Payton," Wanda's husband said. He had the kind of teeth that flash every time their owner smiles. I got the feeling if I wasn't careful they'd jump right out of his mouth and nibble me some place where I wasn't expecting it. That sort of thing can make a girl giggle.

"Hi," I said to both the Paytons. I decided right then that Gregory wasn't my type at all. He had thinning hair and rimless eyeglasses with watery blue eyes behind them. His mouth was soft and feminine-looking. Whatever Wanda saw in him just didn't show at all.

I sat down at the table opposite Wanda, with Fabian Dark on one side of me and Carl on the other. Beside Carl, Mr. Limbo had a chair all to himself. I closed my eyes for a moment and thought: if that dummy starts eating when they serve the soup, I'll scream out loud, I know it.

Edwina rang a little bell she had on the table in front of her, then a woman came in and started to serve the meal. I was really hungry, so I didn't feel like talking, and I guess nobody else did much either. So we got through the food in a morguelike silence which those flickering candles didn't help, either. Edwina passed around a box of cigarettes with the coffee, and I told her no thanks because I don't smoke.

"What a dame!" Mr. Limbo said in his high-pitched cackle. "No vices. I'm hip to a doll with big ideas when it comes to sin!"

"Do you have to indulge in this childish nonsense?" Don asked Carl.

Carl shrugged his shoulders and grinned back at him. "I can't stop Mr. Limbo from expressing an opinion," he said. "This is a democracy, after all. He's entitled to say what he thinks, isn't he?"

"Not about my wife," Don said with sudden violence.

Gregory Payton held up his hand commandingly. "Please," he said. "I find all this most interesting. I'd like to hear more from Mr. Limbo."

"Get him!" Mr. Limbo cackled. "A head-shrinker yet. The first one I ever saw who shrunk his own head first. How else would his hair fall out?"

Gregory colored faintly and concentrated on his coffee for the next few seconds.

Beside me, Fabian Dark chuckled. "You did ask for it, my dear fellow," he said easily. "You really should have known better. Didn't Wanda warn you about Carl at all? He's incorrigible."

"So he can't be bribed," I said. "Well, that's something in his favor, I guess."

There was a dead silence after that. I figured they were all busy realizing I wasn't so dumb after all. Then Edwina rang her little bell again for the servant to clear the table.

"Send not to know for whom the bell tolls; it tolls for thee," Mr. Limbo said in a suddenly deep voice.

"What a happy little family we are," Wanda said. "It only takes a paltry ten million dollars to bring us all together again!"

"Like vultures to the feast," Edwina said bitterly. "As I sit at this table, I can hear the beating of wings."

"But maybe not the wings of vultures?" Fabian Dark suggested. "There are darker wings, you know. Wings that beat more slowly and make less noise, but are far more deadly."

Gregory Payton beamed at him. "Most interesting," he said. "I shall have to bring a notebook with me to the table in the future. I'm going to enjoy my stay here immensely—I can see that already."

"Carl?" Mr. Limbo said in a wistful voice. "You think Wanda would marry me?"

"You have to face up to things, Mr. Limbo," Carl told him gently. "You're only a dummy."

"But she married the head-shrinker, didn't she?" Mr. Limbo complained. "So what's the difference?"

Wanda got onto her feet abruptly. "If we're going to have to endure this sort of thing for the next three days," she said in a strangled voice, "that inheritance is going to be little compensation. I'm going to get myself a drink. Coming, Greg?"

"Of course, my dear," Payton said. He got up from the table and followed her into the living room.

Don glared at his half-brother again. "Won't you ever grow up?" he demanded.

"Is he related to you?" Mr. Limbo asked Carl.

"Half of him is," Carl said. "The half that isn't is commonly know as Spanish Moronic. Strictly on his mother's side, of course."

"I dig that crazy wife of his," Mr. Limbo cackled. "I like big blondes, they're so warm in winter!"

"You want to take a good look at her while you've got the chance, Mr. Limbo," Carl said. "Just in case she vanishes. Don's wives have a habit of not being around for very long."

There was a crash as Don's chair toppled over backwards. He started around the table toward where Carl sat, his hands balled into tight fists. "I've had enough!" he shouted. "I'll take that damned idiot dummy and stuff it down your throat. Maybe that will keep both of you quiet!"

Carl was on his feet by the time Don reached him. Don swung a wild, roundhouse right and Carl ducked easily, then came up close and gave Don a vicious, stiff-fingered jab in the solar plexus. Pain contorted Don's face and he doubled up, going down slowly onto his knees. Then Carl grabbed his hair, forcing Don's head up. I saw his right leg moving swiftly—he was going to smash his knee into Don's face.

I figured it was time for Mavis to get into the act. I didn't want a husband, not even a make-believe husband of three days' duration, with a busted nose and maybe missing four of his front teeth. So I got onto my feet and gave Carl a brisk judo chop to the side of the neck, the way that Marine sergeant taught me.

Carl definitely wilted and turned around slowly to look at me, his eyes popping. He looked kind of crazy right then, so I hit him across the bridge of his nose with the edge of my right hand. The next second he was down on his knees beside Don, and neither of them seemed interested in anything very much.

"Bad blood!" Edwina whispered through the brooding silence. "Ever since they were children. Black hearts and evil minds. Donald got it from that Spanish witch, and Carl from that Southern trollop!"

Fabian Dark still sat at the table, smoking a cigarette and looking completely relaxed. "Come now, Edwina," he said easily, "you're hardly being fair. Their father must have had something to do with it."

"A finer man than Randolph Ebhart never walked this earth!" Edwina said fervently. "They are no sons of his!"

"Randolph was certainly a man, I agree." Fabian said conversationally. "But darkness was something he didn't have to learn from his first wife, or second either, for that matter. A black heart was one thing the boys could inherit from their father. You, of all people, Edwina, should know that."

She stared at him, her eyes widening a fraction. "What do you mean?" she whispered.

Fabian smiled at her, almost benignly. "I was thinking of the cellar," he said. "The candles that used to burn down there so late into the night. You must remember them, Edwina, surely? The candles burning, the masks and the chains? I always thought you helped him. A sort of handmaiden?"

Edwina started to shake uncontrollably. She put her hand to her mouth and bit down savagely on her index finger until the blood spurted. She made a moaning noise, then ran from the room.

"Randolph was a great one for games," Fabian said to me amiably. "All sorts of games." The smile on his face gave me the shudders. I thought if he looked at me much longer I'd start making the same sort of noises Edwina had.

Then I felt a hand on my arm. I swung round, ready to let Carl have it, and saw it was Don. There was pain still etched on his face, but he'd managed to stand up straight again. Carl was still on his knees, a glazed look in his eyes.

31

"I've had enough of this for one night," Don said in a tight voice. "We'll go to bed, Mavis."

"Mr. Ebhart!" I said coldly. "Aren't you presuming just a little? If you think . . ." Then I remembered.

"That's Mavis," Don said to Fabian, forcing a smile onto his face. "Always kidding."

"Of course," Fabian said politely. "I like to see there is still fire in your veins after a year of marriage. I wish you an enchanted evening."

"Thank you," Don said curtly. "Good night."

"Good night, Fabian," I smiled at him. "I hope those old chains you were talking about don't rattle in the night and keep me awake."

"If you are kept awake, my dear," he said, "I'm sure it won't be the chains. You make a charming couple: the dutiful wife and the expectant heir. I envy you."

Don had a tight grip on my elbow as he pushed me toward the door. I took one last look at the dining room as we left it. Mr. Limbo lay lifeless on his chair, that fixed grin still on his face as he stared blankly up at the ceiling. I thought if I had to make a choice between the two of them, I'd take Fabian Dark—chains as well!

When we got to the living room of the suite, Don closed the door carefully behind us. I stood in the middle of the room and waited for him. Then he walked straight across to his bedroom and opened the door. I was just thinking that he was really a caveman type, and the trouble with that unarmed combat training I've got is there's no point in fighting for my honor because I always win, when Don said "Good night," walked into his room, and closed the door behind him.

That didn't leave me much choice, so I went into my own room and sat on the bed, which creaked a little, and began to feel the blues creeping all over me. I mean, nine-thirty in the evening and my first night as Mrs. Ebhart, and he goes into his own room and closes the door behind him. I don't wonder so many girls divorce their husbands for mental cruelty!

I had a shower and got into my shortie nightgown, which is rather cute with lots of lace and much too short for modesty. A pair of lace-edged panties go with it, but when I looked at myself in the mirror, I decided to leave them off. No reason to be shy with myself.

I sat at the dressing table and started to give my hair its routine hundred strokes of the brush. I'd got to ninety-six when there was a knock on the door and the next moment Don walked into the room.

There was a dead silence for about five minutes—or it seemed like five minutes—while he looked at me. "Oh," he said finally. "Sorry."

"That's O.K.," I told him. "You'd see as much if I wasn't wearing anything."

"I wanted to say thank you, Mavis," he said, coming a little closer. "Where did you ever learn to fight like that?"

"Like what?"

"Like the way you handled Carl downstairs." He grinned at me, and somehow he looked very boyish, but not too boyish. "I'd hate to buy into an argument with you!"

So I told him about the Marine sergeant, and by the time I'd finished we were both sitting on the bed and Don had his arm around me.

"You're a fascinating girl, Mavis," he said seriously. His arm tightened suddenly and I wondered how I was going to breathe, but then I thought: who cares about breathing anyway? "You're beautiful," Don went on slowly, "an expert in unarmed combat, you have a perfect figure . . ."

"Brains . . . ?" I said hopefully.

"Nobody has everything, Mavis," he said, and before I could argue, he kissed me.

I never thought being kissed would ever come under the heading of "New Experiences," but you learn something new every day, as the man said when he went home early to see what his wife did on the nights he worked late.

Maybe I always run a high temperature because my resistance is low, somehow. As Don kissed me, it melted away into nothing with a minus sign in front of it. Being kissed by Don was like being sent to the electric chair. As the first shock hit you all your muscles tensed, then suddenly they all relaxed and you just didn't care what happened next.

After about five years, he took his lips away from mine and looked down at me, his eyes shining. "You're the most beautiful girl I've met, Mavis," he said huskily. I guess I should have answered him, but I couldn't, I was too limp. He let go of me gently and three seconds later he took me into his arms again, but this time the lights were out.

"Don?" I managed to whisper.

"You have to remember," he whispered, "we are married, after all."

I knew vaguely there was something wrong about that argument, but I didn't want to think about it right then. I might have remembered.

CHAPTER FIVE

Suddenly I was awake. I just lay there, making purring noises and wondering what it was that woke me in the first place. Then I heard it again and it made me shiver. I reached over and switched on the bedside lamp. My watch said it was three in the morning, and when I looked around I discovered I was by myself again. I guessed Don must have gone back to his own room sometime while I was sleeping.

I listened and couldn't hear anything at all for a few seconds, and I was just starting to relax and think about going to sleep or going to see if Don would like a glass of hot milk or something, when I heard it again. This time there was no mistake—it definitely was the sound of rattling chains. Fabian Dark had said something to Edwina about a cellar and masks and chains. Remembering that didn't help me at all.

Without thinking about it, I found myself at the door

of Don's room. I knocked, then went in without waiting for an answer. "Don?" I said softly, and there was no answer. "Don?" I wailed hopelessly, but there was still no answer. I switched on the light and saw the room was empty. It didn't take much figuring out: he must have heard the chains too, and gone to see what was happening.

I went back to my own room and tried to make up my mind which was worse—wait around on my own for Don to come back, or go looking for him. Then I heard a faint rustling noise in the corner of the room, and my mind was made up right away. I didn't care what those chains meant —I'd face anything rather than a mouse.

Halfway across the room I stopped again. The shortie nightgown was going to look silly if I met anybody else besides Don in the house. Besides, there might be a draft. So I changed into a pair of tapered slacks and a sweater, and put a pair of sandals on my feet. Just thirty seconds to comb my hair and use a little lipstick, and I was ready.

I went through the living room to the door which led into the corridor outside, and opened it cautiously. It was very dark out there, and I wished I had a flashlight with me. I wished I was back in my apartment in L.A., or with Don in . . . well, never mind that. But then I remembered that mouse again, so I stepped out into the corridor and closed the door of the suite behind me.

It was pitch-black outside. I started to move along the corridor slowly toward where I knew the head of the wide staircase started. I couldn't see where I was going, so I walked very slowly with hands held out in front of me. I'd gone maybe ten steps when my right hand touched something, and I stopped.

Whatever it was, it didn't feel like a wall at all. It was smooth but warm to the touch. I felt around it gingerly; there was a sort of bony protrusion, and beneath it I touched something even warmer and softer to the hypersensitiveness of my fingers. Suddenly I realized my fingers were on someone's lips and it was a nose I'd touched a moment before.

I opened my mouth to scream, but before I could, a voice said "Boo!" and then cackled with laughter. My knees were knocking and I was shaking all over—how that sweater didn't bust a seam I'll never know. But I was beginning to feel a little better because I'd recognized the laugh.

"Mr. Limbo," I stuttered. "Don't ever do that to me again!"

A flashlight beam hit me in the eyes, blinding me for a moment, then moved slowly away from my face and even more slowly down the rest of me until it stopped at my sandals.

"What a pity!" Carl's voice said. "You always go to bed dressed, Mavis?"

"Don't change the subject," I told him. "What are you doing standing here in the dark in the middle of the night?"

"I could ask you the same question," Carl said easily.

"Don't worry about that!" Mr. Limbo cackled. "Ask her that one about going to bed dressed, again. That's o[ne] answer I want to hear."

"Why don't you make it easy for yourself, Carl, and stay with the one voice?" I asked him.

"Because there are two of us here," he said. The flashlight beam moved and Mr. Limbo's painted face leered at me from underneath Carl's arm.

"I heard chains rattling," I said. "And Don isn't in his room and——"

"*His* room?" Carl said with a great big query in his voice.

"So I figured he must be out looking for those chains," I said, ignoring the query. "And I thought I'd go looking too, and see if I could find him."

"And the chains?"

"I don't give a——" I took a deep breath—that sweater was getting the hell kicked out of it. "I don't care about the chains: I just want to find Don, that's all."

"The doll is lonely," Mr. Limbo said sorrowfully. "You hear that, Carl? She wants some masculine company. You go on back to bed and I'll take care of Mavis. Look me up next week sometime."

"If you don't keep quiet," I said coldly to Mr. Limbo, "I'll pull your arms off, one at a time!"

"You tell her, Carl," Mr. Limbo said.

"Talking of pulling arms off," Carl said softly, "I should kick your teeth in. You hit me when I wasn't looking!"

"Looking or not," I told him, "it wouldn't have made any difference. I'm an expert."

"I'll believe it," he said wonderingly. "You're the craziest girl I ever met. I still don't see how brother Don ever talked you into marrying him, the slob! Maybe it was that several million dollars he picks up in three days from now, huh?"

"You have a nasty mind as well as a nasty face," I said coldly. "I never met a couple of more repulsive dummies than you, Carl Ebhart! Now, if you'll excuse me, I'm going to find my husband."

"Alone?" Mr. Limbo asked in an eerie whisper.

That threw me just a little. I'd taken one step forward, and I stopped suddenly. "Well," I mumbled, "if . . ."

"What use would it be having a couple of dummies like us along?" Mr. Limbo jeered.

"Don't be rude to the lady," Carl said reprovingly. "If we tag along we might get the chance to slug her while she isn't looking."

There are times in a girl's life when it's better to say nothing, like when you're working late at the office and the boss's wife walks in unexpectedly. I figured this was a good time to say nothing, too.

"So we'll go along," Carl said. "Where do you think your husband has strayed, Mavis?"

"I thought he must have gone to see what was happening." I told him.

"Just where were the chains rattling?" he asked.

"Somewhere downstairs, I think."

"So we'll take a look," he said.

"Yeah," Mr. Limbo cut in. "Maybe it's the old man's ghost come to haunt the eldest son. That I wouldn't miss for all the chorus girls in Las Vegas!"

Carl shone the flashlight ahead of us along the corridor.

37

We walked down the sweeping staircase and stopped in the living room. I blinked again as Carl switched on the lights. He was wearing a dark shirt and a pair of slacks, and I was going to ask him if he slept fully clothed too, but then I thought better of it, because Mr. Limbo would probably answer the question anyway.

"I don't hear any chains," Carl shrugged his shoulders easily. "Maybe the witching hour has come and gone. While we're here we may as well have a drink."

"I'm looking for Don, not a drink," I said.

"We'll find him," Carl said patiently. "A drink will keep out the night air." He walked over to the bar and sat Mr. Limbo on top of the counter, while he made the drinks. "Yours is a gimlet, Mavis?"

"How did you know?"

"Seventh son of a seventh son," he grinned. "Fabian mentioned it."

I had to admit the drink did me good. It started working right after the first sip. I could even look Mr. Limbo in the eye without shuddering.

"Chains," Carl said suddenly over the rim of his glass. "It was Edwina . . . no, Fabian. I don't remember very distinctly because I was down on my knees at the time, having been slugged by a certain female! What was it Fabian said? Something about Edwina should have been used to darkness? 'Candles burning, masks and the chains.' Yeah." He snapped his fingers quickly. "Of course—the cellar!"

"What do you mean: of course, the cellar?" I asked him frigidly. "Is there a Mardi Gras going on down there that nobody told me about?"

"That's what Fabian said," Carl sounded impatient again. "He was talking about the cellar to Edwina: he made some crack about her being a handmaiden, or something."

"I never knew being a maiden had anything to do with your hands before," I said. "All these years I've been thinking that——"

"As I remember," said Carl, obviously not even listen-

38

ing to me, "you get to the cellar from the kitchen. There's a flight of stairs. . . . Let's take a look."

"You take a look," I said hopefully. "I'll wait right here. It's probably damp, and there might be rats or mice down there."

"Your husband might be there," he said, "and if I come back and tell you Don's having a ball in the cellar with Edwina, you won't believe me, so you'd better come look for yourself."

"Don and Edwina?" I laughed nonchalantly. "Why, that's absurd. What would he—— You lead the way!"

From the living room to the kitchen seemed like half a mile. I tagged along behind Carl, who had Mr. Limbo tucked under his arm again. I'd hoped Carl would leave the dummy in the bar, but I was beginning to realize that Mr. Limbo was as much a part of Carl as his right arm.

We got into the kitchen and Carl switched on the lights. He stood looking around for a moment, then pointed to a door in the far wall. "That's it!" he said triumphantly. "The stairs are behind that door."

I didn't have any choice but to follow him. He opened the door and flicked up the light switch on the wall. Nothing happened.

"It should work," Carl said irritably. "We'll use the flashlight, anyway; there's another light in the cellar itself."

"Why don't we just call out from here?" I asked nervously. "Then if Don's down there, he'll answer."

"Not if he's with Edwina," Carl grinned at me. "He may be dumb, but not that dumb!"

"O.K.," I said. "You lead the way."

Carl went down the stairs slowly, holding the flashlight so I could see the stairs as I followed him. When he reached the bottom step, he stopped suddenly, so suddenly that I rammed into his back. "Unholy Toledo!" he said softly.

I regained my balance and hoped my tummy wouldn't show a bruise where I'd bumped him. "Why don't you give hand signals?" I snarled at him.

"Candles," he said, which was the silliest answer I'd ever heard.

"Candles?" I yelped. "Who's talking about candles. I'm talking about——"

Then I stopped right there, because I could see over his shoulder exactly what he was talking about. Candles. Maybe a dozen of them, spread around the cellar and all of them lit. Flickering candles that broke the darkness into a patchy gloom without lighting the place. Thick cobwebs hung down from the ceiling, and there was a horrible musty smell that made me feel sick.

"This place gives me the creeps," I said shakily. "Let's go back to the kitchen, please!"

"Sure," Carl said. "I guess there's nobody—— What's that?"

He shone the flashlight into a corner, and I screamed when I saw it. There was a body lying there in the pool of light. I ran over and knelt down beside it. "It's Don!" I said wildly, and started to cry.

The next moment, Carl was beside me. He turned Don gently over onto his back, then grunted. "Shut up!" he said.

"What?" I bawled.

"I said to shut up! He's not dead—he's breathing quite normally. Probably had a fall. Go up to the kitchen and get some water. Here," he thrust the flashlight into my hand, "you'd better take this with you."

I found a jug in the kitchen and filled it with cold water, then took it down into the cellar again. Carl took the jug out of my hand and tilted it over Don's face so that the water poured down onto him. "You'll put him into shock, doing that!" I said angrily.

"The only shock he'll get will be the taste, after all these years of whisky," Carl said callously.

Don grunted, then opened his eyes slowly. He blinked a couple of times, then groaned. "My head!" he said weakly. "Who hit me?"

I cradled his head in my lap and Carl shone the flashlight down so we could see the top and back of Don's head. There was a large bump just behind his right ear with clotted blood around it.

"You're O.K.," Carl said unsympathetically. "Somebody slugged you, that's all. It's nothing more than a bad headache."

"That's all you know," Don said grittily. "You should feel it."

"Who was it, anyway?" Carl asked him.

"I don't know," Don said dully. "Whoever it was must have been behind me. I never saw anyone."

"What were you doing down here?" Carl persisted.

Don raised himself slowly into a sitting position. He certainly looked a mess. His robe and the legs of his pajamas were stained with the dirt and damp of the cellar floor.

"I woke up and thought I heard chains rattling," he muttered. "And after that I thought I heard somebody scream a long way away. I thought I'd better take a look and see if it was my imagination or not. I remembered Fabian saying something about chains after dinner and——"

"We've already been through that routine," Carl interrupted him. "So you came down here to the cellar. What then?"

"That's all, I'm afraid," Don said. "The light wasn't working over the stairs. I didn't have a flashlight, but I did have some matches. So I sort of fumbled my way down the stairs, striking matches as I went. I missed one step and nearly fell. I swore out loud, so whoever it was down here knew I was coming, and had plenty of time to duck out of sight. I had only just walked in when I was slugged."

"Were the candles lit when you came down?" Carl asked him.

"I don't honestly remember," Don said. He got onto his feet carefully, and groaned again. "Every time I move I feel as if my head's going to fall off."

"Don't worry," Mr. Limbo said, "you'd never miss it!"

"Don't start fooling around with that damned dummy again, Carl!" Don growled. "I'm in no mood for it."

41

"I'm disappointed," Carl said mockingly. "This is definitely anticlimax. I thought at least we were going to find you and Edwina in the middle of an orgy or something: you sure she wasn't here and slugged you because you got fresh?"

"That's not even funny," Don snarled.

"Why don't we all go back to bed?" I said helpfully. "I'll clean up that bump for you, Don, and some sleep and aspirin will be the best cure for it."

"Now I heard everything!" Mr. Limbo said in a reverent sort of voice. "She's even got a little-mother routine! I bet she was a girl scout once and she had badges all over!"

"I told you to stop that!" Don said in an ugly voice.

"Take it easy, half-brother!" Carl told him in a good-humored voice. "You're in no condition to pick another fight, and next time I won't make the mistake of turning my back on your wife."

"Why don't we go upstairs," I said hopelessly, "before I catch cold?"

"I guess so," Carl said. "But somebody slugged your ever-loving husband down here, and somebody must have lit those candles. We might as well take a look around before we leave."

"Why don't you and Mr. Limbo look around while I take Don back upstairs?" I said.

"Only a few seconds," Carl said. "Who knows what we might find? Maybe another will that cuts out Don completely!"

I started to count up to ten, and I thought if Carl hadn't made a move toward the stairs by the time I reached it I was going to slug him over the head, and Mr. Limbo could do the worrying!

Carl played the flashlight along the nearest wall. There was nothing to see until the beam stopped suddenly, and square in the center of it was the most hideous face I'd ever seen outside a nightmare. A face carved out of ebony with evil slanting eyes and a hooked nose. The lips were parted in an insane frenzy which matched the dilated eyes with their green pupils.

Vaguely I could hear someone screaming, and it wasn't until after it stopped abruptly when Carl dug his elbow into my ribs that I realized it must have been me.

"Shut up, Mavis!" Carl said wearily. "It's not real."

"You mean I'm seeing things?" I gurgled.

"It's a mask," he said. The light slid further along the wall and revealed a second face. A female one this time, but even more grotesque. The grotesque face of a witch, with greasy wisps of lank hair hanging down over it. Beneath the thin, cruel lips the chin had been molded into an enormous, obscene deformity.

"You see," Carl said. "There's another one."

"I don't want to see any more," I shuddered, "I won't sleep for the next six months as it is!"

"The candles burning," Carl murmured. "The masks ... Where are the chains?"

The flashlight beam continued its search along the walls. In spite of myself, I had to watch. There were two more masks and then nothing but cobwebs again for the length of the second wall. I began to feel a little better—maybe there was nothing else?

Then the beam stopped for a moment and jumped convulsively, so that the light flickered too much for me to be able to see clearly.

"What is it, Carl?" I asked him.

"The ... chains," he muttered hoarsely.

As the beam steadied, I screamed again. Heavy rust-colored chains had been bolted into the wall. There were four of them, two about five feet from the floor and the other two at floor level. Two that held the wrists and two that held the ankles, supporting her sagging body with ease.

She was completey naked and her body was beautiful, dazzling white under the glare of the flashlight. Her face made a horrible contrast—the lips curled back from the teeth, the tongue protruding blackly.

"Edwina!" Don said in a shrill voice.

"Strangled," Carl whispered deep in his throat. "You were lucky, Don. Just a headache!"

CHAPTER SIX

We sat huddled together in the living room, but somehow we all seemed far apart. I sat next to Don on a couch, and opposite us Wanda and Gregory Payton sat on another couch. Fabian Dark was slumped in an armchair staring blankly at the wall in front of him. Carl was at the bar, making drinks that nobody seemed to have any enthusiasm for, with Mr. Limbo sitting on the counter to keep him company.

I moved a bit closer to Don and saw him wince as my shoulder touched his. "How's the head?" I asked him.

"Lousy," he tried to smile but didn't make it. "But, like Carl said, I guess I'm lucky with only a headache to worry about."

I shuddered. "Don't make me think of it again," I told him. "That poor woman!"

I heard a police officer tramp briskly through the hallway outside. "How long are they going to keep us in here?" I asked Don. "We've been here about twenty minutes already and not one of them's even said 'Hello' yet. You think they've forgotten all about us?"

Don grimaced. "I doubt it. We're all suspects, I imagine. Maybe it's deliberate policy on their part. The longer they leave us alone, the more scared the murderer gets!"

"You think it was one of the people here in this room that did it?" I asked him.

"I don't know," he said. "It's a thought I don't even want to think about."

A glass was dangled under my nose and I took hold of it automatically. "One gimlet," Carl said, "and a Scotch for you, half-brother."

"Thanks," Don said sourly as he took the glass. "How can you sound so bright?"

"It's Mavis," Carl said. "Who can look at her and still feel depressed? Life is for the living, half-brother."

"You ghoul!" Don said.

I heard the click as the door swung open, and looked over my shoulder in time to see the man walk briskly into the room. He was a tall, thin guy, wearing a gray suit and a darker gray hat which looked as if it was glued to his head. He walked right across the room to the bar, then stopped and turned around slowly, so he was facing everyone in the room.

"My name is Frome," he said in a harsh voice. "Lieutenant Frome. You all know a woman has been murdered —strangled to death. I don't think it's going to be hard to find the murderer, but it may take some time. I intend questioning every one of you individually. None of you will leave this room without my permission. One of my men will be at the door. If you have a good reason for wanting to leave the room, tell him, and he'll see me about it."

That sounded kind of stupid to me, because everybody was bound to have a good reason for leaving the room sooner or later, and probably sooner—except Mr. Limbo, of course.

Lieutenant Frome looked at Carl. "I'll take you first, Mr. Ebhart, as it was you called in to report the murder in the first place."

"Whatever you say, Lieutenant," Carl said easily. He finished his drink in one gulp, then picked up Mr. Limbo from the bar counter and tucked him under his arm.

The Lieutenant watched with a blank look on his face as Carl walked toward him. "What do you want that dummy with you for?" he asked.

"It takes a dummy to talk to another dummy," Mr. Limbo snapped. "Besides, I want to leave the room. I got a good reason, too. You want to hear it? I got to go, because I got to——"

"All right!" Frome said, his face brick-red. "Come on!"

he waited until Carl and Mr. Limbo were outside the door, then slammed it shut behind him.

There was that silence again for maybe thirty seconds, then Don grunted. "Sometimes I wonder whether Carl should be put away in a private asylum for his own good," he said.

Gregory Payton leaned forward eagerly, his eyes shining behind their windowpanes. "I don't think it's as bad as that," he said. "I've been studying him ever since we met at dinner. He's very sensitive to the fact that I'm a psychiatrist. You noticed how deliberately rude he was to me?"

"That was Mr. Limbo," I reminded him.

"Most interesting," Gregory said happily.

"Uh?" I said.

"Cause and effect," he said. "You see, you're already beginning to identify Mr. Limbo as a person, a human being. Not only that, but you're talking of Carl and Mr. Limbo as two different people."

"What are you getting at?" Don asked him coldly. "That Carl's crazy? I just said that. You don't have to be a psychiatrist to figure that one out!"

Payton shook his head so vigorously that I felt sure some more of his hair had fallen out. "No, no," he said earnestly, "you're absolutely wrong. There's no question of insanity at all. Merely a personality deficiency, you see?"

"No," Don said. "I don't."

Gregory took off his glasses and polished them furiously with his pocket handkerchief. "Carl uses Mr. Limbo as a crutch—a mental crutch, of course. It is Mr. Limbo, you note, who is always rude, contemptuous, iconoclastic, in his conversation, never Carl. The dummy speaks the real thoughts of the man."

"Hey!" I sat up with a jerk. "I've just been insulted!"

"I still say he's crazy," Don said tensely, "and all that double-talk of yours doesn't alter the fact. He treats that dummy like it was a real person—my guess is Carl really thinks it is."

Gregory shook his head again, even more vigorously.

"No, you are willfully misunderstanding me, Don. It's——"

"You're so damned smart," Don told him. "Have you figured out who killed Edwina yet?"

"That is a stupid question," Gregory said firmly. "I'm no detective."

"You've got Carl all figured out," Don went on, with a grin on his face. "Maybe you've got us all figured out? I bet you've got the murderer taped already, but you won't say so in case you're proved wrong!"

Gregory whipped off his glasses and started to polish them again. "I have no idea who killed Edwina," he said evenly, "but if you insist upon an answer to your question, I'll say this—any one of us was capable of killing her."

Wanda took an interest in the conversation for the first time. "Are you including me, darling?" she asked in a soft voice.

"I'm including you," her husband said, "and myself."

"Thank you," she said. "Don't forget to lock your door when you go to bed in case I get any old-fashioned ideas about sleeping with my husband!"

"I . . ." Gregory almost blushed. "Really, Wanda! You must control——"

The door opened again, and everyone looked around quickly to see who it was, forgetting all about Gregory. A uniformed cop stood there glaring at us. "Mr. Donald Ebhart, please," he said.

Don squeezed my hand for a moment. "I hope this doesn't take too long, Mavis," he said. "I'll get back as soon as I can."

"Sure, Don." I smiled up at him. "How's the head now?"

"Lousy!" he said, and got up from the couch and walked over to the door.

About twenty minutes later the cop came in again and called Fabian Dark. Neither Carl nor Don came back into the room, so I guessed the cops were deliberately keeping them out, so they wouldn't have a chance to talk to the rest of us about the questions they'd been asked, or the answers they'd given.

It left only Wanda, Gregory, and myself in the room, and I thought we might as well talk, anyway, so I said to Wanda: "You don't really want him to lock his door, do you? I mean, I know his hair's falling out, and although his name's Gregory he's no Peck, but you did marry him, didn't you, and after all, a husband——"

"Shut up!" she almost spat at me. And after that there just wasn't any conversation at all. Sometimes I wonder what's the use of trying to be friendly with people. I was awfully glad when the cop came back and called my name the next time.

When I got out of the living room, the cop escorted me into the dining room. Lieutenant Frome was at the end of the table, only this time the lights were on and there weren't any candles burning. I was glad about that: candles were going to give me the screaming mimis for the rest of my life.

The Lieutenant had some papers in front of him, a pencil in his hand and a tired look on his face. "Sit down, Mrs. Ebhart," he said briefly, so I sat down in a chair beside him and waited.

"You tell me what happened," he said in a dull voice.

So I told him all about it, from the time I woke up and saw Don was missing, up to the time we saw Edwina's body in the cellar.

"That checks," he said after I'd finished, but he didn't seem terribly happy about it. "This is about the screwiest setup I ever hit! If anybody should have been murdered, it's your husband, but no, it's the housekeeper who gets it!"

"I'm certainly glad it wasn't Don," I told him. "I'd miss him."

"Yeah." He took another look at me and it must have been the sweater, because he seemed to brighten up a little. "Not as much as he'd miss you," he said thoughtfully. "You have any ideas about who'd want to kill the housekeeper?"

"No," I said truthfully.

"What about this lawyer character, Fabian Dark?" he said. "I heard about him talking to the housekeeper after dinner. He must have known of that setup in the cellar."

"I guess he did," I agreed. "But he was talking about Randolph Ebhart. Maybe he knew that Randolph had put those things in the cellar a long time ago."

Frome closed his eyes for a moment. "You aren't going to tell me she was murdered by a ghost! I'll admit the old man was buried here, but——"

"Buried here!" I gurgled. "You mean right here in the house?"

"For crying out loud!" he grunted. "You're married to the eldest son—what did you think that vault was out near the cliff edge—Fort Knox?"

"I didn't know about it," I said truthfully. "I wish I still didn't."

"Anyway," he said, "you don't have any ideas at all who could have wanted to murder her?"

"None," I told him. "I hardly knew her, anyway. I met her for the first time today—or it's yesterday now, I guess."

"You're so right," he said heavily. "It was yesterday. Nobody can pull the wool over your eyes, can they?" He eyed the sweater again for a moment. "Though I wouldn't mind trying myself," he added.

"You just try," I said coldly, "and I'll break both your arms for you, or my name's not Mavis Seidlitz!"

The Lieutenant blinked at me. "Your name's Clare Ebhart," he said slowly. "Isn't it?"

"Of course it is," I smiled nervously at him. "It was a joke, Lieutenant. I couldn't possibly break both your arms, so of course my name isn't Mavis Seidlitz, see?"

He shook his head. "I never met so many screwballs in the one place, either. A guy who carries a wooden dummy around with him all the time, and when you ask a question, it's the dummy who talks back. Then there's the other one, the guy that looks like he's thinking about shooting himself, and what he's worrying about is the millions of dollars he's going to get in a couple of days' time. Now I've got you, a crazy blonde who isn't sure of her own name yet. Mavis Seidlitz—how did you dream up an oddball name like that?"

"I don't see there's anything odd about it," I told him. "I think it's quite a nice name."

"You must be really nuts," he said, "like the rest of them. O.K., no more questions now. You can go back to your room, but not back to the living room until I've finished questioning the others."

"Thank you," I said stiffly. "And what happens if I get murdered on the way up?"

"I'll make a note of it for my report," he said in a tired voice. "Go away, will you? I've got enough troubles already."

I walked out of the dining room and along to the stairs. The lights were switched on this time, which made me feel a little better, but I was running by the time I reached the suite. I stepped inside, slammed the door shut behind me, and leaned against it getting my breath back.

Don was on the couch with a glass in his hand. He looked at me and raised his eyebrows a fraction. "Somebody chasing you?" he asked.

"No," I said breathlessly. "I just wasn't taking any chances."

"What did the Lieutenant say?"

"Nothing, really." I walked over and sat beside him on the couch. "You never told me your father's buried here."

"I never told you about my childhood, either," he said shortly. "There must be a hell of a lot of things I haven't told you, Mavis."

"So don't bite my head off," I told him. "You go on like this I'll start thinking we really are married."

"I'm jumpy," he muttered. "Sorry. I keep thinking about Edwina and that cellar!"

"Don't!" I shivered and moved even closer to him. "What time is it?"

He glanced at his watch. "Four A.M."

"I just know I'll never sleep," I said.

"There's not much chance of anyone sleeping tonight," Don growled. "After that lieutenant has finished with his questions, Fabian wants to see all of us in the dining room."

"Whatever for?" I stared at him.

Don poured himself another drink carefully before he answered. Then he looked up at me, his face blank. "Some talk about a new will," he said flatly.

CHAPTER SEVEN

I sat with Don at one side of the table, and opposite us were Carl and Mr. Limbo, Wanda and Gregory. Fabian was at the head of the table, where Edwina had sat, a bunch of important-looking papers in front of him.

Lieutenant Frome had finished asking questions about ten minutes before, and had left the house. There were some uniformed officers patrolling the grounds outside the house, but none of them were inside.

Fabian looked kind of nervous, and who didn't blame him? He lit himself a cigarette and puffed at it furiously. Don shifted irritably on the chair beside mine.

"All right, Fabian," Carl said evenly. "What's this all about?"

The lawyer cleared his throat a couple of times, then he said jerkily, "Your father made a second will."

"Why haven't we heard about it before?" Don asked coldly.

Fabian shuffled the papers in front of him. "It was your father's express wish that the existence of the second will should be kept secret until now. As you all know, the first will stipulated that the three beneficiaries had to stay in this house for the seventy-two hours prior to Don's thirtieth birthday. Randolph said the second will should be read to all of you after your first twenty-four hours in this house."

"We've been here only twenty-four hours?" Carl asked. Then he grinned suddenly. "It seems like twenty-four days!"

"After what happened tonight," Fabian said, "I've taken

it upon myself to read you the will now. I think it's only fair to everyone."

"You knew, of course," Don said in a rasping voice, "all the time since Father's death that this second will existed. I'm just a little curious about its authenticity, Fabian!"

"It's a legal document all right," Fabian said coldly, "and it's valid. There is nothing to stop a man making two wills, with the second superseding the first. If you remember, Don, Randolph didn't dispose of any of his assets in the first will. He merely disposed of a portion of the income in allowances to Carl, Wanda, and yourself."

Don grunted and slumped back in his chair. I saw the slow smile spread over Wanda's face as she looked at him. "Getting worried, brother dear," she asked, "in case your take isn't as much the second time round?"

"Just what difference does it make, Fabian?" Carl asked casually.

"Randolph's instructions are that I read the whole thing to you," Fabian said. "I think it will be easier if I do that right away."

"That's what I like about your old man, Carl," Mr. Limbo cackled. "He's dead, but he won't lie down."

"Don't start that again!" Wanda said tautly. "I can't stand it!"

Fabian cleared his throat again, then started to read the will. "I, Randolph Irving Ebhart, being of sound mind and body, do hereby declare this to be my very last will and testament."

"That's a break, anyway," Mr. Limbo cackled again. "I was getting worried it'd be like a radio serial—with a cliff-hanger at the end of each installment!"

"Shut up!" Wanda said tensely. "Go on, Fabian."

The papers rustled in Fabian's hands as he continued. "I trust you will permit me some reflections from the grave. Unless Death has intervened, gathered around the table will be my two sons and daughter, my housekeeper and my lawyer. There will also be my eldest son's wife (under the terms of my first will he has naturally married to insure himself of his inheritance). Perhaps Carl and

Wanda are also married, and their respective partners are also seated at the table.

"It gives me some pleasure to picture the scene. I imagine a certain tenseness in the air, an impatience? One thing I am sure of—after some years of living on an allowance, my children's need for money will be desperate.

"No less desperate will be the needs of my housekeeper and my lawyer—" Fabian's voice faltered for a moment, then went on: "sharing as they do those peculiar and expensive tastes I know so well. I wonder, Fabian, just how much of the trust money from my estate you have embezzled by now? Edwina, is there any silver left in the house?

"Don, how much have you borrowed on the strength of your inheritance already? Carl, how many wildcat schemes of yours urgently need an injection of hard cash? Wanda, how much blackmail have you paid in these years, and how much do you owe at this moment?

"I am sure that all of you have a great and urgent need for money. After this length of time, you have probably forgotten my true feelings for all of you. I find it hard to find words to express those feelings. Contempt is one, amusement another. I was unfortunate in my two marriages, even more unfortunate in the fruit of my unions."

Fabian stopped for a moment to light another cigarette, and I could see the sweat standing out on his forehead.

"Is there much more of this?" Wanda asked in a high-pitched voice. "I don't think I can stand it."

"Not much more," Fabian said softly. "Shall I finish the reading now?"

"Of course!" Don snarled. "If she's feeling squeamish, she doesn't have to listen."

The only sound was the faint rustling of paper again, then Fabian picked up where he'd left off. "The provisions of my final will are simple. Firstly, that nine tenths of my estate shall go to the charities named hereunder."

Fabian looked up. "Do you wish me to read the list of charities that benefit?"

"Nine tenths!" Don muttered wildly. "He's crazy! I'll

contest it—I'll fight it through the Supreme Court, I'll——"

"You can't," Fabian said flatly. "It's legal. Randolph took advice from the best brains in the country before he made this second will."

"The old man would," Carl said. "You know better than that, Don."

"Nine tenths!" Don repeated with a stunned look on his face. "That leaves about a million, at the most."

"Anybody got a dime?" Mr. Limbo asked. "This guy wants to buy a cup of coffee!"

"Let's hear the rest of it," Wanda said. "We must get something!"

Fabian nodded. "I'll read the rest of it. . . . The remaining tenth of my estate is to be divided equally between my children, their wives or husbands, my housekeeper, and my lawyer. Provided that the original terms of my first will are strictly adhered to.

"All of you will remain on the Toledo estate for the remaining forty-eight hours of the seventy-two hour period. At midnight of the last day, you will all go to my vault and spend a period of thirty minutes inside, to pay homage to my earthly remains. I hope to be with you in spirit.

"Should any of you die, or have already died, before that time, their share of the estate will be divided equally among the survivors.

"I shall now leave you to reflect upon the fairness with which you have been treated, and remind you that the Ebhart fortunes were built on the old but good principle of 'survival of the fittest.'"

There was a silence after Fabian had dropped the papers back onto the table. Don rubbed his forehead with a shaking hand. "I want to get this straight," he said hoarsely. "What does this mean to us, Fabian? In money?"

Fabian clasped his hands in front of him primly. "It means there are now six of us to share the remaining tenth of the estate," he said. "Each share is worth something under two hundred thousand dollars."

Wanda laughed suddenly—a harsh, grating sound. "Trust Father!" she said bitterly. "He knew us! He knew just how deep we'd get, thinking we were all going to inherit a fortune. Even with Don getting the lion's share, Carl and I would have got a million. Now we've got to be content with a fifth of that!"

"It's still a lot of money," Fabian said mildly.

"Enough for you to put back what you've embezzled from the trust funds?" Mr. Limbo cackled.

Fabian's face darkened. "Enough to buy you out of your wildcat investments?" he said to Carl.

"Why stop there?" Mr. Limbo said. "Enough for Wanda to meet her blackmail payments? Enough for Don to repay what he's borrowed already?"

"Shut up!" Don said coldly. "What's the damned use of us fighting each other about it? Fabian says the will can't be broken, and that's the end of it. We've got to live out this farce for another forty-eight hours and there's nothing we can do about it!"

"Pay homage to his earthly remains!" Wanda said viciously. "I'd like to set fire to that vault!"

"I wonder," Carl said softly, "whether we're all missing the point of the will, or just pretending we are."

"What do you mean?" Gregory Payton asked him.

"Survival of the fittest," Carl said in a low voice. "We all need more than the amount we'll receive now. The old man provided just one way to get it."

"Go on!" Don told him.

"The remaining tenth is shared among those of us who are living forty-eight hours from now," Carl said. "The less there are alive at the end of the time, the greater the share they'll receive."

"So?" Don said tautly.

"So this will is a classic example of the old man's sense of humor," Carl said. "It's nothing but an invitation to murder!"

"Of course," Gregory said. He took off his glasses and began polishing them with his pocket handkerchief. "We can all see that now. I find it an interesting thought that Fabian, as Mr. Ebhart's lawyer, must have known the

55

contents of the second will all the time. It gave him a definite advantage over the rest of us."

"Just what do you mean by that?" Fabian asked in an ugly voice.

"It possibly gave you plenty of time to make your own preparations," Gregory said. He held his glasses up to the light and squinted at them to make sure the lenses were spotless. "I mean, there's one less to share already, isn't there? Edwina has already been murdered!"

CHAPTER EIGHT

It was six o'clock in the morning and daylight outside when I got to bed. My watch said it was just after two in the afternoon when I woke up again. I felt hungry, but I guessed there wouldn't be much room service after what had happened to Edwina last night, so I'd just have to stay hungry for a while longer.

I had a shower and got dressed. I put on a black skirt and a white transparent blouse. Underneath I wore the black slip that the ad described as "Two thirds lace and one third legion." Under the blouse it was really two thirds Mavis and one third lace, but I figured they couldn't have known I was going to buy one of their slips, could they?

The living room was empty, so I went over and knocked on Don's door. I didn't get any answer, so I opened the door and looked into his room, but he wasn't there.

The house seemed deserted when I got downstairs and looked hopefully into the dining room, but there wasn't anybody around, not even a cloth on the table. So I went into the living room and found somebody—Gregory Payton.

"Good morning," I said, and smiled, because I was glad there was someone around, even if it was only him.

"Hello, Mavis," he said, and then his smile froze as he

stared at me. He looked like one of Kinsey's disciples who's just discovered a brand-new field of research.

"Where is everybody?" I asked him.

"Wanda's resting," he told me. "She's still very much upset by what happened last night. Both Don and Carl have gone out somewhere, I think. Probably walking in the grounds—they can't leave the estate."

"Together?"

He shook his head. "I saw Don leave about an hour ago, and Carl left only ten minutes back. I haven't seen Fabian this morning at all."

"Have we still got the police around?" I asked him.

"They're still here," Gregory said. "There's one of them in the front hall and a carload of them down at the gates, keeping the newspapermen from getting in. Apparently the name Ebhart still has some influence around these parts."

"Oh," I said.

The phone rang shrilly and Gregory moved over to answer it. He spoke a couple of words, then looked across at me. "It's for you," he said.

I walked over and took the phone from him and said "Hello?" into it.

"Mrs. Ebhart?" a man's voice asked.

"Sure," I said, because whoever it was wasn't going to fool me into admitting I was Mavis Seidlitz again.

"This is Sergeant Donavan," he said. "I'm on duty at the gates. There's a guy here claims he's a personal friend of yours and wants to see you. Name of Rio. O.K. to send him up?"

"It certainly is," I said. "And thank you for calling."

I put the phone back and saw Gregory looking at me expectantly. "It's a friend of mine," I explained. He looked at me blankly. "Well," I said impatiently, "you know what a friend is, don't you? Even if you don't have any, you must hear about them from people who lie on that couch of yours all day and want to get adjusted."

Gregory blinked twice. "I know what a friend is," he said slowly.

"You could have said so in the first place," I told him.

"Then we wouldn't have had all this trouble, would we?"

"No," he said slowly, "I guess not."

"That's the trouble with you psychiatrists," I smiled tolerantly at him. "You just have to complicate everything, even the simplest things. Using all those long words when you mean 'Nut!' I've heard of that Freud character, and if you ask me, his trouble was he had a dirty mind!"

"What about Jung and Adler?" Gregory asked in a choked sort of voice.

"I couldn't say," I said. "I never had them. I guess I'm a healthy type of girl. German measles is all I've ever had, really. If you'll excuse me, Greg, I have to go meet Johnny now."

"Johnny?"

"My friend. F-R-E-N-D. Don't let's start that routine again, please!"

I left him standing there and walked out of the room and along to the front hall. The door was open, and there was a uniformed cop standing just outside. He saw me coming and stiffened all over. "I'm Mrs. Ebhart," I told him when I reached the doorway.

"You're a lot more than that, lady," he said hoarsely.

"A friend of mine is coming," I went on, ignoring his glazed eyes. "A Mr. Rio."

"They called me from the gates and said he was on his way," the cop muttered. "Anything I can do?"

"Not a thing," I said, "except maybe you can take that look out of your eye."

"I'd have to be dead to do that, lady," he said, "and even then, I'm not sure."

Johnny's car came into sight then, and I ran past the cop to meet him. It stopped right beside me, and I opened the door for Johnny to get out. He had a worried look on his face and he didn't look at all pleased to see me.

"Where can we talk?" he grunted. "Somewhere private."

"We can go up to my room," I said. "Nobody will disturb us there—Don's gone out for a while."

"Oh, fine!" Johnny said. "How will it look to the rest of

58

them? Your husband's out and another guy visits, so right away you take him up to your room!"

"You've got a nasty mind," I said reprovingly. "Like that Freud."

"Freud? Is he one of the family?" Johnny asked anxiously. Sometimes he can be so dumb, I wonder he remembers to shave himself in the mornings.

"I'm talking about *the* Freud," I said patiently. "The original psychopath who started the whole business."

"I should ask!" Johnny groaned as if he'd got a sudden pain. "Where can we talk?"

"Why don't we talk out here?" I suggested. "We could take a walk around the place. I haven't been outside since we got here."

"O.K.," he said, and took my elbow. "Let's walk."

For the first quarter mile it was more like a run than a walk. I'm not the sort of girl who dislikes exercise: it's good for the figure, but there are limits. Finally Johnny slowed down a little. "Let's hear it," he said.

"What?"

"The murder the headlines are screaming about!" he snarled. "What the hell happened last night?"

"None of your business!" I said tartly, but then I figured he must still be talking about the murder. "The housekeeper, Edwina, was killed," I told him.

"I know that. It was in the papers," he said. "You'd better start from the beginning, and don't leave anything out."

"A girl's entitled to some privacy," I said. "After all, we're a private detective agency, aren't we? I mean, why do we call ourselves that if we don't have any privacy? Isn't that what they call fraud?"

"All right!" he yelped. "You can censor the intimate details, just tell me the rest of it!"

So I told him the rest of it while we kept on walking slowly around the grounds. By the time I'd finished, we were right up to the edge of the cliff, and there was all that blue ocean below us.

Johnny was staring at me with his mouth sagging open, and I knew he was too used to having me around to look that way, even if my skirt *had* lifted around the top of my thighs with the high wind. "What's the matter?" I asked him.

"Let's sit down," he mumbled, so we sat down on the grass and I tried to pull my skirt down a couple of times, but the wind was too fierce, and I thought what the hell, anyway?

With his head resting on his hands, Johnny was staring vaguely out to sea. "Mr. Limbo," he said in a muffled voice. "A psychiatrist and a redheaded wife. A lawyer who knows all about the black arts. . . . Candles and masks and a nude body in chains in the cellar! . . ." He looked at me wildly. "I wouldn't believe it for a moment, except for one thing."

"What's that?" I asked him.

"You told it to me," he said resignedly. "You couldn't have made it up, you don't have that much imagination, Mavis. Your dreams don't go past something a shade over six feet tall with a voice like Gregory Peck's."

"I always fill in more detail than that," I said defensively.

"Never mind," Johnny said abruptly. "What did this Lieutenant—Frome—think about it?"

"I don't know," I said. "He didn't tell me."

"Understandable," Johnny grunted. "You were just one more screwbell in the bunch to him."

"If you dragged me up here just to look at my legs and insult me, Johnny Rio," I said, "I'm——"

"I'm not insulting you," Johnny said patiently. "Neither am I looking at your legs—that I can do almost any time. I don't have to come here and make a production out of it!" He took another look and brightened a little. "Come to think of it, it's a long time since I saw black lace."

I pulled my skirt down hastily and hung onto it. "You're not answering my question," I told him. "I want to know——"

"O.K.," he said, "let's start from the beginning. Don was going to inherit a fortune, had lost two wives, and needed his third wife to be alive and here two days from now if he was going to collect—right?"

Johnny grinned at me. "Why don't we take a look inside?" he asked. "While we're here it seems a pity not to pay our respects to the mortal remains of Randolph Ebhart."

"You can't," I said quickly. "There's a padlock on the door."

"It might not be locked," he persisted. "Let's try it."

He walked around to the door with me following him reluctantly, and tried the padlock. "It's locked all right," Johnny grunted, then he bent down and took a closer look. "But it's been opened recently. Look."

I took a cautious look and saw what he was getting at. There were traces of oil around the lock, and two of the chain links were bright, standing out against the rust of the others.

"So somebody had the same idea," Johnny said. "But they had a key to get inside." He straightened up again. "I don't imagine it's important, anyway. Let's get back to the house. I should be going."

"Johnny!" I said faintly, and clutched his shoulder.

"What's the matter with you?" He turned and looked at me closely. "You feeling ill or something?"

"I was just thinking," I said. "Last night at dinner, Fabian Dark said to Edwina that darkness was something Randolph Ebhart didn't have to learn from his first wife. Then Fabian said he was sure she remembered the candles burning in the cellar, the masks and the chains, and he'd always thought she'd helped Randolph—been a sort of handmaiden."

"Did he now?" Johnny said softly. "I should have remembered that, you told me before."

"Well," I swallowed hard and tried to keep the shivers out of my voice. "You don't suppose . . . that 'I remain'—it couldn't mean that somehow Randolph Ebhart let himself out of this tomb and went to the cellar and . . ."

"Are you crazy?" Johnny asked.

"But if what Fabian Dark said was true, Edwina used to go down to the cellar with Randolph." My voice was really shaking now. "Last night the cellar must have been set up in exactly the same way as it was before he died five years ago. The marks on the chain—you said someone had been inside that tomb recently—what if it was the other way round—someone has been *out* of the tomb recently!"

"What you need is some food," Johnny said soberly. "But I have to admit your thinking is smarter than mine."

"I could have told you that months ago," I said. "I'm not sure if we'll get any food now there isn't a housekeeper any more."

"Too bad," Johnny said. "I'll eat in Santa Barbara."

"Johnny?" I said.

"Yeah?"

"Just what part of my thinking was smarter than yours?"

"Randolph Ebhart, the fun and games he played with Edwina in the cellar—that part."

"But it's Fabian Dark who knew all about that," I said, "not me."

"And I would have forgotten it was Fabian Dark, if you hadn't reminded me," Johnny said. "Let's go."

CHAPTER | NINE

Johnny left me at the front door, and I stood for a moment and watched him drive away.

I felt sorry to see him go, because nobody was going to try and murder him in Santa Barbara, unless he got too fresh with some waitress, and somehow Johnny always knows when to stop, even if it is the last moment.

As I walked inside the house I could feel Sergeant Donavan's eyes boring holes through the back of my blouse. So I wiggled my tail a little, the way the air hostesses do, and I thought if it kept him awake nights it served him right for looking.

The suite was empty, so I guessed Don hadn't got back

yet. I had a nice luxurious bath and then got dressed. The chemise number in black lace with a satin belt just above the knees was the answer to gloom, I figured. The only other decision I had to make was which perfume to wear.

I always carry two: "I Surrender" and "My Sin." That way I'm prepared for any situation. After last night, "I Surrender" seemed a bit obvious, so I dabbed some of "My Sin" in the places where a girl dabs perfume and the details are a secret between us girls.

It was starting to get dark outside, and I was starting to get scared inside. I didn't want to sit around that big suite all on my own, so I went downstairs again and into the living room.

Fabian Dark was the only person in the room, and he was over by the bar, pouring himself a drink. He smiled at me with that catlike smile of his: it made me feel I'd forgotten to put on any clothes at all. "Charming!" he said. "That gown is definitely a morale booster, Mavis. Let me make you a drink."

"Thanks," I told him as I walked over to the bar. "I'll have a gimlet."

Fabian made the drink and handed it to me. "The domestic affairs seem to have been finally organized," he said. "I understand dinner will be at seven-thirty. You weren't in the house for lunch, so you were fortunately spared the horror that masqueraded under the name of beef hash."

"Don't mention food to me," I said wistfully, and drank some of the gimlet.

"Everyone seems to have had some exercise but me." Fabian shrugged his shoulders. "You, Don, and Carl have all been out. The Paytons seem to have kept to themselves—I haven't seen them at all today. Perhaps it's their day for self-analysis: I can understand it keeping them busy."

"Have you heard any more about what happened last night?" I asked him.

"I saw Lieutenant Frome this afternoon," Fabian said easily. "I understand he will be back later tonight. He didn't tell me if he had made any progress at all. Poor

Edwina! I can't think why anyone should want to strangle her."

"Tell me about Randolph Ebhart," I said casually.

"What about him?" Fabian raised his eyebrows slightly.

"Well, what sort of man he was, stuff like that."

Fabian lit himself a cigarette with exaggerated care, then looked at me again. "That's a very complex question, Mavis," he said softly. "To me, there were two things about him that impressed me above all others. He was a very passionate man, and he had a very strong sense of humor."

"I can see what you mean about the passion part," I said. "He and two wives and then there was Edwina. . . ."

"What you really want to ask me is about the cellar." Fabian smiled wickedly at me. "Isn't it? The masks and the chains. . . . There are some people who find pleasure in the abnormal. I don't doubt Gregory Payton has words for them and trite little phrases to explain why. . . . Randolph was one of those people, and Edwina was another."

"You mean she liked being down in that cellar?" I said, and shuddered at the thought.

"But of course," Fabian said. "I would think she liked being in the cellar last night. I would even suggest that when those strong hands fastened around her throat, she ——" He stopped suddenly, and I heard footsteps coming into the room. "Can I get you another drink, Mavis?" Fabian asked smoothly.

"No, thanks," I said breathlessly.

"You can get me one," Carl's voice drawled from behind me. "How about you, Mr. Limbo?"

"No, not for me," Mr. Limbo's strident cackle cut across the room. "I wouldn't trust that creep to pour me a drink—I bet he can just squeeze his finger tips and arsenic drips out!"

Fabian kept the smile on his face, but his lips thinned out almost into a straight line. "Last night," he said conversationally to Carl, "when the police were questioning you, there was an interesting discussion about your sanity. Don thinks you are mad, of course. The only dissenting opinion was Payton's. But then, psychiatrists don't accept madness as a technical term, do they? They have all sorts of more impressive three and four-syllable words for it."

"The little man," Carl said softly, "who so desperately needs a big whip. What frightened you in your youth, Fabian? Your teddy bear?"

Carl walked over to the bar and sat Mr. Limbo down on the counter. Then he looked at Fabian with an easy grin on his face.

"The service here is lousy," Mr. Limbo said suddenly. "I bet that creep don't even know how to pour a drink! What use is he?"

"He'd make a very nice paperweight," Carl answered. "He's around the right size and weight. If we had a desk, we could use him, Mr. Limbo."

Fabian stared dully at Carl for a few seconds longer. Then he suddenly took the ice pick from the counter and swung it over his head in a vicious arc that descended towards Carl's face with savage speed. Carl's right hand shot out and grabbed his wrist, twisting it, so that Fabian cried out in pain and dropped the pick. "You should remember to fasten the chains first," Carl told him.

Then there was a long silence, while Fabian turned away slowly and walked across the room toward the door. The only sound was the click as the door closed behind him.

"I think the broad's changed her mind, from the look on her face," Mr. Limbo said. "Right now, she needs a drink."

"I'll make sure she gets one," Carl said.

The smile on his face when he handed me the drink was a lot different from the one he'd given Fabian. It gave me a kind of defenseless feeling under the chemise. Like the feeling you get when you're standing with your back to the light, and you can't remember whether you're wearing a slip or not.

"I wouldn't let Fabian worry you, Mavis," Carl said quietly. "You could take care of him with one hand tied behind your back."

"Right now, it's not Fabian who worries me," I admitted. "It's you."

"That's interesting," he said. "Let's talk about it for a few thousand words. With any luck, Don might not get back tonight at all."

"Why do you think that?" I asked him nervously.

"Just wishful thinking," he said, "but my luck would never be that good."

"Ask her if they sleep in different rooms," Mr. Limbo whispered hoarsely. "If they do, you still got a chance of sneaking along the balcony in the middle of the night."

"Don't you dare!" I told them both indignantly. "I get nightmares as it is, without having that dummy leering down at me when I wake up."

"She's married to a Don," Mr. Limbo said. "Tell her my full name, Carl. Tell her I'm Don Juan Limbo, and she's crazy about me, and she knows it."

"Be quiet," Carl said severely. "You're not doing me any good at all. You did have an interesting question there. . . . Do you, Mavis?"

"If you mean what I think you mean, then I'm not answering that question," I said flatly.

"Do you sleep in different rooms?" Carl asked patiently.

"Oh," I said. "Of course we do!"

The door opened, and I heard footsteps coming into the room again. Carl muttered something under his breath which sounded rude, even from the tone of his voice.

"Well, well, well!" Mr. Limbo said brightly. "If it isn't the headshrinker and his sleeping partner. Don't look now, Carl, but your schizophrenia is showing."

Wanda and Gregory Payton came up to the bar beside me. Wanda was wearing a dream of a thing in blue silk which someone had painted onto her. That was how it looked, anyway.

"I'm beginning to think you must be frightened of me, Carl," Gregory said pleasantly. "You protest too much about my profession."

"Isn't he something?" Mr. Limbo asked admiringly. "The first time I ever saw a vacuum wearing cheaters!"

"Don't we have enough to contend with right now,

without you fooling around with that dummy and your cheap insults?" Wanda said frigidly to Carl.

"You mustn't let Mr. Limbo upset you, my dear," Greg said gently to her. "Because that's what Mr. Limbo is for —right, Carl?"

Carl shrugged his shoulders. "I must remember to ask him sometime. Make you a drink?"

"Scotch for me," Wanda said. She looked my chemise up and down. "What's the belt for—protection?"

"Some girls need it." I smiled fondly at her. "It must be nice to be like you, Wanda—safe!"

"Happy family," Mr. Limbo sang suddenly in an awful parody of that old number "Happy Holiday." His cracked voice set up echoes around the room. "Happy Family . . . while the merry chains are clinking!"

"I can't stand it any more!" Wanda screamed. She grabbed Mr. Limbo by one leg, then hurled him across the room.

The dummy hit the wall with an awful crash, then fell to the floor. Its head rolled about three feet away from the body and lay there, the face chipped and battered beyond recognition.

Carl moved around the bar, then walked across the room slowly and picked up the head and body of the dummy. "Poor Mr. Limbo!" he said suddenly. "Murdered by a crazy woman. Maybe Edwina got killed the same way."

Wanda ran toward him, sobbing hysterically. Her fists beat a wild tattoo against his chest, until he pushed her away impatiently. She stumbled, lost her balance, and fell heavily to the floor.

"You can't do that!" Greg bleated and pawed uselessly at Carl's shoulder. "Leave my wife alone, you hear me?"

"A pleasure," Carl said. "And you leave *me* alone!" He punched Greg neatly in the stomach.

Greg staggered backwards, doubled up, with both hands clasped to his middle. He collapsed onto the floor beside his wife and sat there, moaning softly.

I heard the click as the door opened again, and a voice asked: "A second murder, Carl? With witnesses?"

Don walked across the room towards him quickly. Carl looked at him, a twisted grin on his face. "Just another demonstration of family affection, half-brother," he said in a soft voice. "You want to ask Wanda about the second murder. She just killed Mr. Limbo."

"I hope he's not repairable," Don said shortly. "That damned dummy was starting to get on my nerves."

"Maybe you've got a guilty conscience, half-brother," Carl said. Then he cradled the remains of the dummy gently in his arms and headed toward the door, talking to the battered wooden pieces in a soft, crooning sort of voice, the kind of voice you use to comfort a child that's been hurt.

The door closed behind him, and Don looked at me, his eyes bulging slightly. "What the hell's going on?" he asked.

I told him the main points, while Wanda climbed back onto her feet and Greg still sat on the floor, nursing his middle.

"I said Carl's crazy," Don grunted. "This act with the dummy only proves it. He should be locked away somewhere."

Greg slowly tottered onto his feet, his face a light green color. "I think perhaps you're right," he said painfully. "I didn't know the violence was so close to the surface."

"You're so damned smart!" Wanda said fiercely. "After it happened! You're not even a head-shrinker, let alone a man!"

"You're upset," Greg said evenly. "Emotionally off balance. Why don't you have that drink?"

"You worm!" Wanda sneered at him, her voice growing stronger. "It makes me sick, right deep down inside me, just to look at you! Get out of my sight!"

Greg looked at Don and me, his eyes blank behind the rimless glasses. "She doesn't know what she's saying," he said politely. "Excuse me." He took a step forward and then slapped Wanda across the side of her face so hard that she staggered and fell to her knees. "Get up!" he said softly. "Get up onto your feet!"

She got up slowly, the imprint of his hand painted in

vivid red across her cheek. There was naked fear showing in her eyes as she looked at him.

Greg smiled at her. "That's better," he said in the same soft voice. "A little silence goes a long way at times like these. Now, you'd better go to your room."

Wanda walked across the room with dragging steps, and Greg waited until the door had closed behind her. Then he looked at us and smiled cheerfully. "It must be nearly time for dinner," he said. "I don't know about you, but I'm hungry!"

Don looked at me and shrugged his shoulders helplessly, and I shrugged mine right back and felt the chemise take up the strain. "I have to say one thing for my family," Don said wonderingly. "They may all be crazy, but they don't make the mistake of marrying into sanity!"

"I really think we should go in to dinner," Greg said mildly. "I understand Lieutenant Frome wishes to see all of us here at eight-thirty. It doesn't leave us much time."

We followed him out of the living room and along to the dining room. I was glad to see the electric light was switched on tonight, so I didn't have to watch the candles flicker all the time. There were only the three of us at the table, the others didn't put in an appearance. They didn't miss anything—the food was awful, like the meal I cooked in my apartment once for a guy I was trying to convince I was a domesticated home-loving girl. The way it turned out, I needn't have bothered. He wasn't interested in a domesticated, homely girl.

After we'd finished dinner, we went back into the living room, and found Lieutenant Frome already waiting for us. Greg Payton joined his wife, sitting not very close to her on one of the couches. Greg looked his usual serene self, but Wanda had the shakes just a little.

Fabian Dark sat by himself, his hands clasped across his stomach, and he smiled amiably at me as we came into the room. We sat on the other couch, and Don pressed his thigh against mine reassuringly—at least, I think that was what it was meant to be. About five minutes later Carl came into the room, and slumped into the nearest armchair.

Lieutenant Frome stood with his back to the bar, and glared at each of us in turn. "All right," he said harshly. "Last night a woman was murdered, and the murderer is right here sitting in this room. I'm going to find out which one of you it is, and you're all going to sit right here until I have!"

He glared at us again, but nobody tried to argue with him, so he cleared his throat and went on talking. "I'm satisfied it had to be someone inside the house," he said. "It would have been impossible for anyone outside to have done it. The closest we can get to the time of the murder is 2:30 A.M. Let's just check again what everybody was doing around that time."

The Lieutenant studied the sheaf of notes he held in his right hand, so I took the opportunity to lift Don's hand from my thigh, because Fabian was watching us with that nasty smile of his, and it made me feel embarrassed.

"According to your statements last night," Frome said, looking up suddenly, "Mr. and Mrs. Payton were in their room asleep. They knew nothing of what happened until they were waked by the police and told to come downstairs. Mr. Dark's story is the same."

He looked at Don and me, then at Carl, who was staring blankly straight ahead of him, without even seeming to hear what the Lieutenant was saying. "The other three of you were much more active," Frome said in a sarcastic voice. "Mr. Donald Ebhart thought he heard a noise in the cellar, so he went to investigate and was hit over the head as he reached the bottom of the stairs.

"Mr. Carl Ebhart also heard a noise and got up to investigate. Mrs. Donald Ebhart woke up hearing noises and found her husband had disappeared, so she went to investigate both the noise and the disappearance. On the way she met Mr. Carl, so the two of them went down to the cellar, discovered her husband, who was still unconscious, and finally the body of the housekeeper as well."

Lieutenant Frome folded his notes carefully and stuffed them into the inside pocket of his jacket. "Anybody want to argue about that—change their story in any way?" he asked.

I guess nobody did, because nobody said anything.

"All right," Frome said again, which was silly. He kept on saying that, and it wasn't. "We'll start with the setup in the cellar. Who knew what it was like down there?"

There was silence for a few seconds, then Carl said, "Fabian Dark," in an expressionless voice. "He reminded Edwina of it last night after dinner. Don and Mavis were there: they heard him say it."

Frome looked at us and I nodded my head. Don grunted a "Yes" at him. So then Frome looked at Fabian coldly.

"Of course I knew about the cellar," Fabian said in a calm voice. "So did the others. By others, I mean Don, Carl, and Wanda. Randolph Ebhart found his pleasures in strange ways. . . . That was one of them."

"It had to be somebody who knew about that cellar who dragged the poor woman down there," Frome said.

Fabian giggled. "Really, Lieutenant. 'Poor woman' is overstating things a little, you know. I don't doubt that Edwina went down to the cellar quite happily and of her own free will. She used to be a very active partner in the amusements when Randolph was alive."

The Lieutenant's face reddened. "You mean to tell me she . . . yeah, it figures! In this house, I guess anything goes!"

"I don't doubt Wanda told her husband about it, and Don told his wife," Fabian said. "So, in fact, all of us knew about the cellar."

"According to your statements last night, none of you know of a motive for the housekeeper's murder," Frome went on. "Anybody had any second thoughts about that?"

"The Ebharts are a strange family," Fabian said. "They always have been. You might have to look beyond the bounds of logic for your motive, Lieutenant."

Frome blinked at him. "You mean I got to find a nut?"

"Exactly," Fabian nodded. "I was wondering. It may be it's impossible to hit yourself over the back of the head, but it's not impossible to hit the back of your head against something—a wall maybe—is it?"

"Go on," Frome told him.

73

"It's only a thought," Fabian said softly. "The body is found in the cellar; a man is also found there. But he gets nothing but sympathy because he has a bruise on the back of his head. Maybe he had just killed Edwina when he heard the others coming down the cellar stairs. He would have no means of escape. Surely, under those circumstances, the obvious thing to do would be to hit his head against the wall, lie on the floor and feign unconsciousness?"

The Lieutenant looked at Don. "What do you say to that, Mr. Ebhart?" he asked.

"It's a lie, of course," Don said coldly. "Fabian's wriggling, Lieutenant. As my half-brother told you, it was Fabian who mentioned the cellar to Edwina last night. According to Mr. Dark, everyone else knew about the cellar—that my father and Edwina used to play games down there. I didn't know it, and I'm sure the others didn't either. I wonder how Fabian knew. I'm wondering if he took my father's place over the last five years. None of the rest of us have been near this house since my father's death. But Fabian would have made regular calls as the administrator of the estate."

"That makes sense to me," Carl said in a wooden voice. "It needn't necessarily be murder, Lieutenant. She could have been killed accidentally in a fit of overenthusiasm. Payton's a psychiatrist—ask him what he thinks. Ask him what those masks and chains add up to."

Frome looked at Greg. "Well?"

Greg smiled aimlessly. "It could be, Lieutenant. It's not that uncommon. Sadism and masochism can often go hand in hand. There are people who derive pleasure from inflicting pain, and some derive pleasure from receiving pain. Carl's suggestion that the death was an accident is a reasonable premise, psychologically speaking."

"If you're looking for one of either breed, Lieutenant," Carl said, "you have a choice. From what happened in here just before dinner, Wanda enjoys being beaten up by her husband, and he enjoys hitting her. If it comes to that, you've only got their word they were in bed asleep when it happened. Maybe there was a threesome in the cellar?"

"You lying——" Wanda shouted. "What were you doing wandering about the house in the middle of the night, anyway? Maybe you'd just come up from the cellar when you met Mavis. Then you had to pretend you'd only just left your room, and go down with her again. You damned near murdered me before dinner. You hit me, and you hit Greg!"

"Just exactly what did happen in here before dinner?" the Lieutenant asked in a mild voice.

Greg told him what had happened when Wanda broke Carl's dummy. "I don't doubt he would have gone to much greater violence," Greg said calmly, "only Don's arrival in the room stopped him. It could be that Edwina said something about the dummy last night that brought on his fury.

"If Fabian's story is true, it wouldn't have been hard for Carl to persuade Edwina to go down to the cellar with him. Once they were down there, it would have been child's play for him to kill her. He could have put her into the chains afterwards to try and throw suspicion onto someone else—Fabian, perhaps?"

"I remember," Wanda said in a tight voice, "Father used to say Don was vicious, but Carl was crazy."

"And he called you a slut," Carl said easily. "And he was right."

Wanda looked at him murderously, then swung around to face her husband. "Are you going to just sit there while he insults me?" she demanded.

"I am," Greg told her. He took off his glasses and started to polish them vigorously. "If you wanted a knight in shining armor, my dear, to defend your honor, you should have married someone else, I'm afraid."

"You coward!" she said contemptuously. "You miserable cockroach! You . . ."

"What a beautiful couple they make!" Fabian chuckled delightedly. "They went to Cuba for their honeymoon, Lieutenant, as I remember. That's where Wanda learned about cockroaches, and Gregory learned about women, I imagine."

"Why don't we stop enjoying ourselves for a moment,"

Carl said quietly, "and tell the Lieutenant the truth?"

"The truth?" Frome asked hopefully.

"About the second will," Carl said. "You're the lawyer, Fabian. You give the Lieutenant the details."

Fabian didn't look enthusiastic about the idea. Then he saw the look on Frome's face, so he shrugged his shoulders and told him the details.

"But that gives everybody an equal motive!" Frome gurgled when Fabian had finished. "That just makes it worse!"

He took a large white handkerchief from his pocket and mopped his face vigorously with it. Then he shook his head a couple of times. He was the first guy I ever saw drowning in the middle of a living-room floor.

CHAPTER TEN

It was eleven o'clock exactly when we got up to the suite. I sat down in an armchair while Don made us a drink. Lieutenant Frome had finally given up asking questions, and from the look on his face when he left, he was going out to shoot himself. I didn't blame him: the more I was around the Ebhart family, the more I felt the same way. With the exception of Don, of course.

Don gave me the drink and took his over to an armchair facing mine. "What a night!" He grinned bleakly at me. "I started to feel sorry for Frome after a while. The way he's going, he doesn't have a hope in hell of finding Edwina's killer!"

"Do you have any ideas, Don?" I asked him.

"Sure," he said. "I did it, then slugged myself over the back of the head when I heard you and Carl coming down the stairs."

"Seriously?"

He shook his head. "No. It doesn't make any sort of

sense to me. If anybody should have been killed, it was you."

"Don," I said hastily. "I'm still alive—don't knock it!"

"The only one who knew about the second will was Fabian, of course," he said slowly, "but I can't imagine Fabian as a cold-blooded killer."

"You know something," I said slowly, "I've been thinking."

"Take it easy, Mavis," he said anxiously. "Don't lose your head the way Mr. Limbo did."

"There's a difference between me and Mr. Limbo," I told him. "I'm no dummy."

"This is not necessarily the opinion of the proprietor," Don grinned. "Go on."

"I think it was Fabian killed her," I said.

"Why?"

"Well, it was him reminded Edwina about the cellar and those things in it last night," I said. "And you can sort of feel it when you're around him. He's unclean, somehow."

"A woman's intuition?" Don raised his eyebrows and looked terribly superior.

"If you don't want to hear about my plan, that's O.K.," I said casually. "I don't really need you. I guess Carl will help me."

"Carl!" Don snarled. "Don't you ever get near him if I'm not somewhere around. What plan? What are you babbling about now?"

"I warn you," I said. "If you keep sounding like Johnny Rio, I won't be able to think about you romantically any more."

"I'm sorry, Mavis, honey," Don said quickly.

He came across and sat on the arm of my chair, then put his arm around my shoulders. It made it hard for me to concentrate.

"Go on, honey," he said softly. "You were saying something about a plan?"

"I was," I said shakily, "but if you keep on, I'll forget all about it."

"Good," he said. "This is all part of my plan."

I pushed his hand away. "Be serious, Don! You know what I think?"

"No," he said in a resigned voice, "but I'm obviously going to any minute from now."

"Look," I said, "if somebody had killed you or me, as your wife, the motive would have been obvious, wouldn't it, under the terms of the first will?"

"The money," he said. "Sure."

"Even if they hired somebody to do it, or promised them part of the inheritance, it would still be obvious."

"I guess so."

I smiled up at him triumphantly, because I knew it was a terrific idea, and it was all mine. "Supposing one of them, or all of them, hired somebody to cheat you out of your inheritance," I said. "And the one they hired was very clever, and very nasty too."

"I guess he'd have to be all of that," Don said. "What are you trying to tell me? One of the family hired an assassin who was so dumb he killed the wrong person?"

"No," I said. "I wish you'd listen, Don! He killed the right person, and now he's going to frame you for the murder."

Don stared at me for a long moment. "I'm not with you, honey," he said finally. "I guess it has been a tiring day. Why don't we go to bed. . . . Well, why don't we?"

I took a deep breath which didn't help Don's concentration, and tried again. "Supposing Carl or Wanda made Fabian a proposition in the first place—a part of the inheritance if he made sure you didn't inherit? Supposing he has been playing games down in the cellar with Edwina ever since your father died. He'd know it would be no trouble to get her down there, and once he'd got those chains around her wrists and ankles, he could kill her easily, couldn't he?"

"I guess so," Don said reluctantly. "But why should he go along with a proposition like that? He'd know he'd never collect from the others, because he knew about the second will."

"That's it!" I said triumphantly. "He knew about it, but the others didn't. He knew that the less of us around, forty-eight hours from now, the more he'd collect. So if he murdered Edwina and had you framed for it, that would be two people out of the way!"

Don shrugged his shoulders. "It sounds reasonable. But how can he frame me for something I didn't do?"

"I thought he was trying pretty hard tonight," I told him. "But Fabian's cunning: he didn't make it too obvious that he was. And don't forget, if my theory's right, there's someone else involved. The one who hired Fabian to get rid of you. If they get together they'll tell Frome a story that could put you right into the gas chamber!"

Don's face hardened. "Maybe that isn't such a crazy idea of yours, after all," he said. "It could just be possible. Sometime tomorrow they could fake some evidence to prove I killed Edwina." He paused a moment. "You said something about a plan, Mavis?"

"I think Fabian's—well—attracted to me," I said modestly.

"Any man in possession of his sight would be," Don said promptly. "I'll accept that."

"Supposing I went to his room in a little while," I said. "I could tell him you were fast asleep, and didn't know I'd gone."

"What then?" Don asked harshly.

"I could tell him how attractive I think he is, and I'm curious about that cellar—sort of make him think I'd like to play games down there myself."

"And?"

"And if I'm right, he'll probably take me down there," I said. "And when we're down there, I could maybe trick him into admitting he killed Edwina. You know—heat of the moment, and all that jazz."

"Fine!" he said. "Then having confessed to you, he strangles you to keep you from talking."

"He could have that idea," I admitted, "but he won't."

"You have one good reason why he won't?"

"The best," I said happily. "You!"

Don looked at me with his mouth sagging open. "What?"

"You," I repeated. "Because when I go to Fabian's

room, you go straight down to the cellar and hide in there. As soon as you hear Fabian confess, you grab him. How about that?"

"It's the craziest idea I ever heard!" he shouted.

Then he simmered down a little. "But it might just work: I guess we don't have anything to lose. All right—but be careful. I know from the way you tossed Carl and myself around last night you could handle Fabian without any trouble. Just don't turn your back on him."

"I won't," I promised.

"How soon do you want to start?" he asked.

"Just as soon as I'm ready," I told him, and got up from the chair and went into my room.

I had to smile to myself as I peeled off the chemise, because Johnny always kids himself he's the brains of our partnership, and I could just imagine the look on his face when he found out I'd been catching a murderer while he'd been fooling around in a Santa Barbara motel.

When I was down to the altogether, I peeked into the mirror and got a private eyeful of Mavis Seidlitz—that's another joke. Then I opened a suitcase and took out my Sunday Punch. It's a very special nightie, gardenia-colored, and I was very gentle with it as I slipped it over my head. It's made of nylon tissue tricot—the nightie, I mean, not my head. It has the Empire line, high-waisted, and on me it's got a high bustline, too, with lace and satin piping on the bodice. They've been taking the fun out of nylon with all this opaque jazz, but this nightie is only just a little opaque, which means you have to get real close before you can make up your mind whether you can see through it or not. That's the sort of service we girls want from a manufacturer.

I put on the matching coat over the nightie and slipped my feet into a pair of high-heeled mules with satin bows across the toes. The last thing added was the perfume, of course, and I went back to "I Surrender," because I felt that "My Sin" might make me too confident.

Don looked at me for what seemed a long time when

I walked out into the living room, then he came closer—and closer. He stopped two feet away from me, then shook his head slowly and sighed. "I'm still not sure," he said huskily. "Can I, or can't I?" He shook his head again. "Maybe you shouldn't wear it, Mavis. Fabian will be setting up searchlights instead of candles in the cellar."

"You think I'll have any trouble?" I asked him, and did a quick turnaround for him the way models do when it looks like they've got one foot nailed to the floor.

"You have only one worry," he said, "—fighting off Fabian until you get him down to the cellar."

"Fine!" I said. "I guess I might as well get started then. Do you know which is Fabian's room?"

"Sure," Don nodded. "The third door down on the left. You'd better give me a couple of minutes to make sure I get down there first. I'll wait for twenty minutes, honey, and if you haven't shown up by then, I'll come looking to find out why."

"O.K.," I said.

"Good luck," he murmured, and kissed me. Finally I had to kick his shins or else we would still have been there. I got out of the room quickly while he was hopping around on one leg, and turned left, then started counting the doors. When I got to three I stopped, and knocked on the door gently.

Fabian didn't open it, so after a while I knocked again. The door was still shut after the third knock, and I was beginning to feel the way Cleopatra must have felt when she was carried into Mark Antony's camp on a litter, and a sentry told her he'd gone fishing for the week end. Fabian just couldn't do this to me.

After the fourth knock, I tried the doorknob, and it turned in my hand. I pushed the door open and stepped quietly into the room. It was dark inside, and I got a frantic urge to scream as I fumbled along the wall for the light switch. After what seemed like a half hour, I found it. The lights came on suddenly, and I began to feel a little better.

The room was empty, the bed still neatly made. I figured Fabian couldn't have gone to sleep yet, which was something. Trouble was, I didn't know where he'd gone, and that was something else again.

I stood there talking to myself about it, looking at the door without really seeing it. The doorknob turned slowly and the door started to inch open. I was still busy talking to myself, so I didn't take much notice. It was halfway open when I did one of those old-hat double-takes, because I wanted to scream again when I figured if the door was opening, there had to be someone behind it, opening it!

By the time he got inside the room I was almost hysterical. When I saw who it was, I sighed heavily with relief. "It's you, Greg," I said in a fluttering sort of voice. "Why didn't you knock?—it would have kept me from having a heart attack." Then I saw the gun in his hand and I nearly did have the heart attack.

Gregory Payton came forward into the room slowly, the gun pointing at me all the time. He had a puzzled look in his eyes. "Mavis?" he said softly. "You were the last person I expected to find here. Where's Fabian?"

"I don't know," I said. "I'm looking for him myself."

He looked around the room suddenly and stared at the bathroom door, which was closed, for a few seconds. A faint smile crossed his face. "Of course," he said with a sneer on his face, "you wouldn't know where he was."

"I certainly wouldn't," I said. "I wish I did."

Greg put the gun into the pocket of his robe. "This really amazes me, Mavis. I was looking for my wife, and I find you. I'm disappointed in you, but I guess you're old enough to know what you're doing."

"I don't know what you're talking about," I told him truthfully. "But Fabian isn't here, you can see that."

"Oh, sure." He looked at the bathroom door again with the sneer still on his face. "I wouldn't interrupt you for the world!" Then he turned around and went outside again, closing the door behind him.

The only thing I could think was they must all be crazy in this house. I sat down in the nearest chair and waited for Fabian to come back. After about five minutes, I thought for all I knew he wasn't coming back until breakfast time, and I had no ambition to sit up all night in a hard chair on my own.

Then I had a bright idea. Why didn't I go down to the cellar and tell Don it wouldn't work because Fabian wasn't in his room? It would save Don waiting around and maybe catching a cold in that damp cellar. And after all, if we couldn't catch a murderer, the whole night didn't have to be wasted anyway.

So I left Fabian's room and walked along to the head of the stairs, then down and through to the kitchen. Those butterflies started jiving in my stomach again as I went down the cellar stairs. I was sure glad that Don was down there, waiting for me.

I reached the bottom of the stairs, and then my heart missed three beats at the one time. It looked exactly as it had the night before. Once again the candles burned, their flickering light casting deep shadows everywhere.

I took about six steps forward into the cellar, then had to stop because I was shaking so hard that if I kept on going I wasn't sure which direction I'd take. In the deep shadows of one corner something moved. I opened my mouth to scream, but couldn't because my throat had dried up completely.

It's Don, I told myself desperately, so stop being silly, Mavis! And for one wonderful moment I thought it was really him. Then the something moved slowly out of the corner toward me, and my knees picked up the beat again. I had a vague impression of a white body with full, firm breasts and long tapering legs, but the face wasn't human. It was the face of the mask on the wall, come to life.

As it moved toward me, the candlelight strengthened, and the shadows fled from the face. I stood petrified as the evil mask came closer to me. The parted lips showed misshapen, pointed teeth, and the huge grotesque chin was near enough for me to reach out and touch it.

Suddenly my legs started working again. I turned and ran for the stairs. I raced up them, three at a time, and got halfway towards the kitchen, when I stopped dead. I saw some feet standing motionless on the top step. They moved slowly down to the second, then the third step. I didn't want to look up, but I knew I had to.

Another white body, male this time, and naked. As I'd known it would have to be, the face was the face of the second mask on the wall, come to life.

I saw the ebony face, the hooked nose, the dilated eyes which stared down into mine. It came closer, and I took one step back and opened my mouth, but before I could scream, sinewy fingers reached out and closed around my throat. The face seemed to float, suspended in midair before my eyes for a moment, before a merciful black cloud blotted it out completely.

The first thing I felt was the pain. I opened my eyes slowly and saw the cellar floor weaving gently in front of me. Whoever it was that gripped my wrists and ankles held them in a cruel, viselike grip of iron. I raised my head slowly, straightening myself up, and the pressure eased a little. Enough for me to be able to move my arms a fraction. There was a clanking noise as I moved them.

Slowly the cellar floor steadied down and I saw that I was in a situation that Emily Post would have called downright embarrassing. The last thing I remembered was being on the cellar stairs and seeing that second horrible face coming toward me, then I must have fainted. Those two masked figures sure hadn't wasted any time while I'd been unconscious.

The grip on my wrists and ankles was made of iron all right. Iron chains that held me to the wall, the way Edwina's body had been chained. Remembering that didn't do anything for my self-confidence at all. And I was dressed the way she had been dressed, too—in nothing at all. They'd taken off my nylon tricot outfit, so when I looked down all I could see was Mavis all the way down to my ankles.

Seeing myself that way in what you could call public made me blush, and I watched myself turn a bright pink practically all the way down to my ankles, too. I guess the only consolation I had was that although being without any clothes on at all was definitely embarrassing, on me it looked pretty good, too.

The candles were still burning and I looked around the cellar to see what those two figures were doing, but I could only see one—the witch. She walked toward me slowly, and in a way it made me feel a little better because she wasn't wearing any clothes, either. She had a good figure, but mine was slightly better by about a couple of vital inches, I decided.

When she got real close, only a couple of feet away from me, she lifted her arms and then took off the mask. It was Wanda, of course, which really didn't surprise me, because she was the only girl left in the house. She walked away and hung the mask on the wall, then came back and stood in front of me.

"You stupid little fool!" she said in an icy voice. "Why didn't you mind your own business?"

"I wish you'd put that mask back on," I told her. "Your face is scaring me to death."

She slapped me hard across the face twice, and I could feel my cheeks flaming. "You're in no position to make amusing remarks, Mavis," she said tautly. "I can do anything I like to you and there's no way you can stop it. If I were you, I'd remember that."

"I'll remember all right," I said. "You wait till I get out of these chains! By the time I've finished with you, you'll need that mask—and an ambulance, too!"

She put her hands on her hips and smiled at me. I didn't like that smile much—I was sure there was nothing in it for Mavis.

"What are you going to do to me?" I asked her.

"I don't know yet," she said. "We'll decide when . . . he gets back."

"If you mean Fabian, why don't you say so?" I asked her.

"Shut up!" she snarled and slapped me again. It was getting to be monotonous, and it hurt, too.

"Are you going to strangle me between you?" I said. "The way you did Edwina?"

"Don't be more of a fool than you can help," she said shortly. "I had nothing to do with Edwina's death."

"Then it was Fabian?" I said. "I'd watch it, if I were you, honey. Maybe he's a guy with an original encore when he's finished his act."

"If he is," she smiled unpleasantly again, "I'd guess it's you that's holding the center of the stage right now, Mavis. You're right where Edwina was, remember?"

"Have you seen your husband lately?" I asked her. "He was looking for you—with a gun in his hand."

"You're crazy!" she said, but there was a worried look in her eyes.

I shook my head firmly. "I was looking for Fabian and I went to his room before I came down here. While I was inside, Greg came in, looking for you. Sooner or later he's going to think of the cellar, honey. Does that mask make you immune from bullets?"

She was all set to slap me again, but a slight noise behind her made her forget it and turn around. Her rear view was certainly tempting. If those chains around my ankles had only been about two feet longer, I could have given her something to remember me by.

The other masked figure stood at the foot of the stairs, looking at us. It was hard to tell exactly whether it was tall or short in the flickering shadows. I hoped he'd come nearer so maybe I could be sure whether it was Fabian or not. But he didn't—he just stood there.

Wanda stalked toward him, jiggling as she went. I'd never seen her jiggle before when she was wearing clothes, so I guess it was for his benefit. Maybe if you jiggle for a psychiatrist, all you get is analysis.

"Lover," she said in a low voice when she reached him, "we should teach her a lesson. She's been insulting me."

The masked figure just stood there, looking at her, without answering.

"Why don't you do something?" Wanda said impatiently. She moved a fraction closer to him. "Answer me! She needs a lesson she'll never forget, lover!" He still didn't answer, and suddenly Wanda's body stiffened.

"Lover?" Her voice faltered and she backed off a pace. "But . . ." Her voice cracked with fear. "You're not——"

His hands reached out then, grabbing her by the throat and choking off the rest of her words. There was nothing I could do but stand there helplessly and watch. I saw Wanda's body writhe desperately, then her heels drummed the floor for what seemed a long time. I could feel my heart beating so loudly I thought it would burst.

There was a haze in front of my eyes. Dimly I could see through it that her heels had stopped drumming the floor and she hung limply in that terrible grip.

The masked figure held her there for maybe another twenty seconds, then slowly relaxed his fingers so that Wanda's body slid down onto the floor. I was glad of the bad light then, so I couldn't see her face.

I wanted to scream, but my throat had dried up again, and all I could manage was a hoarse croak. It sounded like a frog in need of oiling. I didn't need any imagination to know what was coming next.

Slowly the masked figure stepped over Wanda's body and walked toward me. I was trembling so hard the chains started to rattle. I wondered vaguely if Edwina had done the same thing, and that had been the noise that wakened me the night before. My forehead was soaking wet, and I felt as if I was suffocating.

The mask got bigger and bigger as he came closer, blotting out everything else from my sight. The green, slanted eyes bored into mine, and the whole world was nothing but nightmare—a waking nightmare from which there was no escape.

He stopped in front of me and raised his arms slowly. I felt the coldness of his hands as they fondled my breasts, and something clicked inside my head. I fainted again.

CHAPTER ELEVEN

"Mavis," the voice said urgently, "are you all right, Mavis!"

I didn't really want to answer him, I was too comfortable as I was, but his voice kept on and on, so finally I forced my eyes open.

Carl's face was the first thing I saw—looking down at me anxiously. "Are you all right, Mavis?" he repeated in an urgent voice.

"I think so," I said. "Get these chains off me!"

He looked at me blankly. "Chains?"

I struggled up into a sitting position and looked around. I'd been lying on the cellar floor. I tried to figure out how I'd got there, remembering I'd been chained to the wall before I must have fainted again.

Instinctively I twisted my head and looked. For a moment I nearly passed out for a third time. Wanda's body was now chained to the wall, and this time I was near enough to see her face. I turned my head away quickly.

"I'll get you out of here," Carl said. "Do you feel strong enough to stand up?"

"I can try," I said. Carl put his arm around me and helped me up.

We walked up the stairs slowly, one step at a time, until we reached the kitchen. I felt a little better once I was out of the cellar, and the kitchen seemed warm and friendly with the brightness of the electric light after those horrible candles.

"What we need is a drink," Carl said. "You wait here and I'll get us one."

He took a couple of steps toward the door and stopped as it burst open and Don hurtled into the room. There was a big purple bruise on his forehead and a wild look

88

in his eyes. He stopped in front of Carl, then looked at me.

"Hi, honey," I said feebly.

The look in Don's eyes grew wilder and I wondered why for a moment, until I happened to look down. I'd forgotten I still didn't have any clothes on. I could see he was jumping to a conclusion right then, and from the murderous look he gave Carl, it was the wrong one.

"Wait a minute, Don!" I said. "It's not——"

But he wasn't even listening to me. He called Carl a nasty name that's rude even if it's ture. Then he swung a savage punch at him which Carl ducked. The next moment the two of them were wrestling together on the floor.

"All right," a harsh voice barked from the door. "Break it up!"

I looked up and saw Lieutenant Frome standing in the doorway. He saw me about the same time, and his eyes glazed over as he stood there, shaking his head feebly. I blushed modestly and tried to cover myself with my hands, but I guess there was just too much of me to cover.

Besides, it made me feel kind of stupid, like "September Morn" or something, which is a picture my mother used to have in the living room. It shows a girl in the nude trying to do the same thing as I was, but doing it better because she didn't have the development I've got. My mother used to say it was a charming picture of modesty, but I always figured it was just a cold morning and the girl had goose pimples.

Don and Carl rolled apart on the floor, then climbed back onto their feet and stood glaring at each other. Lieutenant Frome made a supreme effort and stopped looking at me. "What's this all about?" he demanded.

"Ask him," Don said, nodding toward Carl. "I'd like to hear the story, too!"

"I heard a noise," Carl said. "I came down here to see what it was. I found Mavis in the cellar. . . . I think you'd better take a look down there, Lieutenant."

"All right," Frome said. "We'll all take a look."

"Please," I said. "I don't want to go down there again. If I have to look at her again I'll go crazy!"

"Her?" Don said.

"Wanda," I said. "She's . . ."

Don turned around to the Lieutenant. "My wife's obviously suffering from shock of some sort," he said. "You can see the state she's in."

"I'd have to be blind not to," Frome said hoarsely.

"Let her go up to her room and get some clothes on," Don said. "If you want to question her afterwards, all right, but——"

"I said we'd all go down there," Frome rasped, "and that's exactly what we're going to do, and she can lead the way!"

"That's what I like about the Lieutenant," Carl said coldly. "He's all heart!"

Don slipped off his robe and gave it to me. "Better put this on, Mavis," he said, "then the Lieutenant can concentrate on being a cop again."

I put the robe on and belted it tight around the waist. Frome's face had a sort of regretful look on it as he watched. Then I grabbed Don's hand and held onto it tightly as I walked toward the stairs again. When we reached the cellar I kept my eyes shut tight and hung onto Don's hand until the Lieutenant said we could go back to the kitchen.

The next ten minutes were chaos, with police officers running everywhere, the Lieutenant asking questions, and Don shouting that he was going to get me a lawyer and I shouldn't answer any questions at all, and Carl telling him not to be a fool: I couldn't possibly have killed Wanda, and the Lieutenant saying why not and Carl telling him he was crazy if he thought I could kill anybody.

It gave me a headache. I sat down on the nearest chair and waited while the three men went on shouting at one another. Finally, Lieutenant Frome smashed his fist down onto the table and made me jump.

"All right!" he yelled. "I've stood enough of it. This place is a madhouse. Two murders in twenty-four hours. I'm taking her down to Headquarters for questioning and you can whistle for a platoon of lawyers!" Then he grabbed my arm, lifted me out of the chair and hustled me through the house to the front door.

I was too tired to argue with him, and anyway, getting out of that house seemed like a good idea right then. The Lieutenant sat next to me in the car without saying anything during the ride.

Police Headquarters was a drab-looking place inside. I told Frome they could certainly use an interior decorator, or even a few flowers would help, but he just grunted, and pushed me along in front of him. He took me into a small room which I thought was a cell, until he told me it was his office. He gave me a chair and I sat down. Two other men came in, then the Lieutenant switched off the overhead light and turned the table lamp so it shone straight into my face.

I turned it around again and he turned it back. We did that three or four times, until he snarled at me not to touch it. "But it's shining straight into my eyes!" I told him. Well, really, you would have thought he could've seen that the first time. How dumb can a cop get?

"Just leave it!" he repeated.

"All right," I said. "But if I have to wear glasses after this, I'm sending you the bill!"

"Shut up!" he told me.

"If you're going to be rude to me, I won't stay," I said firmly. "After all, I didn't want to come here in the first place—it was your idea, remember? And I must say I don't think much of your hospitality. I'd like some coffee or something."

"Just answer the questions!" he growled in a low voice.

"How can I?" I said tersely. "You haven't asked me any yet."

"Shut up and listen!" he said. "Then maybe I'll get a chance to ask some questions."

"O.K." I shrugged my shoulders. "Go ahead."

"That's better," he sighed heavily. "You want to tell us about it?"

"I have," I said, "but it didn't make any difference."

"You what?" he asked.

91

"I told you just now," I said. "You couldn't have been listening."

"So maybe I'm crazy," he muttered. "If it's not too much trouble, would you mind telling me again?"

"Not at all," I said. "It's shining in my eyes."

Nobody said anything for maybe ten seconds. "If she's not crazy then I am for sure," Frome muttered. "What in the name of . . . what are you talking about?"

"The lamp," I said, and moved it again. "That's better."

Then he started talking to himself, but I couldn't hear what he was saying. He went on for some time until one of the other men said: "Would you like me to try, Lieutenant?"

"Why not?" Frome said in a hollow-sounding voice. "Why should it be only me that gets an ulcer?"

"There was a murder," the other guy said to me in a soothing voice. "You remember that, don't you? Mrs. Payton was strangled."

"Will I ever forget it?" I said truthfully.

"Just tell us in your own words what happened," he said.

"Sure I will," I said. "How else could I tell you? If you've got any words of your own I don't mind borrowing them, but if I use my own it'll be better, because I know what they mean, and maybe you use long words I don't understand and the one thing I wouldn't want to do is get you confused."

"You just did!" he gurgled. "By all means use your own words and I won't offer even a one of mine"—his voice jumped a couple of octaves—"but tell it!"

So I told them what had happened from the time I got down to the cellar until the time Lieutenant Frome walked into the kitchen.

"What made you go down to the cellar in the first place?" Frome asked when I'd finished.

I didn't answer right away, because I didn't think it was fair. I mean, it was me that figured out a way to trap Fabian Dark and if I told them now, they'd just go and arrest him and take all the credit, and Johnny would never believe me when I told him it was my idea in the first place. So I hedged a little about the answer.

"Come on!" Frome said impatiently. "Why?"

"I couldn't sleep," I said brightly. "You know how it is, it was just one of those nights, so I thought I'd take a walk and maybe that would tire me enough so I could sleep."

"So you took a walk down into the cellar?"

"That's right," I agreed. "And then the rest of it happened."

"You expect us to believe that?" he shouted. "You're lying!"

"Of course I expect you to believe it," I snapped. "Why else would I say it?"

"Come on!" the third man said harshly. "You killed the dame—admit it!"

"I most definitely did not," I told him. "You think I'd forget a thing like that?"

"You killed her," he repeated monotonously. "You strangled her to death. You chained her to the wall so she couldn't struggle, then you put your hands around her throat and choked the life out of her."

"Then I took my clothes off and fainted?" I said. "You're being a silly police officer!"

"Why did you kill her?" he said, just ignoring all I'd told him. "Jealousy? What had she done to you?"

"Nothing," I said.

"Maybe it was her husband?" he said eagerly. "You were crazy about him, but she stood in the way?"

"Have you seen her husband?" I asked him gently. "If Wanda had stood in his way, you wouldn't have been able to see him. Greg's about as exciting as a Girl Guides' picnic!"

I never knew such a rude trio of men. You'd think they were deaf or something the way they kept on asking the same questions over and over again, and not even listening to the answers.

The questions went on and on and on, until finally they started to tail off and at last they stopped. The silence was a beautiful thing to listen to, and I enjoyed it for a couple of minutes.

"Lieutenant," one of them said hoarsely, "we still got that lie-detector upstairs we don't use. Maybe we could give her a run-through on that?"

"What's the use?" Frome said despairingly. "You know a detector won't work with a moron!"

"What's a moron?" I asked interestedly.

"You should ask!" Frome said. He walked over to the wall and switched on the overhead light again. "I'm going back to the house," he grunted. "Maybe I can get some sense out of the others there, but I doubt it. Book her as a material witness or something—but lock her up!" Then he stamped out of the room, slamming the door behind him.

"All right, lady," one of the others said. "Let's go."

"Where?" I asked him as I stood up.

"We're going to find you a nice, quiet cell for the night," he said.

"That sounds wonderful," I said sincerely. "Would you have somebody bring me some clothes from the house?"

"Huh?"

I pulled the fold of the robe apart and showed him my legs. "I just don't have anything on except the robe," I told him. Then I pulled the robe tight again.

"What did you say?" he said.

So I repeated what I'd said, and showed him my legs again to prove it. He must have been shortsighted or something, because he stared at my legs for at least two minutes before he was convinced.

"O.K.," he said in an awed voice. "I'll get somebody to bring your clothes, but if you ask me, it's a crime!"

They turned me over to a matron who had a hatchet face and a figure it's not a kindness to describe. She looked like a convention of "Overweights Anonymous," all by herself.

She unlocked the cell door and pushed me inside, then locked the door again. "Thank you," I said politely. "If I want you again, I'll press the button."

"If you want anything, sister, you'll wait till morning!" she said in a vinegary voice.

"What time is breakfast?" I asked.

"When you get it," she said.

"If the service is as bad as you say it is," I told her, "I don't think I'll stay"—but she'd already walked away before I'd finished speaking.

So I went to bed. The bunk was a hard wooden board, and there was just one blanket to go with it. One thing about being a girl, at least you carry your own upholstery around with you.

CHAPTER TWELVE

In the morning I had a shower, and someone had brought some clothes for me so I could get dressed. I wouldn't say the breakfast was up to the standard of the Beverly Hills Hotel, but I figured Police Headquarters wouldn't get too many movie stars spending the night anyway.

Around ten o'clock, old hatchet-face came along with a uniformed cop and unlocked my cell. The cop took me upstairs and into Lieutenant Frome's office, and the first guy I saw when I got inside was Johnny Rio. He and the Lieutenant just sat there staring at me, so I stared right back at them. The one thing I'm used to, is stares.

"Mavis," Johnny said finally, "it was all my fault. I must have been crazy to let you loose in that house!"

I just kept on staring at him and didn't answer.

"Mavis?" he said. "Are you deaf or something?"

"Are you talking to me?" I asked him frigidly. "My name is Ebhart—Clare Ebhart."

"Oh, sure," he said. "And tomorrow you'll be one of the Jones boys."

"Mrs. Donald Ebhart," I said, glaring at him. How could

he be so dumb and forget all about the arrangements we'd made with our client? If he kept on acting up this way I'd have to get myself a new partner. Next time I'd go for a guy with muscles, and I'd supply the brains.

Johnny glared right back at me. "You can skip the Mrs. Ebhart routine. The Lieutenant knows the whole story."

"You told him?" I said in a disappointed voice. "What's the matter with you, Johnny?"

"I wouldn't like to see you inside the gas chamber," he said heavily. "It might spoil my day."

"Well!" I said. "After all I've been through, and you just . . . just . . ."

"Spring you from jail and out from under a murder rap," he snarled. "The Lieutenant says you can go now, so let's go before he changes his mind."

"Yeah," Frome said huskily. "Go—far, far away, and please . . . don't ever come back!"

"Very well," I said. "I must say I know when I'm not wanted, and if you don't catch the murderer, please don't blame me. Remember, it was *you* who sent me away!"

The Lieutenant clenched his fist and beat it against his forehead. "Get her out of here, Rio!" he said fiercely. "I never slugged a dame yet, but there's got to be a first time!"

Johnny grabbed my arm and hustled me out of the office and right out of Police Headquarters. He had his car at the curb outside, and bundled me into the front seat. He drove away like he had ten minutes to make L.A. or something.

We stopped at a motel on the waterfront and Johnny led the way to his room, which was on the second story and facing the ocean. I sat down on the comfortable couch and had a look at the television, radio, and comfortable furnishings, while Johnny got some ice from the icebox and made us a drink.

"You sure have had things tough," I said. "I don't know how you've stood up to all this misery the last forty-eight hours. It makes me feel positively guilty, when I think of myself just wallowing in all those corpses and chains and damp cellars and——"

"Ah, nuts!" he said rudely.

He brought the drinks back with him and sat on the couch beside me. "I got news for you, kid," he said nastily. "You don't have to feel unhappy about the whole deal. You're going back to that house and wallow some more."

"Johnny," I said softly. "That Marine-sergeant taught me how to break a man's spinal column with one blow. It's the timing, not the force, that counts. For the first time in my life I've got a feeling I'm going to use that trick."

"Relax, Mavis," he said easily. "Save it for the strangler."

I gulped down some of the drink. "Don't use words like that—I get to feeling nervous again."

"Tell me what happened last night," he said.

"I told those stupid cops what happened until I'm sick of the words," I said. "I don't want to go through it again, Johnny, please."

"Just once more, Mavis," his voice was gentle, "or would you prefer to finish up in a motel room strangled with your own bra?"

So I told him the story once again, about my clever idea of trapping Fabian, and how it misfired because he wasn't in his room when I got there—right up to the time when old hatchet-face locked me in a cell.

Johnny grunted when I'd finished and got up to make himself another drink. "You tell it, I got to believe it," he said.

"Just how did you get to know I was in that cell, anyway?" I asked.

"Don Ebhart called me early this morning," he said. "I went down right away and saw Frome. Confidentially, Mavis, that guy doesn't like you!"

"It's strictly mutual," I assured him. "I never heard anything more stupid than those questions he asked me."

"You should have listened to the answers," he said, and I was still trying to figure that one out when he sat down beside me again.

"There's another thing," I said, remembering suddenly what had caused all my last night's trouble in the first place." I'm going to take Don apart when I get back to the house. He was supposed to be waiting in that cellar when I got down there. If he'd been there, none of those horrible things would have happened to me!"

"It wasn't his fault," Johnny said. "He got slugged."

"Not over the back of the head again?" I asked.

"The front this time," Johnny grinned.

"Now I remember," I said. "He did have a nasty-looking bruise when I saw him in the kitchen. What happened?"

"Gregory Payton," Johnny grunted. "I guess that's the trouble with being a head-shrinker—you know all the real nasty things people can do, because you've read about them in textbooks, so you always figure that's just what they're doing."

"That's what I always say," I agreed, "and I never know what I'm talking about, either. What are you talking about?"

"He walked into Fabian's room expecting to find his wife with Fabian," Johnny said patiently. "But he found you with Fabian instead."

I was just going to say that was stupid, because Fabian hadn't been there, when I remembered how Greg had kept on looking at the bathroom door, so maybe he'd thought Fabian was hiding in there. "So?" I said.

"If Wanda wasn't with you, then maybe she was with Don," Johnny said. "And Greg being the sort of head-shrinker who always thinks the best of people, decided right then that there had to be something more than the normal brother-sister relationship. He busted into your room and, before Don could even ask him what he wanted, Greg slugged him with the butt of his gun."

"And that's why Don never got down to the cellar?"

"For sure," he nodded. "Don was out cold in your room. Greg searched the place, and when he found Wanda wasn't there, he got covered with remorse and went back to his own room. That was his story to the cops, anyway."

"That Fabian!" I said. "I just know it was him wearing that horrible mask!"

"How do you know?"

"Don't be silly, Johnny!" I said irritably. "It had to be Fabian—who else could it be?"

"Carl, for example," Johnny said.

"That's stupid."

"Why? He was the guy who so conveniently found you in the cellar. The last thing you remember before you passed out was the masked character who had just strangled Wanda. You couldn't get out of his way because you were chained to the wall. Right?"

"Right," I admitted, grudgingly.

"Next thing you know, Wanda's body is chained to the wall and Carl is asking if you're all right. You couldn't have taken those chains off your own wrists and ankles, then put Wanda's body into them. Why couldn't it have been Carl?"

"You put it that way, there's no reason it couldn't have been him," I said. "Which one do you think it was, Johnny?"

He lit himself a cigarette and thought about that for a few seconds. "I'm not sure yet," he said. "Maybe we're dealing with a maniac, Mavis. Or maybe a guy who's being awful cute by just pretending he's a maniac."

"I don't get that," I said.

"You don't surprise me," he growled. "Before everyone knew about that second will, there was no apparent reason for Edwina's murder. The logical one to be killed for gain was you, as Don's wife, or Don himself. Fabian was the only one who knew about the will—he could have killed Edwina, knowing he'd get more of the handout." He shrugged his shoulders. "It doesn't get us very far, does it? If Fabian didn't kill the housekeeper, it was a maniac, or she was killed for a motive we don't even know about!"

"I dig that," I said. "What you mean is, you don't have a clue about the murderer at all?"

"One thing," Johnny said, scowling at me, "if anything else is going to happen, it'll happen by midnight tonight.

That's the deadline for the will to come into force, isn't it?"

"That's right," I said hopefully. "If you really want to catch the murderer, Johnny, I'll stay right here; lend you a bra and skirt of mine, and you can go back to the house and play Mavis up till midnight."

"You don't have anything to worry about," he said soothingly. "We'll catch him O.K."

"I have nothing to worry about but my neck!" I said, stroking it tenderly. "And what's with this 'we' business? I don't want to catch a murderer—not after last night: I've resigned!"

"I've got a plan," Johnny said eagerly.

"If getting me strangled is a part of it, I'm still not interested!" I told him.

"You remember the vault?" he asked.

"Don't change the subject," I said firmly.

"Vault tomb, the old man's personal monument. 'Time passes—I remain.' Hell! You must remember—we only saw it yesterday."

"Oh, that!" I said, wrinkling my nose. "I've been trying to forget it!"

"You remember the oil on the lock, and the two bright links on the padlock chain?"

"Like the back of my hand!" I said tartly. "The way I remember last year's television programs!"

"How would you like a square tail?" he snarled.

I blinked at him twice. "Huh?"

"If you don't shut up and listen, I'll beat the curves out of it until it's flat!" he said.

"O.K.," I said meekly. "I'm listening."

Whenever Johnny gets masterful it makes me feel breathless, because I'm sure that one of these days he'll actually make a pass at me, and when he does, I'm going to grab it so fast! Johnny is the one guy who makes me hear wedding bells just by looking at me. The trouble is, he never hears them; all he ever thinks about is business and he says you can't mix business with pleasure, but I don't see why business can't be a pleasure, and that's what I'm hoping for.

"Somebody's been inside that vault recently," Johnny said, "and it's my guess it wasn't to pay their respects to Old Man Ebhart. Now, according to the terms of the new will, all of you have to be there at midnight to pay your respects to him—right?"

"Don't remind me," I shuddered. "Every time I think of it I can feel bats flying through my hair."

"Don't worry about the bats," Johnny said impatiently. "They're just coming home to the belfry. This plan of mine is beautifully simple. As soon as you can, after you get back to the house, you tell all of them you know who the murderer is. But tell them one at a time, huh? You tell them the proof is in that vault, locked inside, and you're going out there to get it one hour before midnight."

"Why don't I just cut my throat at the dinner table tonight?" I asked him bleakly. "That way I can die in comfort."

"If you tell all of them the story," he went on, ignoring my comments, "then you must tell the murderer. The innocent people won't want to go out to that vault twice in one night, so they'll think you're just crazy. But the murderer will be interested. If there is anything in the vault that will give him away, he won't want you finding it. If there isn't, I'll bet his curiosity will overcome him, and he'll still follow you out there at eleven o'clock!"

I closed my eyes and shuddered again. "So, at eleven o'clock tonight I walk out of the house," I said through clenched teeth. "Alone I walk right up to that tomb, whistling gaily while I listen to the footsteps padding along behind me. When I get to the tomb, I just wait for the murderer to catch up with me. Then what do I do— talk him into giving himself up?"

"I'll take care of that end," Johnny said smugly.

"Why, Mr. Rio!" I said. "Don't tell me you've perfected your supersonic death-ray that will kill at a range of ten miles even? You mean you're going to just sit here with your feet up, and at the very moment the strangler's hands creep around my neck, you'll press the button and—phyzzzzzzzzzz!"

One second I was sitting there on the couch, then the

next second a hurricane hit me. I kind of whirled through the air and finished up face down across Johnny's knee.

He kept my head down with his elbow dug into the back of my neck. I wriggled, squealed and yelped, but it didn't make any difference. He slapped me so hard I was sure I'd never sit down again, and for the first time I wished I wore a girdle. Against a hand like Johnny's, nylon is just no protection at all.

After much too long a time, he took his elbow out of my neck and let me scramble up into a sitting position again—and that hurt, too!

"I warned you!" Johnny said grimly. "You asked for it, and you got it!"

"Johnny darling," I smiled gently at him. "You're nothing but a brute. A wonderful, masterful brute!" I leaned my head against his shoulder and lifted my head slowly so my lips came close to his. "I guess it's just no use a girl resisting." I sighed deeply. "It wouldn't make any difference when you're really roused. I surrender, Johnny!"

He let out a yelp and jumped to his feet, leaving me off-balance so that I fell across the couch. "You just cut this out, Mavis!" he said nervously. "We're a business partnership—we agreed on that, remember?"

"No," I said sullenly, and sat up and winced again at the same time. "What's wrong with having a little fun?"

"Not on company time," he said severely. "You stop it, Mavis—stay right where you are, or I'll scream for help, I swear I will!"

"Oh, all right!" I said disgustedly. "I don't know what happened to all that red blood you must have had once."

"Never mind about that!" he yelped. "We're talking about what's going to happen tonight. I'll be there, at the vault, around the side where the inscription is, so you walk around the other side to the door."

"If you think I'm going out to that vault in the middle of the night you're crazier than I know you are, and that's almost impossible!" I said firmly. "I wouldn't go out there if Cary Grant was waiting for me—no girl can say more than that!"

"O.K.," he said casually. "You please yourself."

"You mean you don't care whether I do it or not?" I stared at him suspiciously.

"Please yourself, Mavis," he said casually. "You want to be murdered inside the house where you'll have no chance of being saved, I guess I can't stop you."

"What do you mean—murdered?" I quavered.

"Well," he smiled sadly, "the murderer is certainly not going to stop now! But I shall miss you, Mavis," he went on regretfully. "The office just won't seem the same any more."

I guess I know when I'm licked. "All right," I said hopelessly. "Eleven o'clock at the vault. You make sure you're on time, Johnny Rio! If you're late, I'll never speak to you again!"

Johnny smiled at me cheerfully. "That figures," he said.

CHAPTER THIRTEEN

The house was still there when I got back around four that afternoon. Johnny had driven me as far as the gates and made me walk the rest of the way. He said the exercise would be good for me, but whoever got any fun out of walking?

Sergeant Donavan was on duty at the front door again, and the way he looked at me, I should have charged him admission.

I went upstairs to the suite without meeting anybody on the way, and Don wasn't there either when I got inside. I had a nice hot bath and got dressed again. It looked like it was going to be a busy night, so I put on a cashmere sweater and a pair of matador pants. Then I went downstairs again into the living room.

Carl was there, at the bar, and he smiled when he saw me come into the room. "Welcome home!" he said.

"Those idiot policemen finally realized you weren't a murderer after all?"

"I think so," I said. "I didn't mind them keeping me at headquarters, really, because it gave me time to think."

"How did it feel?" he asked in a sympathetic voice. "I hope it didn't hurt too much, Mavis. It'll get better once you get used to it."

"For that you can pour me a drink," I told him.

He made the drink and handed it to me. "Only a few hours to go and then we're free again," he said. "Midnight is the deadline, Mavis. I don't know about you and Don, but I'm getting out of here at a minute after! Let's drink to that."

"Sure," I said, and drank some of the gimlet he'd made me. "Did I miss anything exciting while I was away?"

"I don't think so," he said. "We got the same treatment you did, I imagine. Questions, questions, and then more questions. The trouble with the police is they don't seem to be able to provide any answers."

"How's Greg?" I asked him.

His face sobered. "I wouldn't know. He seems to be all right. From the way he looks and the way he talks, you wouldn't think his wife had been murdered last night. Poor Wanda! I never exactly cared for her while she was alive, but . . ."

"I know what you mean," I told him. "Have you seen Don?"

"He was around about an hour ago," Carl said. "He's probably still around. Maybe he took a walk down to the front gates or something."

"Thanks," I said. "How about Fabian?"

"He's resting," Carl grimaced. "If somebody had to get murdered, it's a pity he wasn't the murderer's first choice."

"Why do you say that?" I asked him casually.

"He's . . . unclean," Carl said slowly. "I can't put it any clearer than that."

"I think I get your message," I said. "How's poor Mr. Limbo?"

Carl's face was bland. "I buried him last night," he said easily. "After it happened."

"I'm dreadfully sorry," I said softly. "You must miss him terribly."

"I'll get along," he said. "But I think I'm finished with ventriloquism. I don't care to use another dummy, not after him."

"I was thinking about Fabian," I said. "Do you know where he was last night? I mean, when the murder happened and everything?"

"Asleep in bed—so he says." Carl grunted. "No one's made a liar out of him yet. You think he killed both of them, Edwina and Wanda?"

I shrugged my shoulders and tried to look mysterious. "Maybe," I said.

Carl looked at me hard for a moment. "You know something I don't?" he asked.

"I know who the murderer is," I said easily. "Tonight I'm going to prove it."

"I bet this has a very funny punch line," he said slowly.

"It's no gag," I told him. "I mean it."

"All right," he said quietly. "Who is it?"

"I'm not telling, not yet," I said. "Carl, you promise you won't mention it to the others?"

"Cross my heart," he promised.

"I have to wait for the right time and the right place to catch the murderer and get the proof at the same time." I lowered my voice to a confidential murmur. "The proof is in the vault, and the time is one hour before midnight."

"I still think this is a gag!" he said sourly.

"I mean it," I said earnestly, "but it's no use going to the vault before that time."

"Vault?" He frowned for a moment. "Oh, you mean the old man's private morgue. What do you expect to find there?"

"I can't tell you any more, Carl," I said firmly. "And please, whatever you do, don't tell anyone else!"

"My lips are sealed." He grinned at me and shook his

head slowly. "I still can't make up my mind whether you're kidding me or not."

"I'm not," I said, and finished the gimlet. "Thanks for the drink."

I walked out of the living room before he could ask me any more questions. If Don wasn't far away, I thought I might as well go up to the suite and wait for him there. I climbed the stairs and then walked down the corridor to our door. Somewhere behind me I heard another door open. I looked around and saw Gregory Payton standing right behind me.

"You made me jump, Greg!" I told him.

"Did I?" he said softly.

"I don't know how to say this properly," I said, "but I'm dreadfully sorry about Wanda."

"Are you?" His voice was polite. "I'm not."

I just stood there, looking at him. He took off his glasses and started to polish them vigorously. "She got what she deserved," he went on in that flat voice, as if he was talking about a goldfish that jumped out of the bowl. "My only interest now is to find the murderer. Not from a feeling of revenge, you understand, Mavis, but rather from a professional viewpoint. He should make a most interesting study. I'd like him to take analysis."

"If you can keep a secret," I said confidentially, "I think I know who the murderer really is." Then I gave him the pitch about the vault and the "one hour before midnight" routine.

Greg blinked at me from behind his glasses. "Are you sure you're not weaving yourself a fantasy, Mavis?" he said gently.

"Of course I'm sure!" I said determinedly. "You wait and see!"

"I shall," he said. "Definitely. I hope you are right, Mavis. The vault, one hour before midnight . . . poetic justice. The sins of the father revisited on his tomb."

"Well," I said nervously, "if you'll excuse me, Greg, I have to go now."

The lenses magnified the pupils of his eyes into two

muddy swamps. "Did you know she couldn't stand me even touching her?" he said conversationally.

"I really have to go, Greg," I stammered, and pulled the door open at the same time.

Once inside the suite, I slammed the door shut and locked it. I leaned against the door and listened. For the first few seconds the only thing I could hear was my heart beating furiously, but after a couple of minutes, I heard his footsteps as he walked away slowly.

If ever a guy needed a psychiatrist, it was Gregory Payton! I looked around and saw Don still wasn't back yet. I hoped he wouldn't be too long. It was starting to get dark again—another night was coming. I thought of Johnny Rio sitting in that motel, and I could have torn his heart out and used it for fishbait. He was nothing but a 14-karat heel with a billfold instead of a heart.

I was still brooding when there was a knock on the door. I ran over and opened it, thinking it was Don, but it wasn't.

"May I come in?" Fabian Dark asked politely.

"I guess so," I said, and held the door open a little wider.

Fabian walked into the living room, looking around curiously, then sat down in an armchair. I closed the door and walked over to a chair opposite him and sat down.

"I wanted to speak to Don," Fabian said. "Is he here?"

"No," I said. "I'm waiting for him."

"Too bad," Fabian said. "But I shall see him later, I imagine."

"I guess you're sure of that," I smiled at him. "There's a little matter of the estate to be fixed up at midnight, isn't there?"

Fabian smiled that creepy smile of his. "Ah, yes," he nodded. "So there is."

"And something else, too—an hour before," I said, and told him the story about catching the murderer at the vault.

He folded his hands across the beginnings of a paunch, and looked at me. "Can't you tell me any more than that?" he prodded.

"I'm sorry," I said, "but it has to be a secret, Fabian, until I've got the murderer."

"Well," he said, "I wish you luck, my dear. You're certainly a very brave girl."

"Thanks," I said. I wished he hadn't mentioned that "brave" bit.

He got onto his feet and started toward the door. "I shall see you later in the evening, I don't doubt. Tell Don I was looking for him."

"Sure," I said.

He stopped beside my chair. "It has been a privilege and a pleasure to know you, my dear," he said. His hand reached out to touch my arm.

I curled up inside and wanted to scream. I remembered last night, with those cold fingers reaching out to touch me while the dilated eyes stared at me from behind the mask. Then Fabian's fingers gripped my forearm for a moment, and I nearly gasped with surprise. The fingers weren't cold at all—they were warm and slightly moist to the touch.

"A privilege and a pleasure," Fabian repeated softly, "to know a girl named Mavis Seidlitz."

"Huh?" I said weakly.

He took his hand away from my arm and smiled again. "You didn't really think I'd be fooled for long?" he said. "I am a lawyer, after all. I checked on Clare Ebhart very thoroughly, my dear."

I watched him, speechless for once in my life, while he walked to the door and opened it. He turned around and looked at me again. "I'm sorry about Don," he said lightly. "Tell him it was a good try, and I hope he won't miss the money too much." Then the door closed behind him, and I thought the world falling in should make a lot more noise than just a click.

There was nothing I could do about it, I thought miserably. I sat there, thinking it was all my fault because I'd forgotten I was supposed to be Clare Ebhart a couple of times, and had said my real name.

Maybe fifteen or thirty minutes later—I'd lost track of time—Don came into the suite. I got out of the chair and rushed over to him. "Don," I said miserably, "something dreadful's happened!"

"I know," he grinned at me and held out his arms. "I haven't seen you since last night!"

I leaned my head against his chest as he put his arms around me, and then I told him what Fabian had just said. When I'd finished he didn't say anything at all. I didn't have the nerve to look at his face to see how he'd taken it, so I just kept my head buried against his chest.

He still didn't say anything, and I started to worry about whether he was overcome by the shock of losing what was left of his inheritance, or whether he'd been concentrating so much on me he hadn't even heard what I'd said.

"Mavis," he said huskily, "you're wonderful!"

I pushed myself away from him violently. "Be serious!" I told him. "Didn't you hear what I just told you?"

"I heard," he said indifferently. "Don't worry about it, honey. Fabian isn't so smart as he thinks he is."

He started walking toward me again with that gleam in his eyes. I backed off a couple of paces hastily. "Not now," I said. "There are other things more important, Don!"

"Impossible," he said flatly.

So I told him about the vault and catching the murderer an hour before midnight. That did stop him. He stared at me open-mouthed. "Are you serious?"

"Of course I'm serious!" I said. "And I've told all the others, too."

"All right," he said with a rasp in his voice. "Who is the murderer then?"

He looked so serious that I had to laugh. I was still laughing when he slapped my face. The slap jerked my head sideways and I staggered, losing my balance and falling across the chair. "Who is it?" he shouted.

I sat up slowly and rubbed my cheek. "Don, honey!" I said, and I couldn't stop my voice quivering a little. "Take it easy—it's only a gag!"

"A gag?" he said. "You fool around with a thing like murder?"

"It's Johnny's idea," I said.

"Rio?" he stared at me wildly. "What do you mean—it's Rio's idea? Some sort of practical joke?"

"No!" I yelled at him. "Just listen for a moment!"

Then I told him about Johnny discovering that someone had been inside the vault recently, and how he planned on using the vault to capture the murderer, by getting me to tell the story to everyone inside the house.

When I'd finished, Don looked at me, the anger fading out of his eyes. "I'm sorry, Mavis," he said humbly. "Terribly sorry I hit you. I guess this thing has worn my nerves down to a fine edge the same as everyone else's. Please forgive me?"

"Sure," I said. "I know how you feel."

"Then come over here," he said gently.

He took me into his arms and kissed me and I got that electric shock treatment again. After the kiss had finished, I looked at him shakily. "I'll have to sit down," I whispered. "You shouldn't kiss me like that—it makes my knees shake too much!"

So he sat down in the nearest armchair and I sat on his lap because there's no point in using two chairs when one is more interesting.

"I don't like it," he said after a while.

"Well," I said indignantly, "you can put your hand back where it belongs, then!"

"I mean you telling them that story," he said. "It makes you bait to catch the murderer."

"Sure it does," I agreed. "That was Johnny's idea in the first place. That's why he'll be waiting beside the vault when I go out there."

"Suppose the murderer doesn't conveniently wait until then?" Don said.

"What?" I gurgled.

"He could make up his mind you're too dangerous to live right now," he said. "He could decide to kill you before eleven—any time."

"I hadn't thought of that," I said. "That Johnny Rio—big hero!"

"I'm going with you," he said abruptly. "You aren't

walking out to that vault in the middle of the night alone."

"Thanks, Don," I said. "I have to admit I don't exactly like the idea myself."

"We'll stay right here until the time comes," he said fiercely, "and if anybody tries to get at you here, they'll have to deal with me first."

"My hero!" I said fondly, and nibbled his right ear to show how much I appreciated him.

"Not much of a hero," he grinned, "but I've got a gun in my drawer. I brought it with me in case anything happened." He glanced at his watch. "It's seven-thirty now. We've got about another four hours to go. You hungry, Mavis?"

CHAPTER FOURTEEN

A sudden flash of lightning hit the horizon and made me jump. Don stood unmoving, staring out of the window.

"Looks like a storm coming up," he said. "It's a quarter of eleven now. I guess we should be moving."

"Sure," I said, and my throat started to dry up again.

I pulled on a pair of sandals, ran a comb through my hair and used a lipstick, then I was ready. I thought there was no reason I should look like a corpse, even if I was going to be one.

Don turned away from the window and looked at me for a long moment. "You're quite a girl, Mavis," he said softly. "If the others had been like you . . ."

"Others?"

"I guess the difference is between real wives and a pretending one for seventy-two hours," he said.

"Just what are you talking about?" I asked him.

He shrugged his shoulders. "Maybe I inherited too

much from my father—in character, anyway. He never had any luck with his women, either."

"I wish you'd start making sense!" I pleaded with him.

"The Spanish woman who dried up and got old and ugly before her time," he said somberly. "Then the Southern belle with her impossible drawl, the beautiful body and empty head. He never had any luck, not even with Edwina. Maybe she was the worst of them all."

He took the gun out of his pocket and looked at it for a moment. "I've got an idea," he said slowly. "Why don't we take the murderer along with us?"

"Huh?" I said.

"It would be safer," he said. "I'd rather have him along than following behind."

"You're kidding!" I said.

He shook his head. "I don't think so."

A sudden peal of thunder shook the room. Don cocked his head to one side and listened for a moment. "Did you hear that?" he asked.

"The thunder?"

"No, something else," he said. "It sounded like chains rattling."

I shivered. "Don't tell me they're playing our song again!"

"Maybe it was my imagination," he said. "We'd better go, anyway."

"All right," I said and crossed all my fingers.

We went out of the suite into the corridor. Don stopped two doors down and held his finger to his lips. I nodded and waited while he tapped gently on the door.

The door opened a few seconds later and Fabian Dark stood there. "Hello, Don," he said. "I've been wanting to see you to have a talk and——"

"How about a walk first, Fabian?" Don said softly and jabbed the barrel of the gun into his paunch.

Fabian looked down at the gun, then back at Don, his eyes widening a little. "What's the meaning of this?" he quavered.

"We're lonely," Don said. "We'd like company, Fa-

112

bian. We're going for a walk—we thought you'd like to come too."

"A walk?" Fabian looked at me for a moment. "You're really going out to that vault, Mavis? Don't be a fool! It's obviously a trap!"

"That's smart thinking," Don told him. "That's why we're taking you along too. Come on, let's move!"

Fabian looked at him for a moment longer, then shrugged his shoulders and stepped out into the corridor. The three of us went down the stairs and through the kitchen to the back door.

Outside it was pitch dark, and Don shone the flashlight he'd taken from the kitchen, ahead of us. "You go first, Fabian," he said. "Try anything on the way and I'll shoot you. I mean that."

"I don't doubt it," Fabian said coldly.

I hung onto Don's arm as we walked over the grass. Boy! was I glad he'd come along, too. Vivid flashes of lightning split the sky and the thunder was rolling almost continuously. I would have died of fright on my own.

Then a flash, worse than the ones that had gone before, lit up everything around us brighter than day for a moment, and I saw the dark rectangular silhouette of the vault not far ahead of us.

Don stopped a few moments later. "The door is straight ahead of us, Mavis," he said. "You take the gun and the flashlight. Wait at the door with Fabian and keep an eye on him." He raised his voice slightly. "Shoot him if he tries anything! I'll go around the side and collect Rio."

"O.K.," I said nervously.

So I waited at the door to the vault with Fabian, while Don walked around to the side. I kept the flashlight firmly trained on the lawyer, while I held the gun in my right hand. I was glad Fabian couldn't see the gun, because it was jumping around all over the place.

"Mavis," he said in a low voice. "You know what you're doing?"

"Of course I do," I said. "And don't you try anything or I'll shoot you!"

"Don't you understand?" he said hoarsely. "Don't you . . ." Then he sighed gently. "I guess you don't," he said. "And you wouldn't believe me, anyway. Listen . . . can't you hear him . . . laughing?"

"Who?" I said nervously.

"Randolph Ebhart," he said. "I can. From beyond the grave. I know his body is dust inside that tomb, but I can feel his power right now just as strongly as if he was still alive. The powers of darkness, Mavis!"

There was another flash of lightning and then the thunder sounded, wilder than ever. I nearly dropped the gun.

" 'Time passes—I remain,' " Fabian quoted in an eerie whisper. "The dead shall deliver up the dead and there shall be nothing but darkness and the sign of the cloven hoof."

"Stop it!" I told him. "What kind of crazy talk is that?"

"A misquotation, Mavis," Fabian said, his eyes showing white in the glare of the flash. "From the writings of Moloch."

I heard footsteps behind me and jerked around swinging the beam of the flash with me. It was Don, and I nearly collapsed with relief when I saw him. He had a puzzled look on his face. "He's not there," he said.

"Isn't that just like Johnny Rio!" I gritted my teeth hard. "Wait till I see him—I'll give him a piece of my mind, along with some judo lessons, too!"

Don took the gun from me. "I don't think we'll wait," he said. "Let's go inside."

"Where?"

"The vault, of course," he said curtly.

"In . . . there?" I gurgled.

"Don't worry," he said. "I've got a key. You watch Fabian a moment."

Don stepped up to the door and put the key into the padlock, then turned it. The hasp of the lock opened and there was a chinking noise as the chain fell away. Then Don pushed the door and it made a reluctant, creaking noise as it swung open. "All right," he said. "You first, Fabian."

The lawyer walked into the vault slowly, his shoulders slumped as if he'd stopped caring about anything, and I went next with Don coming behind us.

The vault was big inside, much bigger than I'd thought it would be. In the middle of it was a stone slab with a casket resting on top of it. And on top of the casket were four candles standing in silver candlesticks.

"Don," I said, my voice quavering again, "let's get out of here, please!"

"We can't go yet, Mavis," he said evenly. "There are some things that need to be settled first. Light those candles." He handed me a match folder.

I walked over and lit the four candles, then stood there feeling the cold dampness on my face. Don switched off the flashlight, and the flickering flame of the candles began to fill the vault with soft, uncertain light.

"Now," he said, the rasp back in his voice, "we'll settle the question of my share first!"

"You don't get it," Fabian said in a remote voice. "This isn't your real wife, Clare Ebhart. This is Mavis Seidlitz—she's some kind of private detective."

"That's right," Don agreed pleasantly. "What were the conditions?"

"You know them as well as I do," Fabian said.

"I'd like to hear them again," Don told him, his voice soft. "Don't argue with me, Fabian."

"Very well," Fabian said. "You have to be married, naturally, to have a wife, and both of you must have spent the last seventy-two hours in Toledo."

"But Toledo doesn't mean just the house, does it?" Don asked.

"If you want to split hairs," Fabian said in a tired voice, "all right. It means the estate."

"Thank you," Don said.

"What difference does it make?" Fabian shrugged his shoulders.

"A lot," Don told him. "You see, my wife has spent the last seventy-two hours at Toledo. Not in the house, but on the estate."

"I suppose you can prove this?" Fabian sneered. "You would hardly expect me to take your word for it?"

"I can prove it," Don said. "I shall, very soon. I have a statement ready for you to sign, that it's true."

"Under the threat of a gun?" Fabian laughed mirthlessly.

"I'll give you the proof in a little while," Don said. "There are other things to be settled first."

He looked across at the casket with the four candles burning above it. "My father's tomb," he said. "It is right we should be here. I am his son, Fabian. Women were the curse of his life—they dragged him down. They have been the curse of my life, too—flaunting their bodies to hide the evil in their minds! But my father was weak, he submitted to them. I have been stronger."

Don's voice roughened with passion as he went on: "First he had that Spanish witch, my so-called mother, who locked me in a dark closet to teach me obedience. After that there was the empty-headed Southern slut who was more interested in the gardener than her stepson. Finally, there was Edwina with her dirty little mind and her lusts with their vulgar trappings. It was she who warped his mind against me."

His voice broke suddenly. "I loved him, but she turned him against me with her lies, and bewitched him with her evil. But you know all about that, don't you, Fabian?"

"What do you mean?" Fabian asked nervously.

"I mean the cellar," Don said coldly. "The candlelight, the masks and the chains. It wasn't enough for Edwina to seduce my father into taking part in her fantasies. There had to be others. There was you, and that sister of mine with her man-crazed instincts waiting to be let loose."

"You're mad!" Fabian said fearfully.

"Time passes—I remain," Don whispered, "and after his passing, the cellar remained . . . and Edwina remained. So you visited here, Fabian, and so did Wanda. It must have been like old times for the three of you, to light the candles and wear the masks again."

"Lies!" screamed Fabian thinly. "You can't prove——"

Don laughed, and the bitterness of it made me shiver

116

suddenly. "Prove?" he said. "You'll have proof—of everything. You've been living expensively the last five years, Fabian, beyond your income. But you could afford it, so long as you managed my father's estate. At the end there had to be a reckoning, so you planned to avoid it.

"You knew the terms of the second will. You knew you had an equal share of the remaining tenth of the estate, and you saw an opportunity to wipe out all your problems. Edwina was becoming a nuisance, maybe even a blackmailing nuisance. So you killed her, got rid of her danger, and one share of that tenth!

"Wanda was also an ever-increasing danger. She had married a psychiatrist, and there was always the danger of him learning the truth about his wife's relationship to you. So you killed her, removed that danger too, and got another share of the tenth."

Fabian dabbed his forehead with a white linen handkerchief, feverishly. "Look," he said in a trembling voice, "I admit that . . . what you said about the cellar . . . Edwina and Wanda . . . that may be true. But I didn't kill them, ——swear it!"

"You don't expect me to believe that?" Don asked him quietly. "It's too late now to protest your innocence. There's only one thing left I can offer—a quick way out, Fabian. You don't want the horrors of a public trial, a sensitive man like you?

"The headlines," Don went on rapidly, "the photographs! The exposure of your private life and lusts to the eager gaze of the public. And in the end, the wait for the gas chamber!"

There was a rustling sound, then Don said, "Sign both of these papers, Fabian, and you won't have to worry any more."

"Both of them?" Fabian whispered.

"Of course," Don said indifferently. "One is a full confession to the murders, and the other states that my wife has conformed to the terms of the second will, and therefore we are entitled to our share of the estate."

"A confession?" Fabian repeated in a low scream. "I won't sign it—I won't!"

"Remember," Don said, ignoring his outburst, "a quick way out. Peace, Fabian, no fuss, no vulgar publicity." He stopped for a moment. "I nearly forgot. You want your proof first, about my wife having been on the estate for the last seventy-two hours, don't you?"

He switched on the flashlight again. "If you'll just take a look at the far corner?" he said casually.

The beam stabbed down into the far corner of the vault and I screamed. Clare Ebhart was there, her body sagging against the cold stone for support. Her wrists were manacled to an iron chain, and the other end of the chain had been fixed in the wall.

Her eyelids twitched as the flashlight beam hit her face, and she opened her eyes slowly. Her face and her clothes were dirty, her hair unkempt. She stared dully into the blinding beam. "I don't care any more, Don," she said slowly, mouthing each word with extreme care. "Why don't you kill me now and be done with it?"

The flashlight beam snapped off again. "There you are, Fabian," Don said cheerfully. "You've seen my real wife on the estate. She's been here longer than seventy-two hours, actually. I brought her here before I brought Mavis.

"I thought it was an ingenious plan, and like most ingenious plans, it was simple. You remember, under the terms of the first will, I inherited the bulk of the estate? I thought it might have proved too much of a temptation to my sister or half-brother to try and murder my wife during our enforced stay here.

"That's why I hired Mavis's services to pretend she was my real wife. But I wasn't fool enough to take a chance you wouldn't discover Mavis was a fake. So I made sure Clare spent the required time on the estate. Just as well, don't you think, Fabian? Because you did discover Mavis was a fake."

There was an empty silence that lasted for about five seconds, then Don said quietly, "You've had your proof now, Fabian, so you can sign the papers."

Fabian's face crumpled suddenly, and he began to cry like a child.

"Just sign," Don told him in a gentle voice. "Then you have nothing to worry about any more. It will be all over in a few seconds."

"You killed them!" I said hoarsely. "You killed Edwina and Wanda. You're the murderer. It's been you all the time!"

"Of course," Don said easily, "but I'm grateful for your confidences, Mavis. You've been an invaluable help all the way through."

"Johnny!" I shouted desperately. "Johnny! Help!"

I listened frantically for an answer. For a fleeting moment I thought I heard something move outside, but I wasn't sure whether I'd imagined it or not.

"Shout all you want," Don said conversationally. "I must admit I lied to you, Mavis. Rio was there, waiting beside the vault. I made sure he wouldn't interrupt us while we were inside."

I had a sudden sick feeling inside. Maybe he'd killed Johnny, and, anyway, that was my last hope gone.

"We don't want to waste any more time," Don said in a rasping voice. "Sign the papers, Fabian. I can make you sign them, you know."

Fabian was still weeping soundlessly. He took the pen and papers from Don and signed both of them, then handed them back to him.

"Thank you," Don said politely. "That leaves only the final scene to be played out, doesn't it? When your partner recovers, Mavis, he'll find me desolate with grief. Too late I got out here to the vault and discovered Clare's body—and yours too. Both of you strangled.

"But I wasn't too late to catch the murderer, who was still gloating over his last coup. I had a gun, he came at me, and I shot him. Regrettably, I shot him dead. Heat of the moment, you know? I can promise you a bullet through the head, Fabian—you won't even feel it."

He turned and looked at me for a moment. "I haven't forgotten your intriguing knowledge of unarmed combat, Mavis," he said. "So I think you had better be unconscious before I attend to you. Your murder must follow the pattern, you see?"

"What do you mean?" I asked him hoarsely. "The pattern?"

"Strangulation, of course," he said. "It wouldn't do to break the pattern now."

He took a step toward me, his arm raised above his head, holding the gun. "Close your eyes!" he ordered.

"Donald!" a harsh voice said. "No!"

Don stiffened suddenly, his eyeballs dilating. "Who said that?" he asked, his voice suddenly thick.

"Donald!" the voice said again. "I told you No! You disobey me!"

I knew I was going crazy then. I looked around the vault, but there were still only the three of us standing there. Except for Clare, there was nobody else in the vault.

"Donald!" The voice sounded like a whiplash. "You disobey your father!"

Don still stood motionless, his body rigid, the arm upraised. He moaned pitifully and the gun dropped out of his hand. "No," he whimpered. "You're dead! Stay dead! You always interfered in my life when you were alive. You can't come back now and start again!"

"Time passes," the voice said cruelly. "I remain!"

The candles flickered suddenly, and then I had to admit to myself that I knew where the voice came from. I saw Fabian's tear-blotched, terror-stricken face, and I guessed mine must have looked about the same.

The voice came from inside the casket.

For a long moment, the three of us stood without moving. Then the voice said urgently, "Mavis, pick up the gun!"

I reacted instinctively, and bent down grabbing for the gun. My hand touched it and, at the same time, Don's heel ground savagely into the back of my hand. I cried out in pain, and then his fist hit the top of my head, knocking me backwards onto the floor.

I lay there, half-stunned, and saw Don reaching for the gun, his face distorted into a snarl of absolute fury. Someone hurtled into the vault, pushing Fabian violently to one side as he came. He reached Don just as he was straightening up with the gun in his hand.

For a moment they faced one another. "You," Don said thickly, "you and your damned ventriloquism! I should have realized before."

"Half-brother," Carl said softly. "Your time has come."

Don brought the gun up in a swift movement, and Carl's fist thudded down onto his wrist a second later. The gun dropped to the floor and I threw myself onto it.

I heard the blows and the scuffling of their feet as I reached the gun. I grabbed hold of it with my left hand and came up onto my knees. Then I saw I wouldn't need to use it.

Don was down on his knees, sobbing for breath, his face bruised and bleeding, battered almost out of recognition.

"Get up!" Carl told him. "Get onto your feet!"

I felt rather than heard someone beside me, and looked to see Fabian standing there, his eyes shining. "Excuse me," he whispered politely and before I could stop him, he snatched the gun out of my hand.

At the same moment, Carl grabbed hold of Don and dragged him onto his feet. He measured him for a moment, then hit him with a vicious uppercut that drove Don backwards across the floor of the vault until he crashed into the casket, knocking two of the candles from the top.

Don staggered back onto his feet, and stood there swaying, his eyes slightly glazed. The two remaining candles steadied down a little, their flames burning brighter.

"Time passes," Fabian said in a high-pitched treble. "*You* remain."

The sound of the two shots was deafeningly loud inside the vault. Don stiffened as the bullets hit him in the chest. For a moment he stood upright, stark horror staring out of his eyes. Then he slumped backwards across the casket again, and the last two candles went out.

The darkness was absolute. I wanted to scream and keep on screaming. A flashlight beam stabbed out suddenly from the direction of the door, hitting me directly in the eyes and blinding me momentarily.

"Mavis?" Johnny's voice said peevishly. "What the hell goes on in here?"

CHAPTER FIFTEEN

Lieutenant Frome slapped a hand across his face, pinching the jowls tight. "This is the second time I heard it," he growled, "and it still doesn't make any sense."

"Yes, it does, Lieutenant," Greg Payton said softly. "A good deal of sense. It explains Wanda . . . to me. I had suspected before, of course. You remember, Mavis, when I found you in Fabian's room. I thought I'd find Wanda there."

"All I know is," Frome snarled at Johnny, "that I should book you for impersonating a cop! And that crazy dame along with you!" He stabbed his finger at me.

"Don't point, Lieutenant," I said coldly. "It's rude. And don't ask any more silly questions: I've had enough of those."

Frome's face turned a rich red color. "So help me!" he gurgled. "I'll——"

"I don't know what you're beefing about," Johnny said to him. "We found your murderer for you, didn't we?"

"We!" Frome glared at him. "Who's we? You didn't have anything to do with it. You were so smart you got yourself slugged over the head outside the vault!"

Johnny glared at me. "That was my smart partner!" he said nastily. "I didn't know she was going to confide in the murderer and tell him I was there, then bring him along for the ride."

"You should have been honest with me, Johnny," I said defensively. "If you'd told me you suspected Don,

I would never have told him about you waiting beside that vault."

"Yeah?" he sneered. "If I'd told you I suspected him, would you have believed me?"

"I guess not," I said apologetically.

"Anyway," Johnny mumbled, "I didn't suspect him— no more than any of the others, that is."

"If you two will shut up for a moment," Frome bellowed at us, "maybe I can get a word in and make some sense out of it!"

"You can get a word in, Lieutenant," I told him, "but I don't know about the rest of it."

He took another deep breath and looked pleadingly at Carl. "You got any ideas?" he asked.

"Don was obviously insane," Carl said in a low voice. "He must have been that way for a long time. I was wondering about his first two wives . . ."

"Let's not go into that now!" Frome pleaded. "Let's just stay with the three corpses we already got."

"All right," Carl nodded. "You remember, Mavis, when we went down to the cellar, we found Don apparently unconscious, and Edwina's body chained to the wall?"

"Will I ever forget it?" I said dismally.

"He must have deliberately hit his head against something to produce the bruise when he heard us coming," Carl said. He looked across at Fabian. "Were you there with Edwina before she was murdered?"

Fabian nodded, his face bloodless. "Yes," he whispered. "I was there. I left the cellar first and went back to my room. I thought naturally she would go back to hers."

"My guess is Don waited until you'd gone, then went down into the cellar and strangled her," Carl said.

Frome nodded curtly. "What about the second murder?"

"Wanda?" Carl shook his head. "I'm not too sure about that."

"I can figure that one out," Johnny said. "Don got slugged by Payton in his room, remember? So when he came around, he went downstairs to the cellar." He turned and looked at me. "You remember, Mavis, you told me you walked into the cellar and saw Wanda there, wearing one of the masks?"

"Sure," I said. "Why does everybody have to keep repeating my nightmares?"

"You ran up the stairs and met a naked masked figure coming down," Johnny said. "That would have been Fabian, right?" He looked across at Fabian, who nodded slowly.

"So they stripped off your clothes and put you in the chains," Johnny said. "My guess is they were going to have what their idea of fun was with you." He looked across at Fabian again, who dropped his gaze, and stared at the floor.

"So," Johnny continued, "Fabian goes out of the cellar for some reason of his own. Wanda's waiting for him to return. Then you saw the masked figure come back inside, Mavis. You told me Wanda backed away from him, and said something like, 'You're not——' and that was as far as she got before the masked figure strangled her?"

"That's how it was," I agreed.

"It's obvious," Johnny said. "It wasn't Fabian who came back—it was Don."

"He must have been hiding somewhere in the kitchen," Fabian said in a low voice. "I felt his hands around my throat and then I blacked out. When I recovered, I looked down in the cellar for a moment, and saw Wanda's body in the chains, and Mavis stretched out on the floor. I went back to my room then."

"Sure," Johnny said. "The one thing Don could depend on was you not saying anything about having been in that cellar!"

Frome looked at Fabian disgustedly. "What kind of obscenity are you?" he said harshly.

Fabian bit his underlip and stared at the floor again, his head shaking slightly.

"The thing that gets me," Frome still glared at him, "is I don't have a thing on him. He can argue self-defense for shooting Ebhart, and no jury would find him guilty!"

"I wouldn't worry too much, Lieutenant," Carl said softly. "All you have to do is let some of the story leak to the reporters. You could tell them about the lawyer who pranced about naked, wearing a mask, in a cellar that had candles burning and chains hanging from the walls. You do that, and people will pay money just to get a look at him."

Frome grinned his appreciation. "I never thought of that," he said happily. "Thanks for the idea."

Fabian stood up suddenly, then walked toward the door. "If you will excuse me," he said courteously, "I should like to rest for a while." He looked at Carl and a faint smile creased his lips momentarily. "Congratulations," he said. "I see you do have some of your father's blood in you, after all."

"Could be," Carl said casually. "Tell him hello for me, Fabian."

Fabian went out of the room, closing the door behind him carefully. Carl settled back in his chair and lit a cigarette. He looked relaxed, except for the bleak expression on his face.

"How is Clare Ebhart?" I asked Lieutenant Frome. "Is she going to be all right?"

He nodded. "Physically, she's not in bad shape, the doctor said before they took her away in the ambulance. But she's had the hell of a shock, of course. The doc figures she needs a complete rest for at least a month."

"I'll look after her," Carl said. "Maybe if I can prove there's some good blood in the Ebhart family, she'll forget the bad blood quicker. Besides," he grinned briefly, "I always did go for pony-tailed blondes!"

"Yeah," Frome said vaguely. "Well, I guess that just about wraps it up. I'll be——" He stopped suddenly and looked at Carl, his eyes widening. "What was that crack you just made to Dark, something about 'Tell father hello for me'?"

From somewhere upstairs there was the sound of a single shot.

"I think he should be doing that any time now," Carl answered quietly.

125

"You told him to go and kill himself?" Frome shouted despairingly.

Carl shook his head firmly. "I was just playing the odds, Lieutenant," he said. "That's all."

I was annoyed with Johnny. I'd gotten to the office early and he was late and if I'd known he was going to be late I needn't have been early, and I'd snagged one of my nylons, too.

"Good morning, Mavis!" he said brightly as he came into the office. "Beautiful morning."

"I wouldn't know," I told him. "It was still dark outside when I got here."

But he wasn't even listening to me: he'd walked right past me into his office. That's Hollywood for you!

When I first got here I thought I was going to be a great star because I'd won a beauty contest at home. I spent three months talking to agents and talent scouts, and if they didn't get me into pictures, they taught me more about life than I'd learned in twenty years in my home town previously.

When I did get a job at a studio, I wasn't a star even then—only a double for a star. I found out I was the spitting image of Cora Corina, and that fixed my movie career but good. Standing around under those arc lights all day wasn't my idea of living, so I quit and got a job as a stenographer.

And out of all the guys who wanted stenos in Hollywood, I had to pick on Johnny Rio, I thought bitterly. What a character! I'm around his office all day, and I'm a honey blonde with 37-25-36 vital measurements—so when he wants to make me a partner, he's talking about business. And what did I get out of being a partner—a salary cut, that's what!

There was a sudden bloodcurdling whoop from inside the office. The next moment Johnny came running out, waving a piece of paper in the air. "Mavis!" he said excitedly. "You'll never guess what—but something wonderful's happened!"

"From that whoop, it has to do with Indians," I said

coldly. "I know—you just bought Manhattan for a bucketful of beads?"

"Look!" he said, dangling the piece of paper under my nose. "It's a check, Mavis!"

I looked at it and sniffed. "Have you gone crazy? You'll have to take three zeros off that check before you give it to the bank."

"I didn't sign it, you dope!" he said. "Clare Ebhart did—for services rendered."

I shuddered. "Don't mention the name Ebhart," I told him. "Every time I hear that name, my feet start running of their own accord."

"Mavis!" Johnny grabbed my shoulders and shook me violently. "Shut up and listen! It's a check for ten thousand bucks!"

"Ten thou . . . thou . . ." My teeth wouldn't stop chattering. "You sure it's real, Johnny?"

"Sure I'm sure!" he yelped. "We've got to celebrate, Mavis. Shut up shop for the day. We'll have a day out and a night out that Los Angeles will remember, even if *we* don't."

Well, when he said that, I couldn't be mad at him any more, even if he had just busted both my bra straps. Not that it made any appreciable difference to the shape of my sweater, I was proud to note.

"All right, Johnny," I said. "Where do we go?"

"You name it, we go there," he said.

"City Hall?" I said hopefully. "We could get a license there."

"That's my Mavis," Johnny said fondly. "Always kidding! Where do you really want to go?"

I was just going to tell him I wasn't kidding, when the phone rang and I lifted it automatically and said "Rio Investigations."

"I want to hire a detective," a woman's voice said, "to find out what my husband is doing."

"I'm sorry," I said firmly, "we don't handle divorce business."

"Oh, this has nothing to do with divorce," she said

quickly. "It's just that he's been acting queerly lately, and I want to find out what he's doing. . . ."

"I'm sorry," I said, "but right now we're——"

"You see," she went on like a rock-crusher, "we have this big cellar, and all last week he's been working down there and he won't tell me what he's doing. So this morning, after he'd gone to his office, I sneaked down there to take a look. Well, I don't know, but if it's one of his do-it-yourself projects, it doesn't make any sense to me. I mean, what could he be making out of some old chains, a couple of hideous masks and a dozen candles?"

I dropped the phone back onto the rest like it had suddenly got red hot, which it had. Then I grabbed Johnny's arm and hustled him toward the door.

"You finally made up your mind where you want to go, Mavis?" he asked.

"Out!" I gurgled, and pushed him into the corridor.

We rode the elevator down to the first floor, then walked out onto the sidewalk.

"O.K.," Johnny said. "Where do we go now?"

"You sure you don't want to stop off at City Hall?" I asked him.

"Sure!" he said vehemently.

"O.K.," I gave up reluctantly. "Then how about my apartment?"

"Mavis," he said irritably, "this is our big day! We can't live it up at your apartment!"

"Are you kidding?" I said shortly.

Johnny looked at me, and for the first time in his life, he was seeing a honey blonde with the vital statistics already quoted.

"I guess I am kidding," he said slowly. Then he grabbed my arm and hustled me off along the sidewalk. I nearly told him to slow down, but then you never know about Johnny—he might have taken me seriously!

A PRIVATE TRUCE

Following Maranus's movements, Hallam slipped his oar into its rollock and allowed the padded blade to sink into the water. On a whispered command from Breuker both oars began to move noiselessly and with good effect.

After ten minutes or so they could hear the Germans shouting to each other and Hallam thought that the boat could be no more than 150 yards away from either strong point. It struck him as odd that Jacobus had risked this course rather than circling the German positions. He did not have to wait long for the answer.

When they had been rowing for about a quarter of an hour he suddenly noticed that on either side of them was a woodland of tall trees, most of which were well out of the flood. They had, Hallam decided, come across a sort of horseshoe-shaped lagoon which before the flooding had probably been a natural depression in the land surrounded by a belt of trees. The Germans, having placed their gun posts on mounds overlooking the flat countryside, now found themselves on separate islands about a couple of miles from the woods.

They turned the boat so that it followed the line of trees to the right and then Jacobus told them to stop rowing. They brought in the oars, switched on the shaded headlamp, and Hallam saw a small inlet ahead. Jacobus muttered something to Maranus and they both climbed out of the boat, standing in only two feet of water. When Hallam tried to follow them, they told him to remain seated. The Dutchmen tugged the boat into the inlet and soon they had placed its bow on dry land.

They walked in single file through the woodland,

Jacobus leading and lighting up the path with the aid of a hurricane lamp. As they continued, the ground upon which they were walking got progressively harder and then Hallam began to hear a noise like distant thunder which he knew was the pounding of the sea. Soon the trees disappeared and they began to tread the soft and thick sands of the inner slopes of the island's northern dunes. On several occasions the lamp illuminated signs depicting a death's head with the word *Minen* printed below, but they did not seem to bother Jacobus. He merely pointed them out to the other two and then indicated the detour they should make.

Eventually they reached the wooden hut, which was almost completely hidden between the folds of the dunes. Jacobus pulled out a key from his pocket and unlocked the door and they went inside.

It was a room about eighteen feet long by ten feet wide. Its single window was sealed by a wooden shutter. In the dim light Hallam could see that most of the space was taken up by fishing nets, old barrels, and sacks of coarse salt. Along one side of a wall were rolls of rotting sails and coils of rope. In the center was an iron stove still piled high with cold ashes and a mixture of blackened fish bones and scales, which had spewed out onto the wooden floor. Near the stove was a small table and two slatted folding chairs. Pervading everything was the pungent smell of dried fish.

Jacobus's eyes swept around the room and he soon found what he was looking for on a shelf behind some empty sacks. It was another hurricane lamp, which he now lighted and placed on the table. Having done this he shook Maranus's hand and gave him the key to the hut, telling him to lock the door after he had gone. Then he grasped Hallam by the shoulder and wished him well.

"*Veel geluk,* Tommy," he said. "*Pas goed op jezelf, man. Het ga je goed.*"

When he had gone, Maranus took some of the empty sacks and placed them on the floor in two heaps.

"Kom, ve slaap now," he said to Hallam. He blew out the lamp and within minutes both men were in a deep sleep.

Hallam awakened abruptly. A light was shining directly in his face and someone was kicking him. He opened his eyes and was momentarily blinded by the glare of an electric torch.

"Christ," he exclaimed. "You're bloody early. . . ."

He didn't get a chance to say any more. Someone grabbed him by the collar of his flying jacket and pulled him roughly to his feet.

It was only when he felt the muzzle of a rifle being dug into his chest that he realized that it was not Geldof the fisherman. Standing in front of him were two grim-faced German soldiers.

Out of the corner of his eye he saw that Maranus was lying on the floor near the door. He was moaning and bleeding from the mouth. Another German stood over him, pointing an automatic rifle at his head.

At 1650 hours precisely the doors of the dining room of the Hotel Auclair swung open and Colonel John Hollis strode in. Everyone rose from their chairs. As he made his way toward a small table and a covered blackboard facing the audience, he greeted the troop commanders individually and told them that the morning's rehearsal had been a "bloody good show." He beamed at everyone and had a special grin for Sergeant Jackson when he spotted him among the other senior noncommissioned officers. Hollis felt in good form; he always did before going into action, and thought it no bad thing for those around him to know it. He believed that morale, like the measles, was infectious.

The commandos' intensive training program had been completed on schedule and today's final rehearsal with live ammunition had been highly successful. Only the weather remained a source of consternation to Hollis. Generally overcast with high winds, it was anything but ideal for an island invasion in the North Sea.

As soon as he had reached the center of the room, Hollis told everyone to be seated and to smoke if they wished. While there was a general shuffling and the lighting up of pipes and cigarettes, he turned to uncover the blackboard on which was pinned a large-scale map of Walcheren and a series of aerial photographs.

"Gentlemen," he began, "D-day will be Wednesday, November first. Five days from now."

He paused purposely, not just for dramatic effect but to emphasize that this was to be the last briefing.

"You all know by now why the guns of Walcheren have to be silenced," he continued, "why the Scheldt has to be opened up for Allied shipping, and why the port of Antwerp is vital for the final onslaught on Germany. All this is old hat to you and so I'll get to the main purpose of this briefing." He picked up a baton from the table in front of him and pointed to the bottom section of the map.

"It is important now that you should have the complete picture of the assault; not just our own side of the show. There's going to be a two-pronged attack: ours at Westkapelle and the other here at Flushing. Four hours before we go in, Number Four Army Commando with a small detachment of Dutch troops from Number Ten Inter-Allied Commando, will cross the estuary from Breskens and land at Flushing. They will then pave the way for the arrival of the King's Own Scottish Borderers and other units of the One Hundred Fifty-fifth Lowland Brigade. When the One Hundred Fifty-fifth have cleared the town it will advance to Middelburg and Number Four Army Commando will make its way northward along the coast to link up with us. When that happens, gentlemen, Operation Infatuate One can be regarded as having been successfully completed."

Hollis paused again, placed the baton on the table, and lit up a cigarette. It occurred to him that such informality would be frowned upon by some of his more autocratic brother colonels in the Corps, and the thought amused him.

"Right," he continued. "So much for Infatuate One—and God knows who dreamed up that ridiculous name—now for Infatuate Two and our contribution."

There was a ripple of laughter from the audience at his reference to the code name of the operation; it was the first sign of an easing of the tension.

"It's going to be no bloody picnic. The guns we're going to be up against, and there are a hell of a lot of them, are mostly in concrete casements and range from seventy-five-millimeter to two-hundred-twenty-millimeter caliber. They are going to be defended by well-trained and exceptionally dedicated crews backed up by the island's Fortress Battalion and other infantry units. Our immediate objective will be the batteries between Domburg in the north and the second breach made by the RAF in the seawall north of Flushing. Each battery is supported by light gun emplacements, flak positions, pillboxes, and trenches; and all of them are surrounded by minefields and barbed wire."

Hollis went on to give the positions of each of the main gun targets, pointing to each on the map as he spoke: W-17 (Domburg), W-15 (just north of Westkapelle), W-13 (south of the Westkapelle breach), W-11 (between Zouteland and Flushing), and so on. When he had finished, he asked everyone present to come forward and gather around the blackboard so that they could see the detail of the aerial photographs. Some of the pictures showed the curve of the seawall in relation to the village of Westkapelle; others, the top of the wall and the flanking dunes from which could be clearly seen the outlines of the gun emplacements. There was one to which Hollis drew particular attention. It had been taken from a low altitude, probably from a Mosquito aircraft, and showed the entire defense system of the seawall and dunes.

Having given them sufficient time to absorb the photographs, the colonel told his audience to return to their seats. When they had settled down, he began again.

"Walcheren, gentlemen, has often been referred to

A PRIVATE TRUCE

as an enormous saucer, the rim of which is made up of high dunes. These dunes are of loose, soft sand: impossible for vehicles but up which, as Mr. Churchill might say, infantry can be put. But the dunes are not continuous; they are connected by a series of seawalls or dikes like the one at Westkapelle, which, incidentally, happens to be the largest. Timber groynes run out at right angles to the sea and are spaced about one hundred yards apart. The beaches are heavily mined and are covered in barbed-wire stakes. Immediately below the seawall at Westkapelle are underwater obstacles including mines set on top of concrete blocks. At one level on the summit there is a light railway and several rows of barbed wire and steel stakes set in concrete. A little lower down are the gun positions, which are linked to the upper terrace by a series of paths. You will perhaps be happy to hear that there are no mines laid on the top of the wall, so gentlemen, it might have been worse."

There was a groan from the audience which Hollis acknowledged with a smile. He then gave them a detailed interpretation of the aerial photographs, at times pointing out features not immediately discernible to the casual observer. Afterward he called for questions and there were many, mostly concerned with timings, their own armored support, the breakdown of the enemy guns, and the usual minutiae of a military operation. One or two bordered on the facetious and Hollis joined in the good humor they generated. Someone at the back of the room commented that Walcheren sounded like the "arse end of the world" to which another voice added: "Intend passing through, old boy?" The room roared with laughter and Hollis decided that perhaps the briefing should be brought to a close.

When Sergeant Jackson came out of the hotel, he found Lieutenant Mike Crowley, another section leader from Y Troop, waiting for him. Crowley, a tall, handsome twenty-six-year-old veteran wearing the ribbon of the Distinguished Service Medal which he had won as an NCO at Salerno, grinned at the sergeant.

"Well, Ron," he said with a tinge of irony, "seems to be that given a nice sunny day and providing the RAF chaps can see what they're doing, we might just get away with it. What say you?"

Jackson looked up at the black sky and the seven-tenths cloud base overhead and then cocked an eyebrow at Crowley.

"Oh, no doubt abaht it sir," he said matching the young officer's mood. "We're going to be on the pig's back, all the bleeding way."

CHAPTER SEVEN

OCTOBER 27–29

Piet Maranus was dragged to his feet and both he and Hallam were hustled outside. They were bundled into the back of a Horch personnel carrier waiting near the door of the hut. Three of the soldiers got on board with them, the fourth went in front and sat next to the driver.

Hallam, who had been pushed onto a bench facing Maranus, saw that the young Dutchman's top lip had been torn and that two of his teeth were broken. The bleeding had stopped, but he was obviously still in pain. The airman leaned forward to get a better look at the injuries and immediately was struck across the face by the guard who was sitting next to Maranus.

At the beginning the Horch crawled its way over sandy wastes, then through rough open country, bouncing over potholes, corrugations, and water-filled ruts. At times, Hallam sensed that they were passing through woodlands; he could hear the branches of the trees brushing the side of the vehicle. From what he remembered Anna's telling him of Walcheren's unflooded areas, he deduced that they were traveling south toward Domburg.

He occupied the time by asking himself a number of questions concerning their capture. Had it been just bad luck? It was possible that the Germans had made a spot check on the hut. Or had they been observed on the last part of the journey when they were walking through the dunes? There was always the possibility that they had been betrayed, of course. But if so, by whom?

There was only Jacobus and the fisherman, Karel Geldof, whom he had never met. It certainly couldn't have been Jacobus. The farmer had taken far too much trouble to get him to safety in the first place. That only left Geldof, but he had been vouched for by Jacobus. The more he thought about it, the more it seemed likely that it had been bad luck. He thanked God that he was wearing his uniform. At least he couldn't be shot as a spy; the worst that could happen was that he would be made a prisoner of war. But what, he asked himself, would they do with Piet Maranus?

The Dutchman sat with his eyes closed, cursing himself. No wonder they had taken the Tommy and him by surprise. He, Piet Maranus, had not done as he was told. When Jacobus had given him the key before his departure he had warned him to lock the door of the hut and he had forgotten to do so. Instead of having to break the door down and thus give some warning, the bastards had been able to walk in.

They were both aware that the journey was coming to an end when the guards began to put their cigarettes out and button up their greatcoats. The Horch slowed down and swung to the right. They could tell by the swishing noise on either side of the vehicle that they were passing down a short avenue of trees. A moment or so later they felt the carrier's brakes being applied. Hallam winked reassuringly at Maranus, who managed to return a painful smile.

They were pulled from the back of the vehicle and taken across a gravel quadrangle to a single-storied building. Their escorts pushed them up a flight of steps that led to a timbered verandah. Having passed through an open doorway, they found themselves in a long, well-lighted corridor near the end of which they were made to halt. A door to their left was unlocked and flung open. They were taken down a long, spiral staircase. A solitary caged electric light, high up on the concrete wall, relieved the semidarkness through which they were stumbling. Hallam counted the number of steps and worked out that they had already descended about twenty feet and there was, as yet, no sign of the bottom.

When they eventually reached the end of the staircase they saw that they were in a large concrete chamber; on the far side was a large iron-bar gate set in an archway. This appeared to lead to a wide passage on either side of which they could see several steel doors.

Around the walls of the chamber were a number of shelves supporting a variety of small arms including machine pistols and automatic rifles. Against one wall were stacked several rows of small shells, ammunition drums, and wooden packing cases marked with a death's head in red.

A Wehrmacht corporal sitting at a small table near

the archway shouted to the two guards. They responded immediately by removing the handcuffs from the prisoners. The corporal unlocked the gate and they were shoved through.

Seconds later, the steel door of the first cell on the right of the passage was slammed behind them.

Ordinarily, Major Karl Griesel would have carried out his first inspection of the day before breakfast, but today he had overslept. It had been a heavy night in the Mess and the moment he sat up in bed, he realized that he was suffering from a monumental hangover. His temples were throbbing and the bedside light which the batman had just switched on irritated his eyes. His mouth was parched and his tongue felt rough and swollen. He drank the lukewarm coffee that the uniformed servant handed to him, shuddered, and then got up to wash and shave.

Ten minutes later the commandant left his room immaculately groomed, having instructed that breakfast should be served to him in his office. It was fifteen minutes past eight, he was feeling slightly better but still a little fragile. As he walked over to the administration building, perfunctorily returning the salutes given by the sentries and others, he prayed for a quiet, routine day.

He passed the orderly room and could hear the typewriters at work and the loud voice of the sergeant in charge shouting abuse at the clerks. He winced at the noise and, making a mental note to curb the NCO's exuberance, he entered the adjutant's office through which he had access to his own room.

A PRIVATE TRUCE

Oberleutnant Helmut Friederichs, aged fifty-two, had come up from the ranks. He was a small man, rat-faced with a small moustache. He thought Karl Griesel an arrogant fool. On the commandant's entrance he got to his feet.

"Heil Hitler," he said formally.

Griesel walked past without looking in the adjutant's direction. He disliked the little man at the best of times and always kept him at arms' length.

"Heil Hitler. I do not wish to be disturbed this morning," he said as he reached the door of his own room. "You understand, Friderichs? There is an important matter I must take care of for Middelburg. As soon as my breakfast arrives, send it in to me."

He was about to enter his office when Friderichs said:

"Forgive me, Herr Major, but there is an urgent matter I must discuss with you."

Griesel stood by the door, his back toward the adjutant.

"It can wait."

Friderichs braced himself. "No, Herr Major."

Griesel turned around. "What the hell do you mean? I said it could wait."

The adjutant cleared his throat nervously. "And with respect, Herr Major, I said it could not."

Griesel scowled at the older man. One day he would go too far; he was already too big for his boots. It was always the same with these jumped-up bastards commissioned from the ranks. He was about to say as much when it occurred to him, not for the first time, that he'd better be careful; one never knew these days, whether a pest like Friderichs might not be an SS agent. And even if he were not, unlikeable as the man was, he had his uses.

He gave Friderichs a curt nod. "It had better be important. Come in."

The major settled himself behind his desk. "Well?"

Friderichs cleared his throat again. "Three weeks ago, the Naval Flak battery south of Domburg shot down a Lancaster bomber and one of the crew was seen to escape by parachute."

"So?"

"The British flyer was never found in spite of——"

"I know that," Griesel interjected. "Get to the point."

"The point, Herr Major, is that this man is now here. We have him in the cell. He and a Dutchman were apprehended by one of my patrols early this morning."

Griesel stared at Friderichs; he was trying desperately to marshal his thoughts. He was still smarting from the Hendrik van Rijn affair and was convinced that if he had been allowed to conduct matters his way he would have got a confession; he had been so near to that elusive promotion by which he set such store. Now another opportunity had dropped into his lap. He couldn't believe his luck.

He found it difficult to decide what to do first. Should he telephone the OBW colonel at Westkapelle, or should he interrogate the prisoners himself? But, of course, he couldn't interrogate them. One was Dutch and the other English; he spoke neither language. Whether he liked it or not, he would have to consult Neumann, who would come along with that fancy

Dutchwoman of his. While he had been mulling over these matters something else in the back of his mind had irritated him and it was a few moments before he realized what it was.

He barked at Friderichs! "*Your* patrols? What do you mean? *Your* patrols."

Friderichs didn't attempt to hide the smirk on his face. He knew exactly what was bothering Griesel. Already the shit was working out a way to take full credit for the arrests.

"I mean just that, Herr Major. *My* patrols. For some time we've been watching the movements of a fisherman called Geldof. We've suspected that he has been registering only half his catches and hoarding the rest in a hut he uses north of Oranjezicht in the northern dunes. . . ."

"*We?* Who the bloody hell is '*we?*'"

"The burgomaster and myself."

"The burgomaster and *you?* Why was I not informed?"

"I didn't think you could spare the time to be bothered with the activities of such a minor miscreant, Herr Major. Could I have been wrong?"

Griesel ignored the sarcasm. "So, you had the man watched. What's that got to do with the——"

"Everything, Herr Major. Yesterday, Geldof received a visitor, a Dutchman named Breuker who farms near here. We thought that this visit was to negotiate a black market deal. When Geldof was seen to hand over a key to this man, we concluded that there was to be a transfer of fish at the hut that night; so I instructed that the building should be put under surveillance. As it turns out, instead of black marketeers, we have caught the British airman and his Dutch accomplice."

Maranus paced up and down. His mind was far too active to succumb to whatever weariness his body felt. He was still angry with himself for having allowed the Germans to capture them so easily. He looked around the cell and came to the conclusion that escape was impossible. He was contemplating this fact when he heard his name being called from somewhere outside the cell.

Although it was no more than a loud whisper, he immediately recognized the voice. He went to the grill set into the cell door and pressed his face against it, wincing in pain as he did so.

"Hendrik van Rijn, is that you?" he asked softly.

Van Rijn sounded agitated. "Of course it's me. I'm in the next cell. I heard you arrive. What's happened? Have they got Anna as well? Who's that with you?"

"Be quiet, old man," Maranus replied, frightened that they might be overheard by the corporal. "Don't get so excited. The man with me is a Tommy—from the RAF; we were trying to help him escape. We both got caught up near Duinbeek. Anna is all right; she wasn't with us. Are you well, mijnheer?"

"I worry about Sybella."

Van Rijn sounded despondent. Maranus, not normally given to sensitivity, found himself trying to think of something to say that would recharge the old man's spirits.

"Anna says that they'll be letting you go soon, Hendrik," he whispered. "Don't worry. I'm sure you'll be back with Sybella before the end of the month. Anna also says that it's all going to be over very soon. The British will be here and all we'll see of the *Moffen* will be their backsides as they run. Everything's going to be all right from now on. You'll see."

He waited for a moment and when van Rijn did not reply he was surprised to find himself anxious.

"Oom Hendrik, what is wrong?" he asked, for the first time ever showing deference to the older man by using the courtesy title of "uncle" before his name.

"Nothing. I was just thinking how good it would be to see Vierwinden and Sybella again. That farm is our world."

Maranus clenched his fists and struck the cell door in a sudden spate of angry frustration. It was only now that he realized that Hendrik van Rijn was ignorant of the flooding of the island. There was no way that he could have known that his lands were now under several feet of saltwater, that he had lost most of his harvest and all his livestock. Only the house at Vierwinden remained undamaged; built on a rise, it had escaped the flood.

Piet Maranus was not religious—he'd never had any time for superstitions, so he said—but he found himself asking for guidance now. How, for God's sake, how did he tell a man like Hendrik van Rijn that he had lost nearly everything?

"Ah, yes. Major Griesel. I have your signal in front of me at this very moment. You are to be congratulated," said Erik Neumann into the telephone.

He looked over at Anna who, sitting on the other side of the desk, had just read the Domburg message for the third time. Neumann conveyed to her an explicit expression of the displeasure he felt when he had heard the voice at the other end of the wire.

"The Herr Oberst is too kind," replied the commandant obsequiously. "It was a matter of routine detection really. Information which I had received concerning a man called Geldof and the possibility of a black market in fish supplies directed my attention to a certain rendezvous in the northern dunes. I decided to put a surveillance on the area and—er—the English airman and the Dutchman were scooped up in my net. Nothing really, Herr Oberst, just a little intelligent deduction, that's all."

"I am sure the Herr Major is being too modest," said Neumann not bothering to disguise the contempt in his voice. "No doubt you are submitting a report on the matter which I will look forward to reading in due course."

"This is precisely why I have telephoned you, Herr Oberst. I thought that perhaps you would wish to interrogate the prisoners yourself."

"Most thoughtful, Herr Major. However, I will be away from the island for the next three days. I shall have no opportunity to conduct an interrogation before Tuesday, at the earliest. I suggest, therefore, that you question them yourself and have a report waiting for my return when, of course, I will come up to Domburg."

There was a slight pause before Griesel spoke again.

"This would be done exactly as the Herr Oberst directs but for the fact that, while we have people here who speak a little Dutch, our only English interpreter was transferred to divisional headquarters last month."

"Very well, there is nothing we can do until I get back. There is no particular urgency, however, and you could. . . ."

He broke off in midsentence as an idea took shape in his mind. Having thought for a moment he said:

"Just hold the line, Griesel. There is a possibility that we may have a solution."

He then placed his hand over the mouthpiece of the telephone and looked at Anna.

"I want him to question the prisoners, but the idiot says he has no one to interpret for him. It might be helpful if you could go up to Domburg while I am away and help him. Would you be agreeable, *liebchen*?"

Her thoughts began to race ahead as she replied without hesitation.

"Yes, of course. When would you want me to go?"

"Entirely in your hands, my dear. It would be helpful if you were to bring back a record of his interrogation so that it is here for my return on Tuesday."

"Then I shall go there on Monday."

"Good. I will arrange it accordingly."

He took his hand from the mouthpiece and spoke once more to the major.

"Griesel, you are still there? Frau Vermeeren, my own interpreter, will assist you. She will report to you on Monday."

"Excellent, Herr Oberst. You wish that we should send transport for her?"

"No. I will arrange for her to have the use of my own car. Shall we say that she will be with you by 1100 hours?"

"*Jawohl*, Herr Oberst. We shall expect her then; and may I thank the Herr Oberst for his most kind cooperation. Rest assured that the interrogation will be conducted with the utmost——"

"Yes, yes," interposed Neumann impatiently. "Oh, by the way, Herr Major, I am certain that I have no need to emphasize that Frau Vermeeren is most highly regarded and should be accorded every courtesy."

"Of course, Herr Oberst. That is quite understood," Griesel replied.

"Good. I am sure it is," the colonel said. "One last matter, Herr Major. Mijnherr van Rijn. There is insufficient evidence to proceed against him. He is therefore to be set free, but not immediately. Keep him in custody until I return. He will be released after I have had the opportunity to speak with him again."

"As you say, Herr Oberst. But——"

"Herr Major, perhaps I did not make myself clearly understood. I repeat, van Rijn will be released next week."

"Of course, Herr Oberst. Forgive me. I. . . ."

Griesel heard the click as Neumann replaced the receiver.

"Pompous bastard," he exclaimed as he slammed his own receiver back into its hook.

Neumann gazed down at Anna. She was sitting on his bed, propped up against the pillows, reading a newspaper. Even wearing her reading glasses and clothed in an oversize shirt of his, she looked exquisite. She turned toward him and he put an arm around her shoulders and pressed her head against his chest.

After a while she looked up and pulled him down to her so that she could kiss him fully on the lips.

Two hours later she was awakened by his gentle touch on her shoulder. She sat up and saw that he was now in his dressing gown and was sitting on the side of the bed, facing her. He gave her a glass of chilled white wine which he had just poured and picked up another from the side table for himself.

"A toast, *Liebchen*," he said. "To our love. May it always bind us together no matter how long we may be apart."

She touched his glass with her own, and with her other hand she reached out and caressed his cheek.

"*Mijn allerliefster vijand*," she said in Dutch, and when he looked at her questioningly, she translated for him: "My truly beloved enemy," and added: "To our love. Please, please God may it not only survive our parting, but let it withstand the wounds it may receive in the name of duty."

They drank, and when he had drained his glass he laughed.

"*Liebchen*, why so serious? We shall be together again soon. This, I promise."

"I, too, pray that it will be so."

When the Mercedes arrived at the water's edge, Anna could see that the boat, its crew, and the pilot of the Heinkel were already waiting. Neumann leaned over to open the door for her, but she held his arm.

"I will stay here," she said.

He nodded and then took both her hands in his. He noticed that her eyes were moist and he teased her.

"I shall be back on Tuesday. You haven't got rid of

me yet, you know. Come, Anna, this little parting doesn't warrant such a farewell."

She disengaged her hands and flung her arms around him. They squeezed each other hard and then, laughing, he gently pulled her away and got out of the car. For a moment he stood by the open window.

"*Auf wiedersehen, mein liebchen.* I really must go; otherwise we shall demoralize that young Luftwaffe pilot over there; his eyes are already coming out of their sockets. Don't stand any nonsense from Griesel when you are at Domburg on Monday. I shall be thinking of you."

She watched him shake hands with the pilot, step into the boat, and turn finally to wave to her. Only when she had seen the aircraft disappear into the clouds did she tell Weiger to take her to the cottage.

As the car made its way along the emergency embankment she told herself that she could no longer afford any of the recriminations that had already begun to enter her mind. The important thing now was to get David Hallam away. She had no idea how she was going to accomplish it, but somehow the first move had to be made at Domburg on Monday.

It had been arranged for her to have an outboard motor boat and a one-man crew. Earlier, Erik Neumann had proposed that Weiger should take her in the car, but at high tide it was unlikely that a car could get through. They had settled on the boat, and she had been greatly relieved. To have had Weiger in Domburg would have created an additional problem. The only question to which there seemed no answer at the moment was how she was going to take on Griesel and his people without help.

A PRIVATE TRUCE

* * *

She waited for the Mercedes to drive off before beckoning to the man standing in the shadow of the trees near the cottage.

Jacobus Breuker waded across the road. When he reached her she saw that his face looked drawn. He managed a faint smile.

"I've been waiting for you since late last night, mevrouw. I don't think. . . ."

He looked as though he were about to collapse. His hands were shaking and his body swayed.

"Don't say any more, Mijnheer Breuker. Come, let's go into the house and I'll make some coffee." She took his arm and led him to the cottage.

Once inside, she made him take off his boots and jacket. She covered him with a blanket and settled him in a large armchair. By the time she had made the coffee he was in a deep sleep.

He awoke three hours later and found her sitting opposite him.

"Mevrouw, I'm deeply ashamed. I should not have slept. I came because the Englishman and young Maranus were arrested at Oranjezicht yesterday morning. Geldof saw it happen. He was approaching the hut to collect them when he heard a motor vehicle making its way from the road to the side of the dunes. He hid below a ridge in the sand overlooking the hut and saw the *Moffen* go inside and. . . ."

"I know about the arrests," she said. "How did Geldof get the information to you, Jacobus?"

"He sent a message that I was to meet him at midday yesterday, in the woodland near Duinbeek. I knew that something must be wrong because by then he should have been at sea."

"And you met, as he requested?"

"Yes. I took the boat up to the edge of the woods and he was waiting for me."

"Was anyone with him?"

"He was alone. Why do you ask?"

She ignored his question. She recalled that Griesel's report had specifically named Geldof as a suspected black marketeer; it was unlikely, therefore, that the *Moffen* would have ceased to take an interest in him. There could only be one reason for their not having arrested him: They wanted him to lead them to anyone else who might be involved. If she were right, then both Jacobus Breuker and she were in immediate danger.

She went over to the cupboard and brought out a bottle of gin. She poured out two large shots and gave one to the farmer.

"Jacobus," she said, "there is just a remote possibility that you and I could free the Domburg prisoners. Are you willing to help?"

His eyes opened wide and for a moment or two he looked at the glass in his hand. He drank its contents in one quick swallow. His large, bulbous nose wrinkled and his generous mouth broadened into a smile.

"Mevrouw, you are almost a stranger to me and there are many things I do not understand. Why, for instance, you work for the *Moffen* and at the same time help the Englishman."

He waited, expecting her to reply. When she did not do so, his brow furrowed and then he nodded.

A PRIVATE TRUCE

"But I think I trust you. In any case, gin is hard to come by these days."

He laughed and held out his glass. She poured him another shot.

"All right. Now listen carefully, Jacobus. I have a plan which, with a certain amount of luck, might work. First of all, tomorrow I will telephone Herr Major Griesel. . . ."

While Anna was briefing Jacobus, Oberleutnant Friderichs was listening intently to every word being said by the staff sergeant of the security police who was standing in front of his desk. Friderichs had purposely arranged the interview to take place at a time when Griesel would not be there. He seldom stayed in the office after eleven on Saturday morning, and today was no exception. He had told the adjutant he would be in the Mess if he were required.

"You are quite sure of your facts, Feldwebel?" Friderichs asked, having difficulty in subduing his excitement.

"Yes, Herr Oberleutnant. The man Breuker met Geldof again yesterday at midday. The meeting took place at the edge of the woods not far from the hut where we caught the Tommy and his friend."

"Go on," commanded Friderichs. "Tell me again, what did the Dutchman do after that?"

"As I said, Herr Oberleutnant, he went back to his farm and then in the evening he left for Westkapelle. He made his way to a lane at the eastern end of the village and spent the night under cover of some trees near a small cottage. At about 0930 hours this morning, a German officer's car arrived and a woman got out. The car left and the Dutchman approached the woman and together they went into the house."

"And the name of the woman?" demanded Friderichs.

"As I reported earlier, Herr Oberleutnant. Frau Vermeeren, the interpreter," the staff sergeant said triumphantly.

Friderichs sat back and smiled at the senior NCO. "So, we now have a most interesting situation, do we not? The woman Vermeeren, a collaborator as far as her own people are concerned, closely associated with a most highly respected German officer but known to be in contact with those helping a British flyer to escape. I wonder who else she might be in contact with, Feldwebel Hoeffner. Who else?"

The security policeman looked puzzled. "Herr Oberleutnant?"

Friderichs chuckled. "You don't see it, do you? What I am saying, Hoeffner, is that she might also be involved with the people whose activity the same highly respected German officer has been investigating."

Hoeffner stared hard at his superior. "You mean that attack on the train?"

The adjutant nodded. "Yes, I do. But I don't know how we will be able to prove it. I have never had any doubt that van Rijn is guilty. If we could loosen his tongue just a little, we might hear more of Frau Vermeeren."

Hoeffner nodded. "I agree, Herr Oberleutnant, but we are under orders not to go near him. The Herr Major says that he is to be released in the next few days. If it were not for that. . . ."

A PRIVATE TRUCE

Friderichs was no longer listening to the Feldwebel. An idea had just occurred to him. It was a gamble, but if it came off it would pay handsomely.

"Now listen to me carefully, Hoeffner," he said. "We may have been ordered to keep away from van Rijn, but nothing has been said about his wife. I think she knows a great deal more than she has told us so far. We can't bring her in for questioning, but I think it might be most advantageous if you paid her a visit. You speak sufficient Dutch for what we want to know. The farm is accessible?"

"I believe so, Herr Oberleutnant. The house is on dry land and although the road is under water, a light vehicle could get through."

Friderichs grinned. "Good. Then go out there immediately and get Frau van Rijn to talk. I want a signed statement leaving no doubt that the woman Vermeeren is known to the van Rijn family. More if you can get it, but that would be enough to start. Understand?"

The Feldwebel drew back his shoulders and stood to attention. "Understood, Herr Oberleutnant. And, if Frau van Rijn is uncooperative, I am to use a little persuasion?"

The adjutant looked hard at the man facing him. "Don't ask such stupid questions, Hoeffner."

After the staff sergeant had left, Friderichs sat back in his chair, lit a cigarette, and inhaled the smoke deep into his lungs. He had always hoped that one day Griesel might make a mistake big enough to give him an opportunity to strike. Now, with a little luck, he might see him crucified.

* * *

225

The following day, Sunday, at just after two o'clock in the afternoon, Griesel was called to the telephone. He was informed that it was headquarters, Westkapelle.

"Frau Vermeeren, how very nice to hear from you," he said when he realized who was on the other end of the line. "What can I do for you?"

"I must apologize for bothering you, major, but before he left, the Herr Oberst requested that I should contact you about tomorrow. It would. . . ."

"You cannot come?"

"Oh yes, I shall come, Herr Major," she said sweetly, "but subject to your approval, it will be later than we arranged. Herr Oberst Neumann has given me work which he requires completed before his return; it will not be possible for me to arrive in Domburg much before early evening. I hope that will be in order, Herr Major."

"Of course, my dear; the Herr Oberst's work must come first. I shall be delighted to receive you whatever time you arrive."

"You are too kind, Herr Major. I am sure that Herr Oberst Neumann will be most appreciative of your cooperation. Goodbye, Herr Major and thank you again."

"*Auf wiedersehen*, dear lady. *Auf wiedersehen*. . . . Oh, Frau Vermeeren, you are still there? Ah yes, good. I have just thought that if you do not arrive here until the evening perhaps you would like to stay the night and return to Westkapelle on Tuesday morning, yes?"

"That is most thoughtful, Herr Major. Yes, an excellent idea. Thank you."

"Wonderful. I shall look forward to your company at dinner after our work is completed."

"Delightful, Herr Major. Until tomorrow, then. Goodbye."

When he returned to the Mess, Griesel was humming happily. Everything was going his way.

Unteroffizier Joseph Krebb held Sybella's arms tightly behind her back and pulled hard each time Hoeffner asked a question. Unlike the Feldwebel's face, which was distorted with anger, Krebb's expression was bland, almost as though he were totally disinterested in the proceedings.

Sybella was bleeding from the mouth, her face was swelling rapidly, and one eye had begun to close. After an hour of questioning, she still refused to admit that either she or Hendrik knew Anna Vermeeren. Hoeffner, who had begun the interrogation calmly, even courteously, had soon lost patience and resorted to violence. Shortly after he had changed his tactics, he had knocked her to the ground.

For the past ten minutes he had sat in front of her repeating the same questions, coaxing and threatening her. He would have felt better had she cried out, begged for mercy, or even told him to go to hell. It was her continual silence that riled him.

He got up from his chair and lit a cigarette. When he had drawn the smoke into his lungs and expelled it several times, he stood before her, his legs astride, the cigarette dangling from his mouth. Suddenly, he lunged forward and ripped away the front of her blouse, exposing her breasts. She stifled a moan and bent her head as far forward as she could, as if that futile gesture might cover her nakedness. Hoeffner immediately grabbed the long strands of hair and yanked them hard so that her head was jolted backward.

"You lousy cow," he shouted at her. "You'd better talk. If you don't, I'll burn your tits off. Now, for the last time, how long have you and your husband known Anna Vermeeren?"

Trembling with fear, Sybella shook her head. Hoeffner's eyes flashed with rage and he shouted at her in German. At the same time he held the lighted cigarette to the nipple of her left breast. She screamed only once though he burned her five more times. Then she fainted.

Ten minutes later, the two German NCOs walked out of the house. Hoeffner was sweating profusely and pink with rage.

"Well, let that bastard Friderichs complain if he dares. Let him have a go at trying to get her to talk. He won't be any more successful than we've been."

Krebb gave him a sidelong glance. "After what you've done to her, she'll be lucky if she talks to anyone ever again."

CHAPTER EIGHT

OCTOBER 30–31

By the time Anna and Jacobus reached the small emergency jetty it was half-past four and the light was already beginning to fade. As they approached, a young well-built soldier in Wehrmacht uniform with a Gewehr automatic rifle slung over his shoulder appeared. He saluted Anna and looked inquiringly at Jacobus, who stood behind her carrying a suitcase.

"The boat is ready, *meine Frau*," he said quietly. "I was informed that you were to be the only passenger, Frau Vermeeren."

She smiled disarmingly. "This man is a friend of the Reich. He is working on the case which takes me to Domburg for the Herr Oberst, and his presence there has been requested by the commandant. His papers are in my bag. Do you wish to see them?"

"*Nein, meine Frau.* All is in order," the soldier replied.

He helped them both to board the small motor boat and within seconds it was skimming across the dark, murky water. The soldier was seated on a stool in the well of the boat, gripping the steering wheel with one hand and the throttle with the other. His eyes were fixed on the point of land dead ahead, some three-quarters of a mile away.

Behind him, Anna and Jacobus sat facing each other on wood slatted seats which ran along the sides of the boat. At a signal from Anna, Jacobus withdrew a ten-inch stiletto from his jacket. Anna got up and stood beside the German who, having acknowledged her presence, again turned his eyes back to the direction in which the boat was headed. Meanwhile, Jacobus crept up silently and stood directly behind him. He raised the dagger slowly and then plunged it with enormous force into the back of the young soldier's neck.

The German's mouth opened wide, but the only sound emitted was a short gasp. His hands jerked from the wheel, his arms stiffened and then immediately slackened. He slithered to the deck, his legs twitching momentarily. Five seconds later, he was dead.

Anna grabbed the wheel, throttled back the engine, and maintained the course at half-speed. Behind her, Jacobus took a coil of rope from his suitcase. Pulling the corpse back into the well of the boat, he began to strip it of its uniform. When this had been done, he trussed up the body. Dragging forward the boat's anchor, which had been lying on top of the after deck, he lashed it to the feet of the dead man and then with several heaves managed to tip the weighted body over the side.

For a moment or two Jacobus, his breathing heavy, stood staring back at the spot where the body had disappeared. His thoughts were interrupted by Anna's voice. She had turned to see whether he was ready to take over the wheel.

"Hurry. We're approaching Domburg," she shouted.

He nodded and leaned over the side to wash his hands. Drying them on his shirt he proceeded to undress and put on the soldier's uniform. As soon as he was ready, he joined Anna. The tunic was a tight fit but with the automatic rifle slung over his shoulder and the forage cap sitting squarely on his head in typical Wehrmacht style, he looked the part.

The evening light had almost gone and it was beginning to rain. Jacobus took the wheel and Anna went back to the suitcase. She took out her small Walther PPK pistol, checked that it was loaded, and slipped it into her shoulder bag. She then unhooked an Erma 9 mm submachine pistol from its catches inside the case, made sure it too was loaded, and then replaced it. She had just closed the lid when Jacobus turned to her.

"There's a boat coming toward us. Shall I stop?"

"No. Slow down but keep going," she replied, moving forward to join him.

It was a small outboard motor boat and there were two soldiers on board. One was seated at the tiller and the other was standing, holding a rifle which was pointing in their direction. When they were about twenty yards away, Anna told Jacobus to throttle right back and approach to within about twelve feet. The other boat had now stopped and was waiting for them. As soon as Jacobus cut the engine, they heard the man with the gun yelling at them.

"You will please identify yourself."

"I am Frau Vermeeren, civilian employee at the Westkapelle Kommandantur. I am already late for an appointment with the military commander at Domburg. I am accompanied by Gefreiter Schwartz of the 1019th Regiment," Anna shouted back, trying to sound irritated.

Back came the reply. "We will proceed immediately, *meine Frau*. The Herr Major sent us to escort you into Domburg. You will please instruct your man to follow us."

The soldiers from the escort boat were waiting for them at the jetty just below the windmill in Roosjesweg. Self-consciously, they assisted Anna onto the landing stage and took her to a staff car nearby.

Five minutes later she was being greeted by Major Griesel at the steps of the administrative block; his round, cherubic face was beaming.

"Welcome to Domburg, dear lady," he said, and as they mounted the steps to the covered verandah, he added, "Perhaps you would like to be shown to your room. We can deal with the interrogation at your convenience."

Anna smiled at him and slowly extricated her hand from the grasp in which it had been held since he had helped her from the car.

"You are most thoughtful, Herr Major, but I'm certain I have caused you considerable inconvenience by my late arrival. Surely you would prefer, as I would, that we start the interrogation immediately. After all, the quicker we begin the sooner it will be possible for us to relax before dining," she replied.

This hint of promise was successful.

"Dear lady," he said with exaggerated deference,

A PRIVATE TRUCE

"your wish is my command. I will have the prisoners called immediately."

As he spoke he caught sight of Jacobus coming up the steps with the suitcase.

"You," he shouted imperiously. "Wait here and one of my men will show you where to take Frau Vermeeren's case. After that you may go. Report back here tomorrow morning at——"

"If you please, Herr Major," Anna interposed, "I may have need of him later. May he remain nearby for the time being?"

"Of course, my dear. Whatever you wish."

Staring at Jacobus, who was standing in the rain halfway up the steps, he barked out a further order.

"Follow us. There is a bench outside my office. Sit there until you are called."

Other than a single guard, halfway down, who opened an office door on their approach, there was no one else about. It was just as Anna had hoped. Although the gun batteries were fully manned night and day, headquarters staff worked to set office hours. Save for a duty officer and the outside guards, the Domburg administration building was deserted in the evening after six o'clock.

Before ushering Anna into his adjutant's room, Griesel turned to the guard, who was about to return to his post in the corridor.

"The English officer and the young Dutchman are to be brought to me immediately."

It was just his luck, thought Bruno Milch; on the one night he agreed to exchange guard duty that bastard Griesel had decided to work late.

He glanced down at Jacobus as he passed, and just for the hell of it kicked Jacobus's shin as he went by.

"You'd better not let the commandant find you sleeping. He'll have your guts for garters and it won't matter whether you came from Westkapelle or Warsaw," he said unpleasantly.

Unteroffizier Ernst Fleischmann heard Milch's footsteps on the spiral staircase and automatically placed his hand over the pistol lying on top of his desk. When the guard appeared, Fleischmann's hand left the gun and descended on the handle of the right-hand drawer of the table.

"You don't have to tell me," he said to Milch. "You've been told to come and get the Tommy and the Dutchman. I've been expecting you. They told me the interrogation was planned for much earlier. What's caused the delay?"

"The Dutchwoman has only just arrived. Griesel's got her in his office now and I shouldn't wonder if it isn't going to be the shortest interrogation on record. By the look in his eyes, I'd say the major has other more pressing matters on his mind."

Fleischmann opened the drawer and pulled out a large steel ring on which there were a number of keys. He got up from the desk and stood very close to Milch.

"I'm going to give you a word of advice, Milch," he said, prodding the guard's chest with an ironlike finger every third or fourth word. "You're scum and your mind is like a sewer. When you speak to me again, forget the descriptions and give the commandant his correct title. Understood?"

It just wasn't his day. Milch blinked, swallowed

hard, and said that he understood. He followed the corporal to the gate which led to the cells, waited until it was unlocked, and then, before going any further, unslung his rifle.

He stood a few feet away from the steel door as Fleischmann unlocked it. He watched as the NCO walked into the cell and heard him shouting. There was a scuffle and the Englishman came stumbling into the passageway as though he had been flung out of the cell with considerable force. The temptation was too much for the guard. He lashed out at Hallam, the boot of his right foot connecting with the airman's buttocks and the base of his spine.

"Get up, Tommy," Milch commanded. "Get up you bastard or I'll put a boot in your head."

He knew the Englishman didn't understand, but the outburst helped to relieve his feelings.

Hallam managed to get to his knees and after a couple of abortive efforts, he staggered to his feet. Meanwhile, Fleischmann reappeared with Maranus. He was shouting at the Dutchman to move more quickly and with each command he clubbed him on the shoulder with the butt of his pistol.

As Maranus was pushed into the passage, he spun around and caught hold of Fleischmann's wrist at a point where the NCO was about to hit him again with the gun. For a second both men stood glaring at each other. Milch brought up his rifle and dug it in Maranus's back, yelling at him to release Fleischmann's arm. The moment the Dutchman complied, the NCO stepped backward and kicked Maranus hard in the groin.

When Milch arrived back outside the adjutant's office with his two handcuffed prisoners, Jacobus was no longer sitting on the bench. He had seen the three men coming down the corridor and was appalled at the sight of Hallam and Maranus staggering ahead of the guard. They were both covered in sweat and dirt; Maranus's face was caked in dry blood and Hallam was limping.

Milch gave Jacobus a look of hostility and pushed his captives against the wall.

"Watch these bastards while I see the commandant," he ordered.

Seeing him make for the door of the offices, Jacobus guessed what the German had said to him. He immediately took up his rifle and pointed it in the direction of the prisoners, neither of whom gave any indication that they had recognized him. As Milch disappeared inside, Jacobus lowered his gun and whispered, "Hold on for a few minutes longer, *mijn kind*. It won't be long now."

Griesel looked up when Milch opened the communicating door. He was sitting behind his desk regaling Anna with his past military exploits in North Africa and Russia. He seemed to have quite forgotten about the prisoners.

"Yes?" he said querulously to Milch. "What do you want?"

"The prisoners are outside, Herr Major."

"The prisoners? Ah, yes, of course. Why has it taken you so long to get them here?"

Milch cleared his throat. "We had some trouble below, Herr Major. But they're quiet now."

Griesel ignored the guard's reply. He turned to Anna. "I think it would be a good idea if we question the Englishman first, my dear," he said. He turned to stare at Milch.

"Well, you idiot, what are you waiting for? Bring in the British Air Force officer."

Hallam, still wearing the leather flying jacket over his battledress blouse, looked across the desk to where Griesel was sitting. He took no notice of Anna, who was seated by the side of the commandant.

Griesel smiled at Hallam, not unpleasantly. When he spoke, his words were immediately translated into English by Anna.

"Will you please state your full name, rank, and serial number?"

"My name is Hallam. David Hallam. My rank is pilot officer and my number is 124608."

"The number of your squadron?"

Hallam looked straight ahead and repeated his personal details.

"You are being very stupid, pilot officer. You will please reply to my questions correctly," said Griesel.

Still interpreting, Anna got up from her chair, casually placed her hand on the back of her hip, and stretched back her shoulders. Nonchalantly, she positioned herself behind Griesel's chair. She moved casually enough not to arouse the suspicion of Griesel and the guard. She remained motionless for several minutes while she interpreted an argument that had now developed between the commandant and Hallam concerning the rights bestowed on prisoners of war by the Geneva Convention.

Slowly, her right hand went to her shoulder bag, hidden from the guard by Griesel's chair. She opened the catch and drew out the Walther PPK pistol. She waited for the commandant to complete his next question, but instead of interpreting it to Hallam she brought the gun up to Griesel's temple and at the same time spoke to the guard.

"Put your rifle on the floor," she commanded. "Move."

Griesel tried to turn his head and shoulders so that he could face Anna, but she pressed the side of the pistol into his face so that he was forced to look straight ahead. His eyes bulged with terror and his mouth was open. As he tried to speak, saliva trickled down his chin.

"You—you—you're mad," he hissed. "What do you want? The Englishman? You will never get away with it. One shot and every guard on duty will come running. You will be. . . ."

"Shut up, major," Anna retorted as she again pressed the barrel of the pistol into his temple. Addressing the guard, she added:

"I shall not tell you again. Put your rifle on the floor—now."

Milch stared first at Anna and then at the commandant. He felt his hands begin to tremble.

"Do as she says, quickly," Griesel yelled desperately.

Hallam grabbed the rifle as soon as it fell.

"Get the others in here, David," Anna instructed.

The airman nodded and went toward the door. As he was about to go into the outer office, he turned.

"Anna," he said quietly. "You are magnificent."

"Hurry, get Piet and Jacobus," she replied coldly.

A moment later, he returned with Maranus and Jacobus Breuker. In spite of his injuries, Maranus man-

A PRIVATE TRUCE

aged to laugh when he saw the commandant and the guard. He went up to Anna and kissed her on the cheek.

"I knew you would not fail us," he said.

Anna ignored the compliment and began to issue orders to all of them.

"Jacobus, go back to the corridor and watch out for anyone coming into the building. Warn us immediately if there is any sign of trouble. Piet, how many guards are on duty between here and the cells?"

"Only one, and he's down in the basement. Why?"

"I want you to go back, deal with the guard, and bring Hendrik up here. There's a gun in the suitcase over there. Take it."

"It will be a pleasure," replied Maranus, thinking of the kick in the groin he had received from the corporal.

He opened the case which Breuker had placed on the commandant's desk when he had entered the room. Slowly, and with loving care, Maranus unhitched the Erma submachine pistol from its catches. He was about to close the lid when he noticed a broad-bladed knife, sheathed in leather, lying in the bottom of the case. He grinned, picked it up, and slipped it between his belt and trousers.

Anna watched him impatiently. "Piet, don't waste any more time. Go now and get back here as quickly as you can."

When Jacobus and Piet Maranus had left, she turned to Hallam, still keeping her pistol trained on Griesel and the guard.

"David, you'll find cord and some rags in the case. Tie these two up and gag them. Don't worry about making them comfortable; just make sure they're unable to move."

Maranus could not remember when he had felt happier. Even the pain in his crotch and the continual discomfort in his mouth seemed to have vanished.

At the last curve in the staircase before it flattened out into the chamber, he stopped to check the Erma 9 mm. Once satisfied the gun was ready for use, he held it under his arm for a few seconds while he reached inside his jacket and felt for the knife. He pulled the sheath around so that it was now at a point on his waist easy for his right hand to reach without effort. He did not refasten his jacket. Holding the pistol in his left hand, he descended the last few stairs.

Maranus got to within ten feet of the table before Fleischmann looked up from the newspaper he was reading. The German muttered an oath as his hand shot forward in an effort to reach for the pistol on the table in front of him.

In two enormous leaps, Piet Maranus landed on Fleischmann's back and both men fell to the floor. The Unteroffizier, now spread-eagled below the young Dutchman, opened his mouth to scream but the moment he felt the muzzle of the Erma digging into his neck, he ceased to resist.

Maranus got up and dragged the German to his feet. Continuing to hold the pistol under Fleischmann's jaw bone, the Dutchman jerked his head toward the gate.

"Open it, you bastard," he said. Fleischmann had no difficulty in understanding what was required of him. His eyes flashed from Maranus to the table where the keys lay. The Dutchman nodded and permitted him to

A PRIVATE TRUCE

move slowly so that he could pick them up. Still with the pistol dug into his neck, the German walked the few steps to the gate and opened it.

Once inside they both walked down to Hendrik van Rijn's cell and within seconds the Dutch farmer was released. Maranus took no notice of van Rijn's outburst of gratitude; he had other matters on his mind.

"We must be very quick, Hendrik," he said, slipping off his belt and putting the sheath knife in his jacket pocket. "Anna and the others are waiting for us upstairs. Take this belt and tie up the *Moff*'s hands behind his back."

When Hendrik had completed his task, Maranus spoke again.

"Now, Hendrik, I want you to do something else for me while I am attending to this one. All right?"

"Anything, young Piet."

"Good. I saw a canvas sling bag hanging over the chair outside. Take it and stuff it with as many hand grenades as you can. You'll find them in the wooden boxes up against the wall. Can you manage on your own?"

"I can do it, Piet."

When he had gone, Maranus pushed his gun even harder into Fleischmann's neck and told him to enter the cell which van Rijn had occupied. They went in together. The German now looked terrified. Maranus pushed him onto the bed. He pulled a large handkerchief from one of his pockets and stuffed it into Fleischmann's mouth. Placing the pistol on the floor near the door he reached into his pocket and took out the knife.

Fleischmann choked on the handkerchief as he tried

to scream. His head thrashed from side to side. Maranus, his face now contorted in an expression of sadistic pleasure, placed his left foot on the German's chest, pinning him down on the bed. Pulling the knife from its sheath he looked into his victim's bulging eyes.

"*Auf wiedersehen, Mof*," he said mockingly. "At least you'll never know what it feels like to be *kicked* in the balls."

The knife plunged twice into Fleischmann's groin and blood began to seep through his trousers onto the bed. For several minutes Maranus stood hovering over the writhing body. Eventually, a combination of shock and loss of blood caused the German to lose consciousness.

When Maranus and van Rijn reached the ground floor, they found Anna, Hallam, and Jacobus waiting in the corridor. Having embraced van Rijn, Anna looked down at the satchel of grenades he was carrying. She nodded approval, then looking at Piet Maranus, she said:

"Unless we are cornered and there appears to be no chance of escape, there must be no shooting. Is that understood?"

Only Maranus questioned the order. "There are bound to be guards outside. How do we deal with them?"

"Not with guns. One shot would alert the entire detachment. We'll have to use knives," Anna replied.

"Ah good," said Maranus.

"Once we are out of the gate, all we have to do is to cross the main road. On the other side is a track that leads to Roosjesweg and the windmill where the boat is moored. A mile and a half at the most," said Anna.

"And then?" asked Jacobus. "Where do we go?"

Before Anna could reply, Hendrik van Rijn said: "Piet has told me about the flooding, Anna, but could we not go to Vierwinden? There's room enough in the house for everyone."

"I fear not, Oom Hendrik," Anna said. "It's the first place they would look for us. We shall return to Westkapelle," she continued. "They'll not expect us to do that. We'll wait for two days and then make our way across to the east. Once we are near the causeway we can concentrate on getting David over to South Beveland and on to wherever the Canadians may be. When we have accomplished that, we'll hide out in the marshes until the island has been liberated."

"Where in Westkapelle?" van Rijn asked.

"Jandhuizen," replied Anna.

Piet Maranus nodded and put his arm around Hendrik.

"Old man, Anna is right," he said. "The cellars of Jandhuizen are deep and safe."

While the three Dutchmen talked among themselves, Anna drew Hallam aside and told him of her plan.

"And now we must go," she said. "Hendrik, David, and I will go first. Piet, you and Jacobus follow."

The gravel quadrangle outside the administration block was in darkness except for the far left corner where a solitary dimmed lamp lit up the path which led to the Officers' Mess. Apart from the pounding of the sea against the dunes, the only noise they heard came from a gramophone someone was playing and the distant voices of men on their way from their billets to an evening meal. The time was just after seven o'clock.

They kept to the outer perimeter of the square, walking as quietly as the gravel would allow. When they turned into the road leading to the gate, they had the cover of the trees as Anna had predicted. She took the lead on the right of the road; Hallam and van Rijn followed. Breuker came on a little behind them and Maranus kept pace on the opposite side.

There were two masked lights on poles either side of the open gate which illuminated a very small ground area. The guards, one on either side of the roadway, were sheltering from the rain beneath the last of the trees. Anna, her pistol now back in her shoulder bag, walked slowly toward them. She stopped just outside the range of the lighted area, took a deep breath, and shouted at the top of her voice.

"Guards, come quickly. The Herr Major needs your help. The car has broken down."

She stepped forward so that they could see her and she banked on the fact that the element of surprise would confuse them into automatically reacting to her summons. She was right.

When they ran forward, their rifles not even held at the ready, she withdrew into the shadows. Breuker and Maranus were now crouched down on the ground waiting for the Germans to pass. As they did so, the Dutchmen sprang from behind. Their movements were identical. Both guards were knocked to the ground by the momentum of the attack. They had not time to cry out. The knives were driven home almost simultaneously and within seconds they were both dead.

They all helped to pull the bodies off the road and into the ditch by the side of the trees. Maranus picked up both rifles, threw one into the ditch, and handed the other to van Rijn. Now they were all armed as they made their way to the waiting boat.

Oberleutnant Friderichs was alone in the small anteroom of the Officers' Mess. The other members were at dinner, but even if they had still been there, Friderichs would have sat on his own. He was unpopular with his brother officers, who thought him a bore, supercilious, and uncouth. He was well aware of how they felt but it did not worry him in the slightest. The time would come, he told himself, when he would be in a position to make his presence really felt and then, by God, he'd show them what soldiering was all about. Until that day came he was content enough to absorb himself in more important matters.

At first he had been furious when Hoeffner had returned from Vierwinden and had told him of his failure. Although he still had sufficient evidence to arrest Sybella van Rijn, to have been able to extend the charge to terrorism would have completely sealed Griesel's fate. Of course, that was what it was all about—the destruction of the man he hated.

When he heard that Anna Vermeeren was to be Griesel's guest at dinner that night, he recovered from the disappointment of Hoeffner's abortive visit to the van Rijn farm. The plan was now simple. The Dutchwoman's involvement with the British airman's escape would be kept from Griesel. The interrogation, with

Anna Vermeeren as interpreter, would take place as arranged but with one slight change. At the end of the proceedings, he would enter the room and make his arrest. He was already enjoying the anticipation of hearing the inarticulate splutterings of an enraged Griesel, whom he knew would be quick to assess the consequences of the situation. The fool would probably panic and try to get an agreement to some sort of joint report, anything to retrieve his own perilous position. He was going to enjoy Griesel's immediate reaction as much as the telephone call he would make to Neumann on his return from Aremberg. Of course, he had to accept that Neumann himself might not be too pleased, but that was a minor problem.

Friderichs smiled to himself as he contemplated what was about to happen. He stumped out his cigarette, fingered his moustache, and looked at his watch. It was half-past eight. The interrogation was probably nearly over; he had better be on his way.

He hurried down the pathway which led past the back of the administration block and climbed a small flight of steps, took a key from his greatcoat, and let himself into the building through the back door.

For a second or two his eyes blinked in the brightnes of the corridor lights; it was only when he turned from having relocked the door that he sensed that something was wrong. He stood absolutely still and peered down the passageway. He thought he must have been mistaken. At first glance everything looked normal; then he saw that the wooden bench, which should have been resting against the wall opposite the door of his own room, was lying on its side and there

A PRIVATE TRUCE

was no sign of the guard. The man might have been called away by Griesel and in his haste he could have knocked over the bench. All the same, it did not look quite right. Friderichs slowly unbuttoned his coat, drew his gun from its holster, and moved silently down the corridor.

Entering his own office he saw that the communicating door was half open. The light in Griesel's room was on. He paused and thought he could hear a sort of low murmuring and slight movement coming from within. Creeping forward on tip-toe, he peered through the narrow gap on the hinge side of the door.

He saw the guard trussed up on the floor. Raising his eye slightly and shifting his body around to get the desk into view, he also saw Griesel's head and shoulders. The commandant had been tied to his chair and gagged.

Friderichs continued to stare through the gap for several seconds. His immediate thought was to raise the alarm, and he was on the point of doing so when it occurred to him that this would hand the initiative back to Griesel; it would give him an opportunity to cover up his ignorance of Anna Vermeeren's role in the affair. It would also mean that he, Friderichs, would be prevented from making his own report. On the other hand, if he left Griesel tied up until morning, he would not have to wait for Neumann to return before contacting Westkapelle; he would have the option of reporting direct to divisional headquarters. It was, he decided, a chance in a million to finish off Griesel altogether.

Moving backward until he was well away from the door, he replaced the pistol in its holster, turned, and quietly walked through his own room back to the corridor. He left the administration building by the back door and within five minutes he was in his quarters. He took off his coat and cap, undid his tunic, and flopped on his bed. It was only then that he began to relax. He lit a cigarette, caressed his moustache, and began to laugh.

The Heinkel 115 had seen better days. Brought into operational service three years before, it had been one of the Luftwaffe's foremost torpedo-carrying aircraft. It was now used rarely and only for reconnaissance. The roar of its two BMW radial engines was earsplitting, and the floatplane shook violently as the low-lying cumulus buffetted against the leading edge of its wings and fuselage.

Otto Leuschner, the pilot, eased the stick forward slightly and adjusted the tail trim. The aircraft responded and began to lose height, shuddering slightly in the process. As he cleared the cloud base at about two thousand feet, he looked down from the long "greenhouse" canopy of the cockpit. He saw the trumpet-shaped peninsula of South Beveland coming up under the starboard wing and banked the Heinkel slightly to port so as to keep away from land. There was no point in inviting trouble. It was just as easy to approach Walcheren from the Scheldt Estuary, provided he didn't go too far south and fly over the Breskens area on the south bank. The battle was in the throes of being lost there as well, and already Allied flak batteries and heavy artillery were dominating the coastline.

The Heinkel lost further altitude and began to make a starboard turn.

For the first time during the flight, Erik Neumann looked out of the cockpit. Walcheren was immediately below. Destroyed by man and apparently forsaken by God, he thought; it was difficult to believe anyone could survive in such desolation.

Survive. He thought of Anna again. She was surviving down there somewhere. Probably holed up in some derelict farmhouse with her bloody Englishman.

It had been at six o'clock this morning that the batman had awakened him to say that he was to report to the personal aide to the deputy chief of staff before his departure to Walcheren. He had shaved and dressed rapidly and had walked over to the headquarters building where he had been shown into the office of Colonel Werner Arendt.

There had been no formalities. Arendt had immediately shown him the decoded signal from Middelburg. He could remember every word it contained.

> Three suspected terrorists and British Air Force officer taken at gunpoint from custody of Domburg military commandant 2020 hours last night. All those taking part in the raid escaped. Four guards killed. Dutchwoman Anna Vermeeren employed clerical duties Westkapelle headquarters and interpreter for your Colonel Neumann involved. Also believed she implicated in causeway attack September 24. Instructions issued for commandant's arrest and full inquiry to be convened.

When he had finished reading the message, he had heard Arendt speaking to him.

"Your own contact with this woman makes it imperative for all of us that you should bring her in at once, dead or alive. It doesn't matter which. The others, too, of course, but she is the important one. The C-in-C does not want you to return to Aremberg until this matter has been cleared up."

Neumann had nodded and was about to take his leave when Arendt had added: "We have told divisional headquarters that they are to keep this out of the hands of the Gestapo and that you are returning immediately to deal with the matter personally. Do not fail, Herr Oberst; I assure you that you will have no friends here if you do. Oh, by the way, Frederichs, the Domburg adjutant, will be waiting for you at Westkapelle. Listen to what he has to say, use him if you wish, but don't trust the little swine. He is the type who will try and make political capital out of it all, if you see what I mean."

That had been more than three hours ago. Now the aircraft was about to land and soon he would be facing the greatest decision of his life.

He knew he would have to be very careful; Friderichs was no fool. The fellow would have to be sidetracked so that he himself would have a free hand to search for Anna. But where should he start looking? She wouldn't be stupid enough to try and get off the island immediately. She would wait for a few days. Where? Certainly not Middelburg, nor Veere, which she would realize was one of the first places they would look. Flushing was a possibility, but it was much more likely she would choose the one place they would not expect her to hide—her own village of Westkapelle.

When he arrived at headquarters, Neumann was told that Friderichs was waiting to see him. The little man, resplendent in his best uniform, marched into the room, clicked his heels, and gave the Party salute.

"Heil Hitler," he said loudly, and in a quieter but still officious tone, added: "Oberleutnant Friderichs reporting to the Herr Oberst, as ordered."

Neumann stood up and returned the salute, smiled, and walked around the desk. He shook the adjutant's hand warmly. He was not particularly pleased with himself for doing so and hoped that he was not overplaying the part.

"My dear Friderichs, we are all most impressed with the prompt action you took in this unfortunate affair," he said.

Friderich's thin lips parted, producing an ingratiating smile and showing the tips of his ratlike teeth.

"Thank you, Herr Oberst. My only regret is that the arrest of Major Griesel was necessary. It was really bad luck."

Neumann nodded his head sympathetically.

"Yes, quite so. Well, as you can imagine, the fact that the woman Vermeeren worked for me as an interpreter is somewhat embarrassing, to say the least. As an OBW staff officer, I cannot afford to have my name—er—linked with such a person. Naturally, I want to see her—and her friends—arrested without delay."

"Naturally, Herr Oberst."

Already Neumann sensed that his approach was on

the right lines; the mention of his status as an OBW staff officer appeared to be having the desired effect.

"Please, Friderichs, be seated," he said. "I would like to go over the possible escape routes that they might have taken."

Both men sat for a moment, neither speaking. Each was occupied in trying to weigh the other up.

"I will do everything I can to assist," Friderichs said at last. "I have, of course, alerted all naval and military detachments on the island. I would have dispatched detailed descriptions to the Gestapo in Middelburg but for some unknown reason I was instructed by divisional headquarters not to do so."

Neumann smiled. "They'll probably want to deal with those fellows themselves."

Friderichs gave him a long, calculating look. "Perhaps, Herr Oberst—perhaps. In any case, it is my opinion that neither the woman nor her friends will attempt to leave Walcheren, certainly not immediately."

"Really?" Neumann looked mildly surprised. "You interest me. Why do you come to that conclusion?"

"For the simple reason that they will realize we are watching every exit. So, they will wait a week or maybe two, until they feel that we have lost interest or——"

"Or until we are involved in defending the island from attack. Is that what you were going to say?"

Friderichs smiled again. "Exactly, Herr Oberst. I think that they may be hiding in one of the two larger towns. Middelburg, perhaps, but more likely Flushing."

A PRIVATE TRUCE

Neumann hoped that the relief he felt did not show. He grinned back at the Oberleutnant.

"You are so right, my dear chap. I can see that we shall have them all in custody before the week is out. I think we should first concentrate on Flushing."

"Excellent, Herr Oberst."

"There is just one small problem," Neumann said, as though annoyed with himself for only just remembering it. "I have a priority commitment for the divisional commander. It necessitates my presence at a meeting with the commandant of the Fortress Regiment detachment at Veere. It will mean that I shall be unable to leave for Flushing immediately." He pretended to think about the matter for several moments and then added: "It is, of course, imperative that no time whatever is lost in this matter."

Friderichs reacted just as Neumann had hoped.

"Should the Herr Oberst permit, perhaps I could proceed to Flushing and then——"

"I could follow you later? Yes. Splendid idea. How quickly could you be ready to leave?"

"Tomorrow morning, Herr Oberst?"

Neumann looked doubtful. "I see. . . . Would it not be possible for you to get down there this evening? I think it would be as well if you could do so. Would that cause you very much inconvenience, my dear chap?"

"Not at all, Herr Oberst. It shall be as you wish."

"Excellent. Then I will join you as soon as possible. No later than tomorrow night," said Erik Neumann.

* * *

On the afternoon of Tuesday, October 31, four officers met in a large hall in Ostend to discuss only one topic—the weather. They were Admiral Sir Bertram Ramsay, C-in-C Allied Naval Forces, Lieutenant-General G. G. Simmonds, now Commander of the 1st Canadian Army, Captain A. F. Pugsley, RN, Commander of Naval Force T, and Brigadier B. W. Leicester, RM, Commanding 4th Special Service Brigade. Seated around the table in the planning center for Operation Infatuate, each of them was only too aware of the enormity of his responsibility at that moment.

Outside under the gray overcast sky Royal Marine commandos as well as sailors and soldiers making up special detachments, were under embarkation orders.

Buffaloes, Weasels, Flail tanks, Shermans, AVREs, and bulldozers were already in their LCTs. Dominating the fleet and looking both awesome and matronly in the company of such small craft was the battleship HMS *Warspite* with her two Monitors, *Erebus* and *Roberts*.

The four officers passed the latest weather reports to each other. On one point they were all agreed. The air operations scheduled to support the Westkapelle landings tomorrow morning would, at best, be restricted. If the weather worsened, they would more than likely be canceled altogether. For a while they sat in silence. There was really nothing more that could be said. A decision had to be made. Was Operation Infatuate to proceed or not?

Admiral Ramsay and General Simmonds conferred quietly while the other two looked on. Then Ramsay addressed them. "Naval Force T sails," he said, "but if for any reason you are of the opinion that the assault is unlikely to succeed, you are to postpone the attack and return to port."

The meeting ended shortly thereafter and orders confirming troop embarkation went out. At 0315 hours next morning, Wednesday, November 1, the Force sailed out of Ostend.

CHAPTER NINE

NOVEMBER 1

The signal arriving on board the headquarters frigate, *Kingsmill*, stated that the bad weather in the United Kingdom and on the continent of Europe had grounded all aircraft. There could be no air strike prior to the landing, no spotting for the bombardment ships nor protective smoke cover for the assault craft.

Having read its contents with characteristic slowness, the commander of the 4th Special Service Brigade turned down the corners of his firm mouth and stuck out his chin. Eventually, he looked up from the message form, turned to the senior naval officer by his side, and grinned.

"Well," he said, purposely lingering over the word, "it could be a lot worse, couldn't it?"

He pointed to the gray dawn that was attempting to break through the low clouds. It was already apparent that visibility would not be a problem, the sea was relatively calm, and the breeze blowing in from the northwest was light. The naval officer nodded his agreement. For the next few minutes both men stood waiting in silence. Soon it would be daylight and then they would make the final decision.

They were not the only ones waiting. In a fleet of nearly two hundred craft of all shapes and sizes, some five thousand men of a combined operations force were already awake and had started to line the decks. Sergeant Jackson, Alf Frazer, and the other eight men of the section stared silently and apprehensively into the semidarkness toward the east where they knew the great seawall of Westkapelle lay. After a night of considerable discomfort in their landing craft they stretched their aching limbs and were grateful not to have been on one of the larger vessels such as the LCTs where men had been compelled to share the confined space with the enormous Buffalo armored tracked amphibians and their smaller counterpart, the Weasels. Jackson and the others, now dressed in the commando battle uniform of Denison smocks and denim trousers, wore the coveted green beret, as highly respected in the British forces as the red beret of the paratroopers of Arnhem. Each man carried a haversack, an entrenching tool helve, and a fighting knife. Jackson had a Thompson submachine gun with a flat magazine slung over his right shoulder, the others each carried a .303 Lee Enfield rifle, the nine-inch spiked bayonet of which hung at their waists.

Escorting the assault force were twenty-five craft of the Support Squadron Eastern Flank manned by crews of the Royal Navy and Royal Marine gunners. Depending upon their set tasks, the craft were armed with either Oerlikon guns, seventeen-pounders, or rockets. On the northern flank of the convoy were three large naval vessels, the battleship *Warspite* and the Monitors *Roberts* and *Erebus*.

About sixteen miles southeast, artillery units gathered south of the Scheldt near Breskens also waited for the decision. In radio communication with forward observation officers who would land with the commandos, they prepared their guns to bombard the four main batteries on the west coastline of Walcheren. These were to be the same targets for the warships and the initial objectives of the assault troops.

Minute shafts of sunlight were beginning to penetrate the low cloud. The moment of decision had arrived. The commanders had watched dawn break with gathering optimism when one landing craft after another began to take shape in the increasing daylight. Through their binoculars the men on *Kingsmill* now scanned the entire convoy. Although gray and overcast, the morning sky with the calm of the leaden-colored sea offered sufficient promise for the hours ahead. Within seconds of the decision, a single codeword was dispatched to Canadian Army Headquarters. The word was *Nelson* and it meant that the attack was on.

Eleven miles off, on the Westkapelle seawall and the flanking dunes, the day was beginning like any other. In the vast network of concrete casemates, pillboxes, and weapon pits, German naval and army gunners were yawning and stretching as they waited for coffee to brew. Bleary-eyed and unshaven, they peered out to sea from the gun slits and over the tops of sandbagged bunkers. The horizon was clear. All was well.

The bomb-damaged and half-flooded village nestling below the great wall was deserted. A starving dog, eyes bulging and rib cage protruding through a disease-ridden skin, limped along the main street. The dying animal sniffed at the doors of the derelict houses it passed in a feeble endeavor to find its lost home. After a while it no longer had strength even to whimper; its back legs finally gave way and the animal sank to the ground.

At the top of the main street, about a mile from the sea, the German infantry and gunners manning the great lighthouse tower and the wall in which it was enclosed, waited for their relief platoons to arrive. Already some of them were clambering down the stone steps from their gun platforms so that they could make a quick getaway to barracks. Neumann reached the tower at 0730 hours, shortly after the deputy commander, Hauptmann Eugen Krumel, had taken up his duties for the day. It was now common knowledge that the raid on the Domburg jail had taken place and that Anna Vermeeren had been involved, which meant that Neumann was not obliged to give Krumel a long explanation. He was impatient to get on with his search so his orders were crisp and to the point.

"The village is deserted. If they are here, they will show themselves eventually. If they do, keep them under observation and inform me at once. Under no circumstances are they to be intercepted, and there is to be no shooting. Understood?"

Krumel clicked his heels. "Understood, Herr Oberst. And where will you be if we want to make contact?"

Neumann thought for a moment. "I'm not sure.

There are matters I have to attend to first, but later I shall be either at headquarters or with Major Holtz at the command post."

The deputy commander nodded. "I will keep you informed, Herr Oberst."

On his way over to Groebelaan, Neumann tried to visualize what it would be like facing Anna again after all that had happened. Thoughts of her betrayal welled up in his mind, but he pushed them aside. He understood well enough what she must have suffered to make the decision; but neither his love nor his understanding could change the fact that he too had a duty. God help him, he had to make sure that neither she nor those she had with her talked to the Allies.

He was surprised to find the door of her cottage slightly ajar, and when he pushed it open he noticed that the lock had been forced. He walked through the flooded area of the ground floor and could see nothing out of place. He stopped and listened, but there was no untoward sound except the lapping of the water against the walls outside. Nevertheless, he sensed that he was not alone. He called out her name and started to climb the staircase.

When he reached the small landing he stopped again. Once more he called out to her, but there was no reply. He walked over to her bedroom door. It was closed. He gripped the knob and turned it slowly, and as the door opened he saw Oberleutnant Friderichs sitting in the small armchair next to the bed. In his right hand he was holding a pistol which was pointing at Neumann's head.

"Come in, Herr Oberst. I have been waiting for you. You have finished your work at Veere already?

A PRIVATE TRUCE

Good. Then perhaps it is just as well I did not take your orders to go to Flushing too seriously."

Neumann's eyes narrowed. "If you know what's good for you, Friderichs, you'll put that gun down. Have you taken leave of your senses?"

Friderichs continued to smile. "Bluff all you wish, Oberst, if it pleases you, but don't think for one moment you have fooled me. I know why you wanted me out of the way. You are besotted with the Vermeeren woman and you are trying to find her so you can protect her."

Erik Neumann was now standing by the bottom of the bed about four paces from Friderichs. "You are an imbecile, Friderichs. Do you really think anyone will believe you? Put that gun down before it's too late."

Friderichs got up slowly, keeping the pistol pointed at Neumann.

"I have news for you, Herr Oberst. I have witnesses. You see, since we last met I've been over to Veere. I've talked to the innkeeper, to Major Hausen, and several others there. I also had an interesting discussion with the Mess steward here in Westkapelle and then, of course, there was your driver——"

"Weiger?" shouted Neumann, genuinely shocked. He could understand the others would talk if given half a chance, but Weiger was different. Strange that he had not reported for duty this morning.

Friderichs sneered. "Yes. Weiger. He talked a lot before he died. A good chap, as you would say, Oberst; he really felt very badly about telling tales out of school. I think he might have said a lot more but unfortunately his heart wasn't quite strong enough. . . ."

"You bloody bastard!" Neumann leaped forward,

knocking Friderichs off his feet. The little man pulled the trigger of his pistol as he fell backward and Neumann felt the bullet whistle past his temple. They grappled on the floor. Neumann freed his right hand and gripped Friderichs' throat. The distorted face looking up at him began to turn scarlet. Out of the corner of his eye, Neumann saw a sudden movement. Friderichs' right arm was moving slowly, the barrel of the pistol was being edged nearer and nearer to his stomach. Quickly he transferred the grip he had on Friderichs' throat to his left hand and with his right hand caught hold of the man's wrist and began to turn the pistol away from himself. The nose of the barrel was pointing at Friderichs' chest when the gun discharged.

There was a brief pause before Neumann moved. He felt Friderichs' grip on his arms slacken, saw blood beginning to ooze from his torn tunic. He was kneeling astride the body, taking in large gulps of air in an effort to regain normal breathing, and trying to gather his wits when the cottage shook violently from a series of nearby explosions.

Neumann staggered to his feet. He looked down at the lifeless body of Friderichs and felt no remorse. There were more explosions and he knew then that Westkapelle was under bombardment from the sea. Klaxon horn alarms were being sounded from somewhere in the village and from the dike itself. He gave a deep sigh, realizing that what he was listening to was the prelude to invasion. If it hadn't meant that, for the time being anyway, he would have to give up any hope of finding Anna, he would have felt relieved that the waiting was over. As it was, he had better get down to the command post on the seawall and find Holtz.

A few minutes before 0800 hours, the Support Squadron Eastern Flank received orders and began to maneuver into two wings. They were to deliberately draw away the enemy's fire from the landing craft, which would bring in the assault troops. As the fighting ships turned, the infantry and tank landing craft carrying the first wave of commandos formed three parallel lines behind them. The run in to Westkapelle, six miles away, was soon to begin.

Some seven miles behind, *Warspite*, *Erebus*, and *Roberts* took up battle stations. At 8:15 there was a flash and a roar from *Roberts*. A huge cloud of brown cordite smoke bellied out, hung in the air, and slowly turned yellow. Seconds later the detonation of the Monitor's fifteen-inch guns thudded on the eardrums of everyone in the convoy.

The German defenses remained silent. Only three salvoes had been fired at a marker motor launch about twenty minutes before the bombardment had begun. Since then, in spite of the incessant shelling from *Warspite* and *Roberts*, there had been no return of fire. By 0835 hours, when the artillery units opened from the Breskens area across the Scheldt, the entire coastline from Domburg to south of Westkapelle heaved and shook as though in the throes of an extended earthquake.

Pillars of smoke and flame began to soar skyward and every few minutes mountains of sand were catapulted into the air. In the thick concrete casemates German naval gunners were instructed to hold their fire. When they saw for the first time the armada of small ships approaching the coastline, battery commanders had difficulty in containing the eagerness of the crews to bring their guns to bear.

Crews and gunners of the support squadron as well as the assault troops in the landing craft behind could see the lighthouse tower of Westkapelle spearing the motley gray sky. At sea level, it looked as though it was situated on top of the seawall and not much taller than the windmill to its left, the vanes of which stood starkly motionless. They watched with almost detached interest as the orange flashes continued to burst through the clouds of smoke hanging low over the walled-in lowlands.

When the SSEF was eight thousand yards off the coast, its two wings divided. Led by the LCGs and closely followed by flak and support craft, both wings bore down on the enemy gun emplacements either side of the gap. Behind them were the rocket craft. The leading LCGs opened fire with their 4.7-inch guns and immediately the north and south shoreline was peppered with explosions.

The order to the German gunners to return fire was given almost simultaneously in every battery, and within minutes the support squadron was under extremely heavy and accurate shelling. The LCGs took the heaviest punishment but, undaunted, they sailed in closer and took on the main batteries. Red tracers streaked from the flak ships into enemy pillboxes; ships were trailing smoke and flames and the air was filled with the smell of cordite and death.

Behind the sea battle now raging within two thousand yards of the seawall, unscathed and apparently ignored by the German gunners, wallowed the flat-bottomed landing craft of the assault troops. The gallant action of the small support craft of the SSEF appeared to be achieving their objective; but those observing the situation from *Kingsmill* wondered how long the squadron could hold out against such odds.

The ruins of Jandhuizen were hidden from the Westkapelle-Domburg road by a large clump of oaks and undergrowth in the middle of a large field, north of the village. On high ground, the derelict walls and the cellars beneath them had escaped the flood.

Built in 1784 by a retired wine merchant from Rotterdam, the house, imposing in its setting of formal gardens and oak trees, flourished until the French occupation of the island. In 1807, a marauding patrol of Republican soldiers, most of them drunk, attacked Jandhuizen. After murdering its occupants and plundering its possessions, they set it on fire.

Well hidden beneath the undergrowth and surrounded by fallen masonry, was the iron trap door to the cellars which had once opened up from the kitchen. A flight of stone steps led down to three large rooms where the merchant had stored his plentiful stocks of vintage wines. It was in the center room, slightly larger than the others, that Anna Vermeeren and the four men now listened incredulously as the shells exploded not more than half a mile away.

The stone floor beneath them began to tremble and, as the shelling gained in intensity, cracks started to appear in the ceiling. Plaster crumbled from the ancient walls.

They all began to talk at once. Maranus, shouting

excitedly, slapped Hallam on the back and began to praise the Royal Air Force. Van Rijn and Breuker agreed that the target was the main Westkapelle battery northwest of the village and they began to count the explosions. David Hallam shook his head and his eyes conveyed to Anna the doubt which she felt herself.

"They are not bomb explosions," Hallam said with conviction. "Listen. Apart from anything else, can you hear any aircraft?"

"No, I can't," replied Anna, mystified at first and then suddenly realizing what it might be. "David, if they are not bombs, they must be shells—from the sea. That could mean. . . ."

"An invasion?"

"No, not an invasion. That's the act of an enemy. A landing. Walcheren is going to be liberated. Oh David, don't you see? We are going to be free. . . ."

Her voice had become progressively more excited; for a moment she covered her mouth with her hands. Maranus, van Rijn, and Breuker ceased to talk among themselves. Although they had not understood all that she had said to Hallam, they were in no doubt of the essence of her words. They gathered around her, facing Hallam. Van Rijn put his arm around her shoulders, but she was unaware of his nearness, nor did she hear the others asking her to repeat what she had just said to the airman. Not even the continual pounding of the bombardment interrupted the thoughts that were now racing through her mind.

In the initial excitement she had momentarily forgotten that Erik Neumann would by now have returned from Aremburg. It was bad enough that he would know that she had betrayed his trust, but he would be in danger and there was nothing she could do to help. Please God, she prayed, keep him safe and please, please make it possible for us to be together when it is over. Make him understand.

She looked across at Hallam, who was trying to explain what was happening to the others; she smiled at the efforts he made with his limited Dutch vocabulary and indicated that she would take over.

Anna and the three men became involved in an animated discussion at the end of which the Dutchmen disappeared into the adjoining room, leaving Hallam and Anna alone.

"We have decided that we must leave here immediately," she told Hallam. "There's just a chance that we could be useful, but in any case it is imperative that we get you to a senior officer as soon as the Allies have landed. Nothing, absolutely nothing, must stop you from passing on the information I gave you."

Hallam looked irritated.

"But why me? If you are correct and the British, or whoever they are, have come to Walcheren, you can tell them yourself. You don't need me to . . ."

"David, listen to me very carefully and please don't argue; there is no time for long explanations. I have a very strong personal reason for not wishing to approach the Allies with the information myself. If you knew what was in my mind you'd probably say I was being—how do you say it in English—irrational? No doubt you'd be right, but it does not alter the fact that my mind is made up."

"Is it because *he* told you?" Hallam asked quietly.

Her eyes flashed. "What do you mean?"

"The colonel, Anna. Your colonel."

She shook her head. "I don't know what you are talking about. I——"

"Anna. My dear Anna," he said softly, clasping her hand. "You once told me how much you were in love with someone else and later . . . well, even though I couldn't understand everything he said, Piet Maranus talked a lot about you and the German colonel. It wasn't difficult to guess what the score was; I've known for a long time what hell you must have been going through. And yes, of course, I'll do whatever you want me to."

"Thank you." She put her head on his shoulder and held onto him for a moment or two. "Oh, David—what am I going to do?"

"My dearest Anna, you'll do whatever has to be done, and you'll do it bloody well."

A few moments later van Rijn and Breuker brought in a number of wooden boxes, cartridge belts, and haversacks which they heaved onto the table in the center of the room. When Piet Maranus returned he was carrying several Schmeisser machine pistols. He placed them by the side of the boxes.

Anna briefed them. She spoke first in Dutch and then in English for Hallam. They would take the boat due east for a short distance and then across the flooded polders behind the tower. Once at the far edge of the village they would make their way along the southern boundary toward the gap.

"Two questions, Anna," Hallam said. The answers did not matter all that much to him. He wanted only to clear the air of the emotion with which it had been charged a few minutes earlier.

"Yes?"

From the half-smile she gave him he knew that she understood.

"That tower. It'll be crawling with Germans. How do we get past without being seen? And if we do—and we reach the gap—what next?"

Anna shrugged. "If it's a seaborne landing, as I'm sure it is, the attention of every *Moff* on and around the tower will be drawn to the village and the seawall."

Hallam nodded. "All right. We get to the gap or somewhere near it. What then?"

"We have guns," replied Anna quickly and—pointing to the table—"plenty of ammunition, grenades, and plastic explosives. If we go now, we'll probably get to the gap before the landing takes place."

"We don't know that there will be a landing yet," Hallam said argumentatively.

She ignored the interruption. "We'll work our way along the village side of the dike, climb up on the embankment, and get above and behind the pillboxes and small bunkers overlooking the north corner of the gap. When the *Moffen* are occupied with the landing forces, we'll attack from the rear."

"Sounds fair enough," said Hallam, "but I was under the impression that the entire seawall was heavily mined."

"Not the top nor the inside embankment near the breach," she replied impatiently.

They made their way from the ruins of Jandhuizen down to the water's edge where their boat was moored. Maranus was a few minutes behind the rest as he walked slowly and with great care, nursing a satchel containing explosives and fuse wire. Behind them the bombardment continued.

They were almost parallel with the lighthouse tower, no more than five hundred yards away on their right, when Anna cut the boat's engine. Hallam and Maranus engaged the oars into the rollocks and began to row. As they passed the tower they could hear the Germans shouting to each other but, as Anna had predicted, the rear of the strong point was deserted.

It was not until they were almost opposite the partly submerged houses on the southern extremity of the village that Hallam and Maranus noticed that they were making little headway in spite of their increased pull on the oars. They were now in the main stream flowing in from the breached seawall. The tide had only recently turned, but it was already running hard against the bows of the boat.

"It's no good," Hallam yelled to Anna. "We can't do any more with these bloody oars. Start up the engine. It won't be heard against this racket. Then get into the side by those houses over there."

Anna switched on the engine, swung the helm hard over. Both men hauled in the oars, got to the front of the boat, and waited.

When they had got out of the current, Anna cut the engine and nudged the boat through what had once been a trim little back garden. They climbed out and were immediately waist high in muddy gray water. Maranus tied the boat's painter to a fence pole. Holding their guns and haversacks shoulder high, they followed Anna in single file up a slope and along the side of the house. She halted abruptly when she reached the far corner of the wall. Without turning, she indicated with an outstretched hand that everyone was to remain still. By now they were treading only mud.

Once certain that the way ahead was clear, Anna beckoned everyone to follow. In front of the house there was a wide path on the other side of which were several houses and outbuildings; these gave them the cover they required. Crouching, they ran toward them, knowing that as they did so they would be in view from the top of the tower. Seconds later, they were safely across and had regrouped in front of a large dilapidated warehouse.

They were about to move off again when, during a brief pause in the shelling, they heard the excited commands of German NCOs and the sound of vehicles coming from Zuidstraat on the other side of the warehouse. It was apparent that reinforcements were being rushed up to the tower. For a moment Anna hesitated. Then, signaling to the others to wait, she crept forward to the corner where a wide lane ran at right angles into the main street of the village.

She peered around to see whether the enemy troops had passed. The lane was less than two hundred feet long and she had a clear view into Zuidstraat. There were no Germans to be seen. She waited several seconds to be certain and then dashed across the opening to take cover in the doorway of another derelict building. Once there, she edged her way back to the corner and looked down the lane again. It was clear.

One by one they started to cross at her command. First Hallam and then van Rijn, followed by Maranus. Only Breuker was to come. She had already lifted her arm to wave him across when she heard a movement at the end of the lane. Her immediate reaction was to step back under cover and at the same time to hold up her hand, warning Jacobus to stay where he was, but she was not in time to stop him.

He started his run across the lane. Simultaneously, there came a command in German to halt and a burst of automatic rifle fire. The Dutchman had taken only three steps from his corner when he was hit in the head and throat. With his arms outstretched toward his friends, his lifeless body pitched forward into the mud.

Hallam was the first to move. He pushed past Anna with his machine pistol ready to fire. Before he could step into the lane, van Rijn grabbed him by the collar and swung him around so that his back slammed against the building. Maranus helped van Rijn to pin Hallam against the wall; Anna, her face stern and showing little emotion, whispered, "Do you want to get us all killed? If you start shooting now, you'll alert every German in the village. Jacobus is dead. There's nothing we can do to bring him back. Come on. We've got to get away from here quickly."

Hallam's eyes were smarting; there was a tightness in his throat, but he nodded and the others released their hold on him. Anna pointed to a mountainous pile of rubble about twenty yards ahead, the result of the October air raids. They raced to it and managed to hide behind some large blocks of masonry from where they watched three Wehrmacht infantrymen appear at the end of the lane.

One of the Germans turned Breuker's body over with the toe of his boot and then bent down to search it. Another picked up the machine pistol lying nearby, inspected it for several seconds, and shouted to the third who was looking closely at the ground where they had all been standing when Breuker had been killed.

After a brief discussion the soldier who had been searching the ground pointed in their direction and for a moment it looked as though they would be forced to start shooting. Then the one in charge shook his head and the Germans walked away.

They waited for several minutes, but the Germans did not reappear.

"They know we're here, but they're not sure how many of us there are," whispered Anna. "They've gone to report to the tower."

"So? What do we do now?" asked Hallam, almost certain of the answer.

"We go to the dike, of course. Are you ready?"

Hallam nodded.

As they approached the north shoulder of the gap, they were compelled to run over open ground pitted with bomb and shell craters. The ground shook beneath their feet as shells burst two hundred yards ahead of them. Spaced about twenty feet apart, they ran as fast as they could, with Anna still in the lead. Several times they had to throw themselves onto the muddy path when there was a deafening explosion and the world seemed to erupt around them.

They regrouped behind a disused workshop, the last of the buildings before the ground began to slope up toward the village side of the seawall. About fifty feet ahead of them was their objective, the north shoulder. Out of breath, they gratefully sank to the ground for a brief rest. Their clothes already soaked, they hardly noticed the mud in which they sat.

Anna stood up, ready to lead the last run up to the shoulder. As she did so there was a series of thunderous detonations from the main Westkapelle battery, followed immediately by the firing of numerous light and medium heavy weapons.

"You know what that means," said van Rijn flatly.

"The ships. The Allied ships are getting near," Maranus shouted.

Anna looked at Hallam. "I don't think we've much time," she said. "We'd better hurry."

They burst from cover and this time ran together in line abreast. Van Rijn, on the right flank, kept his eyes and his pistol trained on the village as they rushed the embankment. They reached the top without trouble and peered over the stone ledge. They were about twenty yards from the nearest pillbox which was perched almost on the tip of the break in the seawall to their left. To their right, and slightly below the top of the embankment, were a line of weapon pits. Further on, there were other pillboxes and about four hundred yards away they could just see the first casemate of the Westkapelle main battery.

Having surveyed the scene on the dike below they slipped back and hugged the side of the embankment, flinching involuntarily as the continual fire power of the German guns created a cacophony around them. Hallam was the first to lift his head again to look over the ledge. This time he looked directly out to sea.

"Christ Almighty," he exclaimed. "I don't believe it. I don't bloody believe it."

They tried to pull him down as Anna shouted:

A PRIVATE TRUCE

"What is it, David?"

He pulled his arm away from their hands. "Come up here and see for yourselves," he yelled. "Look out to sea. . . ."

When they did so, no one spoke. From as far as the horizon, the slightly white-capped sea was bristling with landing craft. They were everywhere. Lines of them, some zig-zagging, others pointing directly toward the coast. In the immediate foreground, a little more than a mile away, two columns of small gray vessels, with guns firing defiantly and battle ensigns fluttering, came straight for either side of the gap. Suddenly, a withering fire from the battery south of the breach began to take its toll of them.

Anna slithered back below the top of the embankment and was immediately joined by the others. Maranus knew what was in her mind. "If we make a run for it and we don't worry about taking cover, ten minutes at the most," he said.

"Good. The battery the *Moffen* call Rebhahn is doing more damage than any of the others put together. I think that is where we should try and give some assistance. We could take the boat to the other side and climb over the dunes. We've got explosives and grenades. We might not be able to do much, but we could be more useful there than down here."

"It's worth a try," said Hallam when she had translated what she had said to the others.

Neumann and Sigfried Holtz in the command post were mesmerized by the action of the small-gun craft which continued to close on the coastal defense batteries. Some of the German naval guns were now fully depressed and yet the British craft were coming in one after the other with their small guns blazing. They were suffering enormous casualties and their own armor was obviously far too light to penetrate the concrete casemates of the coastal guns.

"What the hell do they think they are doing?" asked Holtz irritably. He had been caught outside on the wall when the bombardment had started and was still suffering from concussion and a minor head wound.

Neumann, his eyes still glued to the sea, laughed. "They're being clever, Holtz. Bloody clever—we are falling for it."

Holtz rubbed his forehead lightly hoping that it would brush away the pain.

"What are you talking about? What are we falling for?"

Neumann turned to face him. "They know that they've got nothing that will stop our guns, so the next best thing is to dictate where we point them."

The commandant, normally a rational man and a clear thinker, did not appreciate Neumann's cryptic observations.

"I'm sorry, but I don't see the point."

The colonel shrugged. "It's quite simple. While our gunners hit back at those little ships because they seem to be the obvious target, somewhere out there maybe two or three miles away at present, our real enemy is coming in unmolested. That's what's so clever, my dear Holtz—and I think it is about time we did something about it."

Holtz still looked bemused.

"Very well," said Neumann, "I'll put it another way. While we knock hell out of the gun ships the boats bringing in the troops will be landing before we have fired a shot at them."

"What would you have our gun crews do?" asked Holtz, far from understanding Neumann's point.

"They should hold hard. Take whatever is thrown at them, wait for the troop carriers, and then blast the lot out of the sea."

It was Holtz's turn to laugh. "Every gun emplacement, every bunker and pillbox from Domburg to Zouteland is being hit by these bastards and you, Herr Oberst, you say there should be no retaliation?"

Neumann gave the commandant an angry stare. "Don't be a bloody fool, Holtz; this sort of reaction is exactly what the enemy is banking on. Believe me, we can afford to lose some of the bunkers and pillboxes to these gun ships, but we can't afford to let one Tommy step ashore from the troop carriers. If we don't stop them from landing, we have lost the battle."

Holtz sighed. He was becoming tired of the discussion and his head was hurting.

"Very well, Herr Oberst. I accept what you say, but the battery commanders are going to find it difficult to understand. What is it you want me to do?"

Neumann looked relieved. "Contact Rheingold, Waffenschmeidt, Rebhahn, and Kleist at once. Order them to concentrate their fire immediately on——"

Behind them one of the field telephones began to ring and a corporal clerk answered it.

"Forgive me, Herr Oberst," said the NCO holding out the receiver. "It is Hauptmann Krumel asking for you. He says it's urgent."

The line was bad and Neumann could hardly hear the voice at the other end above the reverberations of the shells and gunfire outside. He listened without interruption except to request that certain words should be repeated. When Krumel had finished, Neumann made a supreme effort to sound calm.

"Let me get this absolutely clear," he said. "Five of them? A girl? One of them killed. How the hell did that happen—I said there was to be no shooting. What? Yes, I see. And you have the rest under observation now?"

"Yes, Herr Oberst. Our people here spotted them as soon as they ran for cover immediately below the seawall."

"And now. Where are they now?"

"They are still there. At the top of the dike near the north shoulder of the gap."

Neumann said nothing. He wanted time to think, but there was no time. Krumel, eager to please, waited for a few seconds and then added: "It is the Herr Oberst's wish that I should send a section to intercept them?"

"No. I will deal with the matter myself, from here. In any case, you will soon want every man you can get your hands on up there."

Small beads of sweat were beginning to form on Neumann's brow. He looked in the direction of Holtz. Neither he nor the clerks seemed to be interested in his conversation. Nevertheless, he lowered his voice.

"You've done a good job, Krumel. Now leave it at that. If any of them, any of them, return to your end of the village, do not open fire. Is that understood? Do not open fire. I want every one of them alive for interrogation."

"It is understood, Herr Oberst. But——"

A PRIVATE TRUCE

"No buts, Krumel. Maintain observation—nothing more. If I need your help again, I will call you. As from now, do not try and contact me here. Wait for me to get back to you."

Neumann found his cap, did up the buttons of his tunic, and announced to Holtz that he was going up to the tower.

The major looked up from the table and held out a sheet of paper.

"Latest situation report just going off to Middelburg. Do you wish to see it before it goes?"

Neumann shook his head. "No. But get on to the batteries and make them concentrate on those troop carriers. If it makes you feel any better, tell Middelburg that I have ordered you to do so."

After Neumann had left, one of the clerks, blinking behind steel-rimmed glasses, stood diffidently before Holtz.

"Does the Herr Major wish me to get the coastal batteries on the field telephone?" he asked.

Holtz, now slumped in a chair with his head resting on folded arms across the table, looked up. His eyes were half-closed. The pain in his head was severe.

"The batteries? Why? What for?"

"The Herr Oberst's orders. . . ."

Holtz shook his head even though it hurt to do so.

"No, my tenacious little friend, the batteries have enough to contend with at present without our interference. In any case, they are the navy's responsibility, not ours."

"But, Herr Major. . . ."

Holtz glared at the clerk. "Yes?"

"It was just that the Herr Oberst said that——"

"The Herr Oberst doesn't know what he's talking about. How could he? He's just a lousy infantryman."

On either side of the 380-yard gap in the seawall, the heaviest of the gun craft continued to slam shells at the main defenses. The Royal Marine gunners worked like men possessed.

The entire support squadron, both wings, were now in action at close quarters with a stubborn and determined enemy. The sea was a huge forest of mountainous water plumes almost hiding one craft from another. There was hardly a deck without its dead and wounded.

A flak craft came at full speed out of the center of the battle area and closed the north side, firing its guns. For several minutes red tracers streaked inland scoring hits on the line of pillboxes. The craft had almost completed her run when suddenly there was a mighty burst of fire and smoke and she disintegrated.

Nearby, another flak ship, thrusting in close, was straddled by shells. Immediately she made smoke and went full ahead, but the battery had her measure. She was hit astern, a near miss swamped her bridge and upper works, two hits forward blew away her bows and the forward magazine. The survivors took to their rafts and paddled toward the shore. They had got only a few yards when German machine gunners opened up on them.

Erik Neumann ran along the top of the dike, stopping every few minutes either to throw himself on the ground or take cover in a shell hole as the earth erupted around him. His eyes were smarting from the thick layer of smoke that hung over the area and the last blast in which he had been caught had temporarily deafened him.

Although he was preoccupied with the thought of finding Anna, he saw with dismay that the guns were still firing at the attack craft and were ignoring the lines of landing craft far out at sea.

"God damn you for being fools," he shouted. "You could have beaten them. But not now. . . ."

Lying flat on his stomach he watched, fascinated, as three LCGs came out of the smoke and spray and bore down on the dike almost immediately below him. For several minutes there was utter chaos. A weapon pit nearby received a direct hit. Sand, stone, and broken bodies cascaded into the air. Shells ricocheted from a concrete pillbox and whined as they spun crazily overhead. One of the craft received three shells amidships and for a second or two appeared to maintain course. Then two more shells slammed into her stern and she sank immediately. A number of the crew managed to jump into the sea as she went.

The other two craft slightly ahead turned and came alongside the survivors. While the heavy guns kept the ships at bay, machine guns raked the sea. Within minutes both craft had been hit and, trailing smoke, they retreated seaward; behind them they left the bodies of the men they had tried to rescue.

Sickened by what he had seen and angered by what he believed was the wasted fury of the German gunners, Neumann's eyes followed the progress of the two damaged gun ships. He knew without doubt that the defense of Westkapelle had failed. About midway between the horizon and the shore were the lines of flat-bottomed landing craft. They were coming in between the two groups of fighting ships. He doubted whether there was a battery commander on the seawall or in the dunes who had even noticed them.

The end of the dike was in sight. He ran toward it. Suddenly the same apprehension he had felt earlier dominated his thoughts. What would they say to each other when they met? So as not to alarm them by approaching from the seawall, he climbed down the fifteen feet of embankment to the road running along the outskirts of the village. He walked quickly to the corner where Krumel said they had been observed. He climbed through a wire fence and crawled onto the open ground beyond where it swept up again to the dike. The area was deserted.

They had worked their way up the land side of the dunes, giving the radar station and the pillboxes near the south corner of the gap a wide berth. Even though Maranus and Anna knew where and how to avoid the mass of mine fields and wire fencing, it had been slow going.

Now they were about thirty feet below the crest of the high dunes behind the battery the Germans called Rebhahn and which to Naval Force T was known as W-13. As they crawled through the last of the low scrub bush growing halfway up the dunes, they realized that they had reached their objective. Not only could they hear the heavy pounding of the guns on the other side but about six hundred yards further on, and nearly a hundred feet below the level on which they were standing, they saw the battery's administration huts. There were about a dozen buildings and they were very close to the floodwater.

Five minutes later they were on the crest of the dune huddled against the side of the battery's concrete observation tower. They knew that while they remained immediately below its wide embrasures they would be safe.

Looking down, they could see the entire battery in a cataclysmic eruption of fire power. The defenses along the north shoulder of the gap which they had seen in action earlier were nothing compared with what they saw and heard now. Their voices were drowned in the continuous roar and pounding of the four guns. The flashes were so frequent that the entire area seemed to be under a constant arc of orange light.

Lifting their eyes seaward they watched as support craft, badly mauled, still came on to face their adversary at the closest possible range. Eventually, they forced themselves to look beyond the human drama of the battle and to concentrate on their immediate concern, the layout of the battery. Each of them tried to retain a mental picture of the positions of the casemates and gun emplacements.

Below the tower, strung out about a hundred yards apart, were the huge concrete covered casemates. They looked newly constructed and were about forty feet long and thirty-five feet wide. Each was half sunk into the dune, which appeared to be the magazine serving all four guns. From it a line of steel rails ran along a concrete apron with small spurs turning off into the narrow incline entrances to each of the emplacements. At either end of the battery was an Oerlikon gun in an open position. In the front and at the sides were a series of machine-gun and mortar posts.

Anna edged as close as she could to Hallam and placed both hands to his ear so that he might hear her above the gunfire.

"We'll go for the magazine. Maybe one of the guns as well—but only one. There'll be no time for anything else."

She noticed Hallam's eyes glance anxiously toward the tower above them. She shook her head.

"There won't be many of them in there. Anyway, they're too preoccupied to notice us. We have about two hundred yards to run. We'll have to be quick."

He nodded and she continued.

"Two of us, you and me, will go for the magazine. Piet and Hendrik can take on the gun. Let's hope we don't need covering fire."

David Hallam watched impatiently as she explained the plan to Maranus and van Rijn. Meanwhile, the duel between the battery and the small ships continued unabated.

"They understand and agree," Anna said eventually. "Piet says he has about thirty yards of fuse wire."

Hallam frowned. "That won't be enough. From the inside of that magazine to the door of the casemate must be all of eighty feet. Then we need another fifty at least for the lead. Maybe Maranus has some ideas?"

Having spoken to Maranus, Anna yelled to Hallam.

"No, he hasn't; but he says we should do as I've suggested. He thinks that once he's in the gun house he may think of something."

Hallam grimaced and raised himself into a crouching position. "That's not much help."

"All right," Anna shouted in English. "What are we waiting for? Come on."

They climbed over the top of the dune together and ran down the steep slope as fast as the loose sand would allow. When they reached the upper corner of the magazine they flung themselves against its side wall and looked up at the tower.

Anna held her breath. There was someone at the aperture. She told the others to keep in close to the wall and lifted her machine pistol to her shoulder. A moment later she relaxed. The German naval officer in the tower had his binoculars trained on the sea and was obviously unaware of the movement below him.

A slight rise in the dune to their right hid them from the Oerlikon gun crew two hundred yards off on the northern flank of the battery. They crept forward, half crouched, hugging the wall until they reached the lower corner. Anna remembered that from the top of the dune the wall appeared to be merely an extension of the side of the magazine, about thirty yards long. Opposite, but some six yards to the left of where they were standing, was the concrete incline with its steel rails running down to the entrance of the first gun casemate.

Telling van Rijn to make sure that they all kept well back, Anna peered around the corner of the wall. She took in the scene immediately ahead, along the apron behind the four casemates. Two empty ammunition trucks accompanied by about a dozen men were proceeding at a snail's pace along the tracks toward the magazine. She estimated that it would be at least six or seven minutes before they arrived at the ammunition store. She then turned her head and looked up the inner side of the wall.

As she had imagined, the building was set a long way back from the corner where she was standing. Its double doors were half open and she saw that just inside were two guards armed with automatic rifles. It was difficult to see very much behind them, but she thought she could discern other movement.

She described what she had seen to the others. It was not going to be easy, but they agreed on a plan. Fortunately, the incessant gunfire would drown the noise of their own weapons. Leaving Maranus with two packs of the plastic explosive she took the other two and all the fuse wire.

"Piet and Hendrik must make a run for it first," she shouted, "then we'll get up the inner side of the wall as far as possible before the *Moffen* spot us. There's a broken-down truck off the rails standing near the far corner where the wall meets the front of the magazine. This might give us some cover, but not much. We'll make for that. From there we ought to be able to deal with the guards."

Hallam nodded. "Then tell them to get ready to cross over. And tell Maranus that as soon as we've got our stuff in position we'll come down to the gun with the fuse lead; it will reach there but not much further."

After she had explained what was to happen, the young Dutchman grinned and replied immediately.

Anna smiled. "He bets you two guilders, David, that he will be here waiting for us when we come out of the magazine."

"Right. Tell him he's on," replied Hallam. Then he looked directly at both Dutchmen.

"*Veel geluk,*" he added. Even if his accent had not been perfect he sensed that wishing them luck in their own language had been the right thing to do.

As soon as Maranus and van Rijn had crossed the apron and were on their way down the incline of the casemate, Anna asked Hallam if he were ready. He nodded. They quickly slipped around the corner and made their way toward the disused truck which stood a few yards to the left of the entrance to the magazine, as Anna had previously described.

Hallam glanced several times to his right and was relieved to see that the two trucks were still a long way off. The men pushing them were far too occupied to look up in their direction and they were constantly having to take cover from nearby shell bursts.

The guards just inside the entrance to the building were also distracted by the attack and were more concerned with their safety than keeping watch outside. By the time that Anna and Hallam had reached the empty truck, both Germans were at the far side of the entrance talking to a third man in overalls.

Anna pointed to the lefthand door. They ran up to it. The German guards had their backs turned, but the man in overalls saw them. His eyes and mouth opened wide but before the guards could react, Anna had opened fire and the three men went down in a hail of bullets.

Anna ran on into the building. In the center was a low stack of shells which seemed to cover the entire floor space. There was a sudden movement in front of her. She threw herself to the floor and rolled over several times until she had cover from behind a steel cupboard standing against the wall. She had just got there when a machine pistol opened up from the other side of the magazine and bullets tore into the cupboard. She knew that she dare not move.

The shooting had suddenly stopped. Anna waited for several seconds and then slowly lifted her head from the floor. As she did so she felt a heavy blow on her right shoulder and the machine pistol spun out of her hand. Two German soldiers were standing over her, their guns pointing at her head. The one that had kicked her was grinning. He bent down and picked up her pistol.

As he got up, Hallam fired a short burst of fire from the doorway and both men were killed instantly. He ran to Anna and helped her up. For a fleeting moment he held her in his arms. Then he broke away and they both turned to the task of laying the explosives among the shells.

When Maranus and van Rijn reached the entrance of the gun casemate they waited for a few seconds, one at either side of the open doorway. At a signal from Maranus they rushed in, firing their machine pistols.

A young naval lieutenant was standing with his back to the doorway, earphones on his head and a mouthpiece strapped to his chest. He spun around, stared incredulously into Maranus's black eyes, and fumbled for his pistol. He was shot through the head before he had time to release the gun from its holster. One of the loaders, a fair-haired youngster, stood petrified and threw up his hands in surrender. He and

A PRIVATE TRUCE

the other three members of the crew died instantly as bullets ripped into their bodies.

It was van Rijn who found the guncotton slabs, the primers, and fuse wire. They were in a large steel box standing against the wall near the entrance. He and Maranus had known that all German gun casemates were supplied with them as an ultimate insurance against the guns falling into enemy hands.

Maranus's hands now moved deftly at the breach of the 150-mm gun. He slipped a small round primer into the center hole of each of the two slabs. Next he connected the fuse wire. Very carefully, he placed both the guncotton blocks into the breach, purposely leaving it open; an explosion in a closed breach would not be so effective.

While Piet Maranus had been preparing the charge in the gun, van Rijn had fused up the explosives and had placed both packs among the small supply of shells nearby. He now handed over the end of the wire to Maranus, who connected it to the guncotton lead. Their work completed, they made a final check of the connections and, with Maranus paying out the fuse wire from a small drum as he went, they left the casemate and ran up the incline.

When they reached the top they looked down to the right and saw the empty ammunition trucks were now almost opposite the second casemate along the apron.

"Old man, we have a choice," shouted Maranus. "We can try and get across to Anna and the *Engelsman* and get shot at maybe—or we can stay here and wait for them to come to us."

Hendrik van Rijn had already started his run across

289

the apron. Making certain that the fuse wire was still running freely from the drum, Maranus followed. When they had reached the other side, van Rijn put his arm around the younger man.

"Choice? There was no choice, was there?" he asked innocently.

"No," murmured Maranus. "Not really."

They reached the door of the magazine about a minute before Anna and Hallam appeared. Maranus told them how he and van Rijn had found the guncotton and proudly held out the now almost empty drum of fuse wire.

Anna looked at it and then the wall above them.

"How far have the trucks got?" she asked.

Van Rijn told her where they had seen them. She nodded. "Right. That means we've got no more than three or four minutes. Piet, you connect up our fuse to that wire and then throw the drum over the wall. There's just enough spare to reach the other side. Hendrik, you come with David and me. We'll go down to the corner of the wall and cover Piet as he comes down."

They reached the end of the wall within seconds and did not stop to look for the ammunition detail. As no shots followed their progress to the other side, they knew that so far all was well. Two minutes later, van Rijn, who had been told to watch, shouted that the drum of wire had come over the wall. Anna and Hallam looked and saw it on the sand about twenty feet up the slope of the dune. By now, Maranus would have started his run down from the magazine.

Hallam put his head around the corner and then brought it back quickly.

A PRIVATE TRUCE

"The bastards are here," he yelled. "Come on. Hit them now before they have a chance to. . . ."

There was a burst of automatic rifle fire from the other side of the wall. Hallam immediately came out of cover but before he could fire a shot, Piet Maranus staggered past him. The young Dutchman collapsed in the arms of Anna and Hendrik van Rijn. Blood was flowing freely from a large wound in his chest.

"Get back here, van Rijn. Leave him to Anna," yelled Hallam, who was by now firing at the ammunition detail, some of whom had spread out along the apron while others had taken cover both in and around the two trucks. Their guns were blazing at the corner of the wall. Bullets were whistling past Hallam and some were slamming into the brickwork by his side.

Anna and van Rijn joined him and their concerted fire seemed to have its effect after a short time. The men who had taken up positions in front of the truck on the apron now retreated to the back. Four had been hit and lay motionless.

Hallam looked over his shoulder and saw that Maranus was now bleeding from the mouth. While van Rijn kept up an intensive fire against the German detail, Hallam and Anna went over to the young Dutchman. They could see that he was dying. Anna held his hand while Hallam wiped the blood from his mouth. For a moment he raised his head slightly and his eyes looked at Hallam.

"*Engelsman* . . . you owe . . . me . . . two guil . . ."

There was just a glimmer of a smile on his blood-stained lips when he died.

They told van Rijn between bursts of shooting. He said nothing but went over to the body and unhitched the two stick grenades that Maranus had tied to his belt. Then he untied the two he was carrying himself.

"There's only one way we are going to get out of this. You take the Englishman and get up to the fuse. I will hold the *Moffen* with these. Light the fuse and get out. I will follow."

"No, Oom Hendrik," Anna cried. "I will stay with you. . . ."

"Don't argue with me, girl," he screamed angrily. "Go, now."

Anna told Hallam what Hendrik wanted. Still firing his gun he yelled back to her. "He's right. It's the only way out. Who stays behind doesn't matter. If it works, we'll all get out anyway. If it doesn't, then we'll all be finished."

They got to the fuse within seconds and Hallam had the match ready. He signaled down to Hendrik van Rijn and waited for him to throw the first grenade. He did so. They saw the explosion and Hallam struck the match, cupped it in his hands, and put the flame to the end of the wire. The fuse took immediately and began to hiss and sputter, burning at the rate of two feet per second. Hallam reckoned that they now had less than a minute before the magazine went up and another twenty-five seconds for the gun casemate to go.

When van Rijn had thrown the grenade, it had fallen about twenty feet short of the trucks and had exploded harmlessly. He knew that Hallam would now have lighted the fuse. He also knew that it would be quite impossible for him to throw the other grenades any further than the first. Either he would be shot in the back as he ran or be blown up with the magazine.

He looked up at Anna, and for a moment he felt guilty for the worry he knew he would cause her. He waved, but he could not tell whether she had seen him. He picked up the remaining three grenades, put two in his left hand, and held one in his right. His mind was calm and completely composed when he ran out from the cover of the wall.

He got to within fifteen feet of the trucks and the detail before the first bullet hit him. His headlong rush toward them had taken the Germans by surprise and at first those that fired did so wildly. It was only when they saw the first grenade coming for them that all their guns concentrated on him. He sank to his knees, got up again, and then staggered three more paces. He tossed the last two grenades as more bullets ripped into his body. They exploded four seconds later, killing five of the Germans and wounding the rest. Before van Rijn died, he mouthed the name of Sybella and asked her forgiveness.

Once he was certain that the fuse had taken, Hallam turned, expecting to see Hendrik coming up from the concrete apron. Instead, he saw that Anna had started to run back to the corner of the wall. He leaped forward and caught her before she had gone more than a few feet. He spun her around angrily. She was screaming, calling Hendrik's name. Hallam glanced back at the fuse. It was now at the top of the wall. Through her sobs Anna shouted out what had happened.

There was no time to comfort her. He shook her,

hard, and started to pull her forward. They had thirty seconds to get to the top of the dune.

Flinging themselves over the crest of the sand hill they lay waiting, their eyes riveted on the magazine and the casemate below them. The seconds passed and Hallam glanced anxiously at Anna.

"The bloody fuses. Something's gone wrong," he shouted.

She thought it ironical. Jacobus Breuker, Piet Maranus, her beloved Hendrik all dead—and now he was saying that something was wrong.

There was a renewed attack by the gun ships and retaliatory firing. Flashing through Hallam's mind were all the moves they had made to connect up the explosives. Somewhere they must have made a mistake and the fuses had burned out.

"Oh Christ, don't let it have been all for nothing," he shouted. "Please. . . ."

He got no further. The top of the dune suddenly shuddered violently and at the same time there was a thunderous repercussion which was clearly distinguishable from the noise of the gun duel still in progress.

They both stared at the magazine as the center of its concrete roof appeared to bulge momentarily and then subside. Huge cracks formed in the structure and from them smoke began to pour. Within a matter of seconds, flames were leaping from the front of the building and from a large hole in its side. The wall which had given them their cover moments before had crumbled as if struck by an earthquake.

Neither Anna nor Hallam spoke. Their hearts beat fast as they waited and watched for the second explosion. Hallam silently counted off the seconds and Anna, now thinking rationally, began to reconcile the deaths of van Rijn and the others with what was being accomplished. Hallam had got up to twenty-eight when it happened.

There was another tremor, smaller than the last, followed immediately by a loud reverberation. They saw the thick concrete slab on top of the gun casemate split into two as if it had been a wooden box struck by an ax. Both slabs of concrete collapsed into the center of the gun house and large cracks appeared on the sides of the building. A second column of smoke spiraled into the air.

"By God, Anna, we've done it. We've done it," Hallam yelled, throwing his arm around her.

Her mind went back to another occasion when she had heard Piet Maranus shouting out something similar; the night they had attacked the train. It seemed a lifetime ago. She pulled herself together. What was it Erik Neumann had said to her on that afternoon in Veere? "We cannot change the past, just as none of us can escape our destiny. Remember that, *liebchen*, and the present will be more tolerable."

She laughed out loud and held on to Hallam as he swooped her off her feet and swung her around and around. Thrusting her face forward she rested her chin on his shoulder so that he could not see the tears in her eyes.

He released her suddenly. "Anna, I'm sorry about Jacobus, Piet, and Hendrik. I know how much they all meant to you, especially Hendrik. I wish——"

She put her finger to his lips.

"No, don't be sorry. There's no need. I was very

wrong to have behaved as I did. Hendrik and the others died fighting for something they believed in. There's no reason to be sorry about that."

He sighed. "No, I suppose not. . . ."

"David," she interjected, "Listen. Can you hear?"

He listened for a moment and then grinned. "The guns. The guns have stopped firing."

They went back to the crest of the dune and looked over the top. There was pandemonium below. Men were running from one casemate to another. Others were rushing up and down the concrete apron and there were fire parties working around the magazine and the emplacement that had been destroyed. Only the two Oerlikon guns were now operating against the gun craft.

Hallam's excitement gradually gained momentum as he shouted: "Do you know what I think? I think the bastards have run out of ammunition. By blowing that magazine, we've virtually silenced the entire battery. It's incredible, but that's what has happened. Look. . . ."

They waited several minutes to make sure. The guns remained silent and the shelling from the sea became more intense and the attack more audacious.

They had just decided that the time had come for them to get back to the north side of the gap when three events occurred almost simultaneously. It was Anna who saw two of them first. They both saw and heard the third together.

She had been watching the LCGs coming into the shore when her eyes caught sight of a large number of landing craft about a quarter of a mile out at sea; they seemed to be moving slowly but directly for the breach in the seawall. She pointed them out to Hallam and as they watched their progress they also saw in the distance five small ships in line abreast that seemed to cover themselves in smoke. Seconds later the sea around the landing craft, and some of the support ships ahead of them, was peppered with what seemed to be small caliber shell bursts.

"Christ!" exclaimed Hallam. "They were rockets. And they came from our own ships. They must have got the range mucked up. They were meant for Westkapelle. Look what's happening to the landing craft now." The LCIs among which the rockets had fallen had immediately taken evasive action and were already zig-zagging away from the direction in which they had been heading.

They heard the aircraft before they saw them. They were preparing to start their journey back down the other side of the dune when the air was filled with the high-pitched sound of single-engine aircraft. At first it was like an enormous swarm of bees approaching. As they got nearer the humming changed to a roar. They came in from the southeast and, as they swooped, they belched out both rocket and cannon fire plastering the already crippled battery with high explosives.

"Typhoons," Hallam yelled. "Let's get out of here. Come on. Run for it before they start on the tower."

They did not stop running until they reached the line of scrub bush at the bottom of the dunes. By this time they were out of breath and they both slumped down to rest in a small clearing. More aircraft were swooping in from the sea. They could hear them strafing the coastline immediately behind them and the batteries near Westkapelle and Domburg.

Anna stretched out on her back. Her eyes were closed and she was now breathing evenly. She tried to blot out the sound of war which seemed to envelop them. Her arms lay limply by her side, her hands were relaxed. The machine pistol she had carried lay rejected for the moment.

Hallam, too excited, too elated to relax, sat on his haunches nearby watching the Typhoons in the distance as they swept up from their low-level attacks near the village.

He looked down at Anna and smiled. This was the first time he had ever seen her so composed.

"About time we got going," he said. "Wake up!"

"I wasn't asleep," she replied. "I was trying to make believe that the war was over and Walcheren was as it used to be. With all this going on around us, that was stupid wasn't it?" She opened her eyes and smiled.

"Well, it won't be long now. A few more weeks, perhaps. Probably all over and done with by Christmas," he said, stretching across to pick up his gun.

There was a light footstep behind them and before they could turn, a heavily accented voice said in English:

"That, my young friend, is a matter of opinion. No. Leave the gun where it is. Now, both of you, get up and turn around slowly."

When they obeyed the command, Anna gasped. Erik Neumann was standing ten feet away and he was pointing a Luger pistol directly at Hallam's chest.

CHAPTER TEN

November 1, continued

"Well, Anna. Have you nothing to say?" Neumann asked in German. His face was stern, but his eyes softened as he looked at her.

Anna pushed back her hair, which was being tousled by the strong wind that had begun to blow over the dunes.

"What do you want me to say? That I am sorry—that I regret having betrayed you?"

Neumann smiled. "I fear that if you did, I would not believe you."

"Exactly," she retorted. "So there is nothing either of us can say."

His expression changed. "Nothing? Are you sure?"

"Nothing."

"So. You want me to believe that our love no longer exists, that it has been swept away? Perhaps you are suggesting that it never happened?"

"No! But how can I begin to make you understand. . . ."

He shook his head. "I understand only one thing,

liebchen. Now that I have found you, I will never lose you again."

While they had been talking, Hallam had been edging closer to Anna.

Neumann had noticed and he jerked the Luger at the Englishman. "Stand away from her," he commanded.

Hallam sneered. "How the hell did you find us?"

Neumann ignored the question. He looked hard at the scrubland either side of where they were standing. "There were more of you," he said in English. "Where are the others?"

"Killed," replied Hallam.

"How?"

Hallam's eyes flashed. "They died fighting—to rid their island of dirty krauts like you."

"I see," Neumann said softly.

"No, you don't," Hallam yelled back angrily. "You don't see a damned thing. You don't even see that you've lost the bloody war. . . ."

Anna interjected, her voice harsh. "David, be quiet. You don't know what you are saying."

She switched to German as she turned to Neumann. "Erik, he's very young and headstrong. He has no idea—he doesn't know what he is saying."

Neumann smiled at her but said nothing. Hallam saw the look that passed between them and tried unsuccessfully to suppress his jealousy. He turned on Neumann again.

"Why don't you stop playing games, you arrogant bastard?" He pointed toward the dunes and the sea. "Our lot are out there. If they haven't landed already, it's only a matter of time before you are put where you belong. If you harm either her or me now, you won't have a bloody chance——"

Anna shouted to him again. "David, you are being very stupid. Don't say any more."

He looked at her angrily. "I'll say what I like. If you think that because you've been his whore he'll go easy on you, you'd better think again."

Then to Neumann he added, "You've got only one chance. Give me that gun and let me take you in. It's your only hope, and you'd better believe it."

Erik Neumann regarded him coolly. "I will tell you what I believe. I believe that if I had not caught up with you and you had got back to your own people, you would have had a very interesting report to make, is that not so?"

Hallam shook his head. "I don't know what you are talking about."

Neumann gave him a wry look. "I think you do. I think you would have felt obliged to pass on the information which an extremely foolish German officer let slip, and that you would have enjoyed telling the bit about the beautiful Dutch girl who betrayed him. Yes, I think you know exactly what I am talking about."

Hallam seemed rather less sure of himself. "Look don't waste time," he said nervously. "Give me the gun."

Neumann shook his head. "I think not. It is now time for you to stop playing games. Put your hands on your head and don't move."

Hallam obeyed. The bluff had failed. There was nothing more he could say. For some unknown reason he didn't feel particularly afraid, although he knew pretty well what the German's next move would be.

The only hope he had now was to make a run for it and he began to speculate on his chances if he were to try. Then, suddenly, it occurred to him that there *was* an alternative. He had forgotten the Schmeisser which he had left where he had been sitting before the German had arrived. His eyes glanced down and began to search the ground to his left.

Anna and Neumann were talking in German again.

"Erik, I know what is in your mind," she said. "Don't do it. He is very young. He said what he did out of jealousy."

"Jealousy?"

"Yes, he knows about us."

"But why should he be jealous?"

"Because he is very young and believes that he is in love with me."

Neumann thought for a moment, but then shook his head. "I am sorry, Anna, it is impossible. I cannot let him go. He knows too much."

She stared at him coldly. "I know all that he knows. Would you kill me too?"

A Typhoon flew low overhead and was quickly followed by a second. Both aircraft had made a frontal attack on the dune defenses from the sea and were making climbing turns over Westkapelle. Neumann waited for them to pass before he answered her.

"Anna, do not say such a thing. Have I not told you that I love you?"

She looked at him appealingly. "Yes, and I believe you. But, Erik, because of that love, I beg you—let him go. You have my word that neither he nor I will speak of the plan to anyone."

The Typhoons were now turning back out to sea,

north of the village. Hallam had followed their flight with no special interest until an idea suddenly occurred to him. The air attack had come to an end, but he could still hear isolated aircraft in the vicinity. If another came over as low as the previous two and the German's attention was distracted even for a split second, as it had before, there might be just sufficient time to make a grab for the machine pistol.

Neumann stared hard at Hallam. He had no wish to kill the young idiot. If only it were possible to accept a promise of silence from him. Turning to Anna, he said: "Even if he gave his word not to talk, how could I be certain that he would keep it? After all, it is his duty as an officer to tell the British what he knows."

Anna closed her eyes and breathed deeply. At last there was hope.

"Because he's a romantic, and is involved in something he doesn't really understand. Don't you see, Erik, he'll do anything I ask of him."

She could tell from the look on Neumann's face that he wanted to be convinced; she felt sadness as well as relief. She hated to deceive him again. There was no doubt in her mind that she could extract a promise from Hallam, but she was equally sure that he would not keep his word once he had got away from Neumann. He would talk, no question of it, both because he was obliged to do so and because he would believe that he was settling a personal score with Neumann. Her only hope was that by the time Hallam had passed on the information Erik would be a prisoner of war, safe until it was all over and they could be reunited.

"And you?" Neumann asked. "You do not love him?"

"He is a boy. Surely you know now that I could never love anyone but you."

"I have never wanted to believe anything more in all my life," he replied.

His eyes switched to Hallam; he appeared to be wrestling with the problem.

"Very well, we will talk to him. If he will give me his word. . . ."

The Typhoon came over the dune like a rocket. Its nose tilted skyward and its single engine roared at full throttle. If anything, it was lower than the other two had been.

Hallam flung himself to the ground, rolled over once, and scooped up the Schmeisser. He got up, aimed at Neumann, and pulled the trigger. Nothing happened—sand had jammed the firing mechanism.

Neumann's reflex action was quick. "Put the bloody thing down," he screamed. As Hallam had raised the gun he had shouted: "It's all right. There's no need. . . ."

Then he saw the airman's trigger finger move again.

"No," he yelled. "You idiot. Stop. . . ."

Anna too had turned toward Hallam. "David, don't for God's sake. Don't. . . ."

But Hallam heard neither of them. His face was contorted, his lips curled back, and his eyes flashed with hatred.

"Bastard!' he shouted, then pulled the trigger again. This time the machine pistol worked, but in his rage Hallam had neither taken careful aim nor had he a firm grip on the gun. The shots went wild.

A PRIVATE TRUCE

Neumann fired the Luger twice. Both bullets struck Hallam in the chest. He fell to his knees; the Schmeisser dropped from his hand. The expression on his face as he looked up at Anna was one of astonishment. He held out his arms toward her, but before she could reach down to him, he pitched forward.

She fell to the ground beside him. His eyes, no longer focusing, were glassy and blood trickled from a corner of his mouth. For a brief moment Hallam seemed to recognize her and his lips began to move slowly. Anna placed her head close to his pallid face, but all she heard through the gasps was the sound of her own name. A few seconds later he died.

Neumann lifted her to her feet and held her in his arms. Although she was not weeping, he knew she was near the breaking point. If only the young fool had not opened fire on him. He had had to fire back in self-defense. He clung on to Anna, as much in need of her comfort as she was of his. When he had found them together he had been prepared to kill the airman without question; now he felt guilty. His hands trembled and his mind was confused.

After a while he held Anna at arm's length. He looked into her face. There were no tears. He wished there had been, for they might have helped to overcome the despair and exhaustion reflected with such intensity in her eyes.

"What can I say, *liebchen?* I did not want it to happen. I had to fire. . . ."

She shook her head very slowly. "I know, Erik. I know. He was to blame, not you."

He pulled her gently toward him again and kissed her. "Thank God," he whispered hoarsely.

She broke away and went to where Hallam's body lay. Her head bent in prayer, she was momentarily oblivious of Erik Neumann's presence.

Watching every move she made, his thoughts went back to their first meeting. What an unlikely pair of lovers they had become. She, hostile and a sworn enemy of everything that was German; he, unbending and self-centered. Yet from such a strange amalgam they had discovered a need for each other and eventually a deep and ecstatic love. Until he had met her, his life had been uncomplicated, set in the well-ordered mold of a professional soldier. There had been other women, of course, but none that he had ever taken seriously. He had loved life to the full but always within the confines of a discipline that placed duty first at all times, a duty the validity of which he had only recently had such cause to doubt. Even now, in spite of their love, the same duty was demanding that he should prevent Anna from talking to the Allies. He glanced down at the pistol still in his hand. Perhaps it was the only way out—for both of them. He tried unsuccessfully to stem the flood of memories: their lovemaking, their hopes and plans for the future. The anguish burned deeply, its pain more acute than any bullet wound.

When Anna returned to him her voice was stronger, her eyes more alert.

"And now? What now?"

Neumann's expression was a mixture of sadness and indecision. Their eyes met and at that moment he knew that she was aware of what troubled him. At the same time he came to a final and irrevocable decision. He and Anna were more important than anything else.

The question of duty and loyalty to his country was misplaced—it belonged to the past, to a life which even now was rapidly drawing to a close. If that was merely an excuse to salve his conscience, then so be it. To hell with the past; it was the future, their future, that really mattered. He replaced the Luger in its holster.

"We survive, Anna," he replied, looking deeply into her eyes. "We shall survive the whole mess, you and I. We have the rest of our lives to look forward to, and by God nothing is going to keep us apart."

She gave him a nervous smile and placed her hand on the side of his face.

"I will of course surrender to the British," said Neumann. "But you, Anna? What will you do?"

"Me? I don't understand, Erik."

"You have a clear obligation to inform the Allies of all you know."

She did not reply immediately. She gazed up at the dunes towering behind them, listened to the gunfire from the sea and Westkapelle. Duty. So much had already been sacrificed for such a small word, she thought. Could anyone be certain that the sacrifices were truly meaningful, that without them the final outcome would be so very different? Almost as soon as it came into her mind she dismissed the thought as a feeble attempt to justify the reply she knew that Erik Neumann wanted. Yet she wondered whether in the years ahead anyone would know or care why people like Hendrik, Jacobus Breuker, Piet Maranaus, and yes, David Hallam, had died.

She looked directly into Neumann's eyes. "I shall

not speak of the Ardennes to anyone. You have my word."

He smiled and put his arm around her shoulders. "Good. Then we must get back to Westkapelle. I have a boat tied up not far from here."

He led her down the lower slope of the dune. When they reached the edge of the floodwater where he had moored the small outboard motor boat, he said: "Have courage, *liebchen*. Have courage."

"I have you. I need nothing more," she replied.

The flat-bottomed infantry landing craft carrying Y Troop came through an inferno of smoke and flames. Passing the support squadron's burning and sinking ships, they approached the dike just north of the gap.

German guns from a nearby pillbox had them in their sights. As the leading craft reached the dike it was hit and a section officer killed. His place was immediately taken by a senior noncommissioned officer who, without a moment's hesitation, dashed forward and captured the pillbox single-handed.

Jackson and Crowley with their two sections landed seconds later. They leaped onto the beach and charged up the seawall. Although the first pillbox on the dike had been silenced, a sandbagged machine-gun position had opened up some forty yards further along. For several minutes the commandos were pinned down.

Instructing his men to remain where they were, Jackson yelled to Crowley a few yards away: "Give me covering fire, sir, and I'll get the bastards."

Crowley nodded and shouted orders to both his and Jackson's men. As the sergeant raised himself from the ground the two sections blasted the enemy position with rapid fire. Jackson ran, his body crouched, zigzagging toward the gun pit. He fired his Tommy gun from the hip as he went. Two-thirds of the way he dropped to the ground and unclipped two grenades. Releasing the pins, he threw the bombs with superb accuracy and then pressed home the attack, his submachine gun blazing.

A few moments later he stood in what was left of the gun position, the barrel of his gun pointing menacingly at the sole survivor. He waved to the sections to come forward and it was only when they joined him that he was told Crowley had been killed. Apparently, having instructed everyone else to keep down, he had ignored the danger himself in order to make the covering fire more effective. He had been shot through the head.

Once a foothold on the dike had been established, the major commanding the first wave of commandos quickly dispersed his men. There were three key positions to cover and a troop consisting of approximately forty men was sent to each. One was established on the edge of the dike west of the village; a second made its way forward to the north where it immediately engaged the gun battery W-15 with small-arms fire; the third positioned itself along the south side of Westkapelle.

While the north side of the gap was being assaulted another commando troop landed to the south. They roared ashore from tank landing craft in their amphibious Buffaloes and Weasels. Oerlikons mounted on the LCTs, Polsens and Brownings on the Buffaloes, fired at the pillboxes and weapon pits in the dunes that towered over the landing area.

This commando troop had two immediate objectives. The first was to capture the concrete strongpoints on the shoulder of the breach and the second was to clear a radar station nearby. It was then to advance on the gun battery W-13. Even before the second wave had arrived in support, men of the original landing party had secured the beach and were working their way south along the dunes destroying enemy positions and taking prisoners.

While both commando troops were advancing on their respective sides of the breach in the seawall, the shelling of its approaches and the landing areas was if anything intensified. The German gunners saw the landing craft touching down and realized their initial mistake. Through the smoke haze of burning support ships they watched as more and more LCTs and LCIs carrying the second and third waves of assault troops made their way to the beaches. Guns all along the seawall and the nearby dunes began to change direction and elevation.

Four LCTs carrying tanks and assault vehicles arrived in two waves north of the gap. They were soon under heavy fire from the guns of W-15, the battery slightly north of the village. Time and time again, the LCTs tried to touch down on the dike but were driven away. One was so badly hit that it withdrew altogether; the other three backed off and ran through the gap, beaching in the soft clay beneath the north shoulder. Many of the vehicles could not be driven off the craft, others became bogged down in the mud on disembarkation to be destroyed by more shelling or drowned by the fast incoming tide. In spite of the crews' heroic efforts to get the tanks into action only eight out of twenty-two on board the landing craft managed to reach the top of the dike.

In sacrificing itself to cover the landing, only six of the Support Squadron's original twenty-five small ships were still battle-worthy; of these, two were running low on ammunition, two more had engine trouble and, though operational, were limping from one action to another. Half of the squadron's casualties had been inflicted by the Rebhahn battery.

The latest casualty state of the Support Squadron had just been received on the bridge of *Kingsmill*. With eighty percent of its ships either sunk or out of action, Leicester and Pugsley knew that it could only be a matter of time before the enemy directed its fire onto the landing craft.

Earlier, when it had been seen that the Squadron had successfully drawn the fire of the German gunners, someone on the bridge had said that it had been nothing short of a miracle. Now, while both commanders were preoccupied with the possibility of an adverse turn in the tide of the battle, the second miracle of the morning occurred.

First there were three, then six, and finally the entire sky appeared to be filled with Typhoons of the Royal Air Force. These were the aircraft that *Kingsmill* had been told would not be taking part in the operation because of bad weather. Originally, they had been scheduled to be on Cab-rank duty over the headquarters frigate to take on prearranged targets.

Now, having taken advantage of a sudden break in the weather at their bases, they roared overhead with what appeared to be an uncanny and splendid sense of timing. They requested permission to go into the attack.

An immediate order went out from *Kingsmill* to all rocket craft to cease fire. Seconds later, when that signal had been acknowledged, another order was transmitted, this time to the pilots of the Typhoons: Attack. Attack without delay.

Over the dike and the dunes at two hundred feet, their rockets and cannon shells ripped into the defenses. As soon as they had flown over the assault area the pilots realized the critical situation below. They knew that while their rockets and cannon shells were no match for the concrete casemates and other emplacements of the main batteries, there was one critical task they could perform. They could take over from what was left of the navy and keep the enemy gunners occupied while the commandos were approaching the landing areas. Not until every rocket bomb and cannon shell had been expended at point-blank range and their fuel was running out, did the pilots of the Typhoons leave their targets.

The last aircraft to depart flew low over *Kingsmill*, dipped its wings in a salute, and then disappeared into the clouds.

Jackson's section had been separated from the remainder of the troop and instructed to reconnoiter the southern outskirts of the village along which the floodwater was now flowing. They trudged through the slimy ooze of the embankment, making the most of the sparse cover afforded them by the occasional deserted building.

About two hundred yards from the seawall Jackson signaled his men to freeze. Something midstream in the throat of the gap had caught his eye. It was a small outboard motorboat.

"Well, I'll be buggered," he said quietly to himself. Then he called in the section.

"We're about to take our first prisoner," he said when the men had gathered around him. "There's a Kraut and a girl in the boat over there. God knows what they think they're up to, but since this isn't the bloody Henley Regatta we'd better find out."

"They're going to come in up there," said Frazer, pointing to the side of the floodwater about two hundred yards from where they were standing. "We could get a bit nearer and knock the bastard off as he gets out of the boat."

"We'll take him in—and the girl," replied Jackson sharply. "Understood? No one knocks off anyone until I say so. Right?"

"Right, sergeant," replied Frazer.

They took cover some distance from where Jackson estimated the boat would land. The NCO then gave his orders. The section was to split up. He and four men would make their approach below the embankment along the water's edge while the other five were to go to the left in an outflanking movement and head off the couple should they attempt to escape. They were about to move off when they heard the first sounds of heavy fighting coming from the eastern end of the village.

"Hold it," commanded Jackson.

The men stopped in their tracks and waited.

"Shit! The boys are up at the tower already," the NCO added.

"Wasn't we supposed to be up there on the right flank, sergeant?" asked Frazer.

"Yes," Jackson snapped back, thinking hard at the same time. "Right, you lot. Make like the Seventh fucking Cavalry and follow me. The Kraut and the girl can wait. We'll pick them up later; they can't get very far. Move! On the bloody double."

They ran along the embankment, not even glancing back at the boat carrying Neumann and Anna to shore. In a matter of minutes they were turning into the main street of the village.

The outboard motor was throbbing noisily as the propeller of the small boat fought against the strong current of the fast flowing tide sweeping in from the sea. A strong wind sprayed them with a mixture of light rain and salt floodwater. For a moment Anna averted her eyes from the stark line of the ruined village ahead to gaze at Neumann sitting beside her. His face was grim and strained.

A sudden panicky thought flashed through her mind. She almost screamed at him to make herself heard.

"Erik, how—how are we going to find each other when it is finished—when the war is over? We have never talked of this."

"I will find you—I will come back to Walcheren."

She shook her head violently. "When? It could be months. Years. Anything might happen. Erik, you must write as soon as you have settled wherever they take you. The Red Cross—they help prisoners of war, don't they? They'll make sure I get your letters. And I will write to you the moment I know where you are."

"But, Anna, how—how shall I know where you are to address such a letter?"

She put a hand to her mouth and bit hard on her clenched fingers. "I don't know."

He swung the tiller to the right; they were approaching the embankment. "The main post office in Middelburg," he shouted to her. "Post Restante. That's the answer. Yes. I *will* write to you, Anna. And you must get to the post office at Middelburg as often as you can until my first letter arrives. You will do this?"

She nodded.

"Of course," Neumann added seriously, "there is a danger. It might not be good for you to be seen and heard asking for a letter from a German. . . ."

Anna pushed the damp strands of hair back from her forehead. "That's a risk I will happily take," she said simply.

When he had beached the boat, Neumann carried her to the slope of the embankment. From the nearness of the gunfire he realized that Westkapelle itself was now under attack. He wondered how Holz and the others had fared at the seawall. Holding Anna in his arms, he slipped and slithered in the mud as he climbed the rise from the water's edge. Reaching the top he fell heavily on one knee but managed to maintain his balance and keep a hold on Anna. His uniform was drenched and his boots covered in slime.

Once on dry ground he put Anna down and they staggered to the other side of the embankment and into the village. Just as they reached the line of ruins that had once been houses fronting onto the main street, there was a sudden thunderous roar of gunfire; Neumann knew it came from the vicinity of the tower. Long raucous bursts of heavy machine guns and the continuous crackling of automatic rifles and other small arms were accompanied by grenades and shell bursts.

They crawled across debris and crouched behind what had been a window sill. Further along to their right, in doorways, behind trees blasted by bombs and gunfire, among the ruins of the houses, Royal Marine commandos were giving covering fire to others whom Neumann assumed were making a frontal attack on the tower at the end of the road.

He backed away from the half wall and guided Anna to a less exposed position. They slumped onto a pile of timber, their backs protected by a huge mound of bricks and masonry, and waited for the battle to end.

The square red-brick lighthouse tower of Westkapelle which stood at the far end of Zuidstraat was more than one hundred and fifty feet high. Dominating the village and the countryside for miles around since 1818, it had stood as a silent sentinel flashing its warning lights to passing ships at sea. It had been built in Gothic style on the site of a fifteenth-century church and had withstood the ravages of fire, floods, and the destructive gales that yearly lashed the Walcheren coastline. On November 1, 1944, however, it was no longer the mute guardian of the seas but the Germans' main observation post from which they were now making their final stand against the assault on Westkapelle. From the parapet at the top the defenders' guns and grenades had pinned down the assault troops of the Royal Marine Commando in the road intersection below.

The commandos had entered what was left of the village under cover of machine-gunners and mortarmen who had set up their weapons on the ridge of the seawall. Slowly, they had worked their way up Zuidstraat, over the piles of rubble, through shell and bomb craters. It was only when they came within range of the tower that they came under heavy fire.

By the time that Sergeant Jackson and his section reached the main road a full-scale battle was in progress. The NCO and his men stood with their backs to the front wall of a shell-scarred house and stared ahead.

Jackson uttered an oath and then yelled to his men. "All right, you lucky lads, now's your chance to be bleeding 'eroes. Keep close to me and keep your bloody 'eads down."

They ran down the middle of the road, zig-zagging to dodge the hail of bullets which came at them from the top of the tower. Jackson saw two of his men go down. He turned and saw them lying motionless. He and the rest of the section hugged the ground while the man at the rear crawled back to investigate. Jackson waited. He saw the marine snake from one body to the other and then signal to him that both were dead.

The section went forward and within a few minutes had joined the commando troop which was pinned down at the road junction. Without slowing down the rate of fire from his Thompson submachine gun a young lieutenant with a bushy moustache glanced casually at Jackson and his men.

"Good morning," he shouted. "Glad you could come to the party. Help yourselves to whatever's going."

The sergeant and his section were already exchanging rapid fire with a platoon of German infantry positioned behind the stone wall.

"Thanks for nothing," Jackson replied sarcastically under his breath. He need not have worried that his voice would carry over the gunfire; the lieutenant was now with the forward troops shouting commands and words of encouragement to them.

A few minutes later, Jackson heard a cheer go up from the marines nearest to the wall. A Piat mortar team was racing across the bullet-swept ground in front of them. As they dodged the concentrated fire of the German defenders, the young lieutenant who had welcomed Jackson and his men directed his troop to give maximum cover. This resulted in a deafening eruption of small-arms fire at the end of which the mortar team, completely unscathed, arrived on the right flank only twenty yards from the tower. They opened up a devastating attack on the west side of the fortress which immediately reduced the fire power of the defenders.

It was shortly after the Piat mortar team had arrived on the scene that one of the few tanks which had managed to get to the top of the seawall opened fire. It scored several direct hits on the tower. Within a matter of minutes, all shooting stopped, a white flag hung from one of the embrasures, and with bricks and masonry falling around them two German defenders

A PRIVATE TRUCE

came out to surrender. The battle for the village of Westkapelle was virtually at an end.

Sergeant Jackson and his section sat on their haunches at the side of the road smoking their cigarettes. They had been ordered to stand by to take part in an attack on one of the guns north of the village. They were to move out in fifteen minutes' time.

None of them, not even Frazer, wanted to talk. They just sat, smoked, and stared ahead to where the prisoners were being lined up in the middle of the road junction. Jackson took a long look at the Germans. Most of them showed signs of battle fatigue. They stood in long lines, their hands on their heads, shaken and demoralized.

Eventually it was Frazer who broke the silence. "What about that Kraut and his fraulein, sarge?"

Jackson shrugged. "Not much we can do about them now. I suppose I'd better report it to the lieutenant, though."

Frazer winked at the others. "We should have finished the sod off when we had the chance, sarge."

Jackson's face creased in disgust. "You're a nasty bastard, Frazer."

He got up, brushed the dust off the seat of his denims, adjusted his webbing, and slung his Tommy-gun over his shoulder.

"Right, you lot, push off and join the troop; I won't be long. I'm going down the road to check on Minton and Boyce. After that, I'll see the lieutenant about the Kraut."

He watched them slope off toward the southern boundary of the village and then turned away and walked briskly down Zuidstraat where the bodies of the two dead commandos lay.

Now that the battle for the tower at the top of Zuidstraat was over, the road where the bodies lay was silent and deserted. The pounding of the heavy guns in the distance was the only indication that the assault on the island was still in progress.

Jackson looked down at the dead marines. Despite his constant proximity to violent death he had never been able to accept it as easily as some of his comrades. The boy called Boyce was lying on his back; the top half of his face and most of his head had been shot away. Minton, a few yards off, had fallen forward and from the gaping hole in his back it was obvious that he too had been killed instantly.

Crouched on one knee and with his hand shaking slightly, Jackson opened up Boyce's collar and checked that the boy had been wearing his dog tags. He pulled a knife from his webbing and cut one of the disks off and put it in his pocket leaving the other around the marine's neck for the burial detail to find. He then searched the dead marine's pockets to make certain that he had not been carrying any personal possessions; he wasn't supposed to, but you never could be sure with the younger ones. Satisfied that the pockets were empty, he picked up the bloodstained green beret lying nearby and placed it over the marine's disfigured face.

He went over to the other body and went through the same ritual. Having completed his melancholy duty, the sergeant let out a deep breath and stood up. He was about to make his way back to the tower

A PRIVATE TRUCE

when his eyes registered a sudden movement about two hundred yards down the road.

Two figures had emerged from the ruins on the south side of the street. Even at that distance, Jackson recognized them immediately. It was the German officer and the girl. When he saw them hesitate, he realized that they had seen him. He unslung the submachine gun at his shoulder, flicked off the safety catch, and walked toward them.

They saw Jackson as soon as they had reached the roadside. Neumann immediately withdrew his Luger from its holster.

Anna was horrified. "No, Erik! You said you would give yourself up."

Without taking his eyes from the man in the camouflaged battledress who was now walking toward them, Neumann gave a short laugh and handed the gun to Anna.

"Take it quickly," he said sharply. "He's already seen us; we have very little time."

She stepped back, shaking her head and pushing the pistol away.

"But why? We agreed that——"

"Do as I say, Anna," he interjected fiercely. "Hurry before the fellow can see what we're doing."

Reluctantly, she took the gun and stared at Neumann, still bewildered by his request.

He sighed heavily and looked relieved. "Good. Don't you see, Anna, it is important that I appear to be your prisoner. You can say that you captured me up at the Rebhahn battery this morning. No one will accuse you of treachery as they might if we were brought in together in any other circumstances."

Anna's mind was in turmoil. While she had always accepted that there would have to be a parting, now that the time had come she was afraid. She tried to lean her head against his shoulder. In this way she might hide the panic which she knew he would see in her eyes, but he resisted and pushed her gently away.

"Erik, I cannot let you go like this. Hold me once again, please."

The man with the submachine gun was getting near. Neumann looked apprehensive.

"Anna, for God's sake, be strong. Do you think that it is any easier for me? Come now, where's that courage I know and admire so much? Hold the pistol to my back, quickly. Good. Now, keep it there. I will put up my hands—so. And now, *liebchen*, we have a rendezvous with that destiny of ours. No tears. You must promise."

She wiped her eyes with her free hand, threw back her head, and held herself erect.

"There are no tears," she replied.

Anna made her way through the devastation that was Westkapelle. A wind was blowing in from the sea and rain clouds darkened the sky. Until now she had never known what it was like to be utterly alone.

In the village not a single house was intact; the streets seemed to echo with the ghostly cries of those who had gone forever. There was a hollowness, a deep aching in her heart, when she thought of them. Had it really only been this morning that they had fought together for the last time?

A PRIVATE TRUCE

Memories continued to tug at her no matter how hard she tried to force them from her mind. Just a short time ago she and Erik had made love in his quarters, which had stood very near to where she now walked. The building was no longer there; it had been blasted away with the rest of the village in the name of liberation. And Erik? Her beloved enemy? He had gone, too, and until he came back her life would stand still. What would she do? It would be months, perhaps a year or more, before he was released. She looked around at the desolation surrounding her. There was nothing more for her on Walcheren, but then there could be nothing anywhere without him.

With a heavy heart she contemplated these thoughts for a long time, but found no answer. Now she was near the seawall and could see several isolated groups of commandos setting up their camps. It vaguely occurred to her that she should find a place to spend the night.

It was when she had reached the road that ran below the dike that she heard footsteps. They were immediately behind her, light and faltering. She was about to turn when she heard her name being called.

"Anna. Anna, is it you? Anna, my dear?"

Standing in front of her, barefooted, her clothes sodden, her face pale and drawn, was Sybella van Rijn.

"Hendrik? My Hendrik? Where is my Hendrik, Anna?" Her voice was strangely remote. It was clear that she was in a state of shock. When Anna looked into her face she saw for the first time the contusions, the scars, and the drooping mouth. It was then that she knew she had found the answer she had been seeking. She had been wrong. There *was* more to be done on Walcheren, not only for herself but everyone.

She ran to the older woman and put her arms around her, crying with happiness.

"Come, Sybella. Let's go home to Vierwinden. I think we are going to have need of each other, you and I."

HISTORICAL NOTE

On June 5, 1944, Allied forces landed in Normandy. The British Second Army, led by the famous 11th Armored Division, eventually broke out from the Seine and at the highwater mark of their thunderous advance across France and Belgium they captured the great port of Antwerp on September 4th.

Between those two dates, American and British forces outran their supply systems and by August the situation was critical. Unable to build up any reserves, the armies were consuming everything as it was received. Although air lifts were in operation, the bulk of fuel, equipment, and rations was still being transported by road from Normandy, hundreds of miles each day.

Antwerp, fifty miles from the sea, accessible to shipping by way of the River Scheldt and its wide estuary, had a potential intake of forty thousand tons a day and it was only a hundred miles from the Rhine. When its docks were captured intact by the 11th Armored Division on September 4th, the supply problem should have been swept away.

There was only one stumbling block. The Germans still held the mouth of the Scheldt. From Zeebrugge to Breskens on the southern shore of the estuary, and opposite on the island of Walcheren, their heavy coastal guns ensured that Antwerp remained closed to Allied ships.

Generals Montgomery and Eisenhower acknowledged the importance of Antwerp, but appear to have ignored the urgency of clearing the Scheldt to make possible the use of its docks. The significance of the port had first been mentioned in August by Montgomery and thereafter emphasized constantly by Eisenhower. Even when approving the Arnhem plan, the Supreme Commander was aware that it would delay the clearance of the Scheldt, but he continued to underline the importance of its being opened up.

Incredible as it may seem, only the enemy appeared to recognize how urgent it was for the Allies to take immediate action. Even a warning given to SHAEF and the Admiralty by Admiral Sir Bertram Ramsay, Commander-in-Chief of the Allied Naval Forces, on the day of Antwerp's capture went unheeded.

Not only would the clearing of the Scheldt early in September have provided the answer to the supply problem but it would have prevented the retreat of the German Fifteenth Army cut off in the South. As it happened, divisions of this enemy formation were ferried across the estuary from Breskens and made good their escape to the mainland of Holland via Walcheren and the South Beveland Peninsula. Ironically, on their arrival they were almost immediately engaged in opposing Montgomery's attempted thrust to the Rhine at Arnhem.

It was not until late October that, after a bitter struggle, the south bank of the estuary, and to the

A PRIVATE TRUCE

north the long narrow isthmus of South Beveland, were finally cleared. Then the fortress island of Walcheren with its powerful coastal guns were all that lay between the Allies and their free use of the port of Antwerp.

The battle for Walcheren ended on November 7, when Royal Marine Commandos, supported by fighter-bombers of No. 84 Group of the Royal Air Force, flushed out the remnants of a German strong point holding out in the north of the island.

Domburg fell to the commandos in the evening of the day of the Westkapelle landing. Zouteland surrendered on November 2. Some of the fiercest fighting took place at Flushing, which was finally captured on November 4 by No. 4 Army Commando and the 155th Brigade. Two days later, Veere capitulated to the 156th Brigade.

On October 31, the day before the commandos' assault on the west coast, the Royal Regiment of Canada had liquidated the German pocket at the eastern end of the causeway, and the Canadian Black Watch had then gone forward. They had faced heavy opposition and particularly deadly mortar fire, but early in the afternoon the Black Watch were only seventy-five yards from the Walcheren end. That night, the Calgary Highlanders had passed through and after bitter fighting had established a shallow bridge-head. In the face of continued opposition they could not enlarge it and the same evening a sudden and violent counterattack by the German defenders threw them back along the causeway.[*]

[*] Colonel C. P. Stacey, *The Canadian Army 1939–1945*

On November 2, Le Regiment de Maisonneuves took over and re-established the bridge head, but enemy resistance continued to be bitter, heavy shelling supplementing machine-gun and mortar fire. The Maisonneuves handed over their foothold the same day to the 52nd (Lowland) Division and after being continuously engaged since leaving Dieppe, the 2nd Canadian Division was withdrawn to rest. In thirty-four days since it crossed the Antwerp-Turnhout Canal, the Division had captured 5,200 Germans and killed many more. Its own casualties, 207 officers and 3,443 other ranks, testified sufficiently to the fierceness of the fighting it had seen.

Within hours of the capture of Walcheren, the minesweepers went in clearing the Scheldt for the great convoys of merchantmen to follow and to fill the miles of Antwerp's deserted docks.

On November 28, an historic ceremony took place when the first Allied convoy came up the Scheldt and entered the port. Although no one had thought of inviting an official representative of the Canadian Army, appropriately enough, the convoy's leading ship was the Canadian-built "Fort Cataraqui."

From the day of its opening to VE day, six months later, the port of Antwerp handled 5,250,000 tons of stores, 1,280,000 tons of gasoline, and tens of thousands of military vehicles. It was this great mass of armor and supplies which built up the irresistible striking power of the Allied armies for the Battle of the Rhine.*

The German counteroffensive on the Ardennes

---

*The Royal Marine Museum.

front came early in the morning of Sunday, December 16. It took the American forces by surprise and it was some time before they or the British understood its real significance.

For the first few days the American position was highly critical but by December 24, the German advance had come to a feeble end. Two days later, they suffered another serious defeat when General Patton's Third Army fought its way through to Bastogne and relieved the garrison that had been holding out against the enemy vastly superior in numbers.

Allied air activities contributed greatly to the failure of the German counteroffensive, although the cost to both the RAF and the USAAF was high. Throughout the battle, more than 63,000 sorties were flown by both air forces, 71,000 tons of bombs were dropped and 650 aircraft were lost.

As predicted by Field Marshal Gerd von Rundstedt on that day in Aremburg when he had first heard of Hitler's plan, nothing was achieved and the cost was extremely high. German casualties were estimated at 81,000, of whom 12,000 were killed. A further 50,000 men were made prisoners.[†]

Most of the events which take place in this book are imaginary, but the accounts of the breaching of the seawalls of Walcheren by the Royal Air Force and the landing of the Royal Marine Commandos are based on fact. So, too, is the tragedy which occurred at Abraham Theune's mill. The sole survivor, Kornelia Janisse Theune, then aged one year, still lives in Westkapelle.

[†]Ellis and Warhurst (HMSO), *Victory in the West*

As far as I am aware, there are no such places as Oranjezicht and Welghuevel on Walcheren, nor is there a Groebelaan or Linschotenstraat in Westkapelle.

The raid on gun battery W-13 prior to the landings did not really take place. But at about the time when the first craft touched down there occurred what a report of the Army Operational Research Group described later as "probably the most important single event of the operation." W-13 which, between 0945 and 1017 hours had disabled nine of the twenty-five support craft of Naval Force T, ran out of ammunition. My interpretation of this incident and the description of the battery has been tempered with artistic license. I hope that it will not prove too unacceptable to any student of military history who may happen to read it.

—A. L.

Acknowledgments

I would like to record my gratitude to Group Captain E. S. Haslam and Mr. E. H. Turner of the Air Historical Branch, Ministry of Defense, as well as members of their staff who helped me to locate the appropriate RAF Command Papers relating to Operations Infatuate I and II. At the Royal Air Force Museum, Mr. D. E. Brech, Head of Archives, and his assistants gave me invaluable advice and I would thank them for permitting me to spend so much time with S-sugar, their very special Lancaster. I am particularly grateful to ex-Flight Lieutenant Charles Weir, a veteran officer of Bomber Command and one-time member of No. 218 Squadron, who guided me through the technicalities of a war-time operation.

My warmest thanks are due to Major A. J. Donald, the former Corps Archivist of the Royal Marines, for providing me with background material including the War Diaries of Nos. 47 and 48 Commandos. In addition, I found his own vast fund of knowledge concerning the Corps of great assistance. I am also mindful of the amount of time Mr. H. Playford, Research Assistant, Royal Marines, devoted to my many questions relating to landing craft. To him and to Miss B. Spiers I am indeed grateful. I must also thank Major Frank Blackah, RM, of the Department of the Commandant General for his encouragement and cooperation in the early days, and Captain D. A. Oakley, RM, editor of *The Globe and Laurel*, official journal of the Royal Marines, for his permission to make use of published articles and for a remarkably lucid three-minute lesson on the use of guncotton.

Major W. R. Sendall, RM (Retired), who took part in the landing at Westkapelle, has permitted me to make full use of articles he wrote after the operation. For this and for his guidance in other matters pertaining to the assault on Walcheren, I thank him.

Staff at the Imperial War Museum's Department of Printed Books could not have been more helpful and I am greatly indebted to Mr. D. B. Nash and Mr. G. Clout for their assistance and advice. The ease and efficiency with which the department always produced rare books appropriate to a particular aspect of research at just the right time was outstanding.

Mr. F. F. Lambert of the Public Records Office must also be thanked for his unstinting and generous cooperation.

I thank the Minister of Supply and Services, Canada, for permission to reproduce information concerning the Canadian Army taken from C. P. Stacey's *The Canadian Army 1939–1945*. I am also obliged to Her Majesty's Stationery Office for permission to use material contained in Ellis and Warhurst's *Victory in the West*.

My old chief and good friend David Symington, CSI, CIE, exercised a scholarly vigilance over this book and made a number of helpful suggestions. For these and for his enthusiasm and encouragement, I could not be more grateful.

During a visit to Walcheren I talked to so many people that it would be impossible to mention them all by name. The courtesy and cooperation I received was quite overwhelming. My special thanks, however, must go to Mnr. J. P. de Regt, Director of VVV, Zeeland, for his invaluable guidance and charming hospitality; Junkvrouw I. F. den Beer Poortugael for the delightful interlude I spent with her and her late husband when we talked about the old days in Veere; Mnr. M. P. de Bruin, Head of Documentation Center, Zeeland Provincial Archives; Mnr. L. M. Moermond (the burgomaster) and Mnr. W. Dielman of Westkapelle; Mnr. Willem Vreeke and Mevrouw A.M.S. Schenkel-Vreeke of Domburg; Mervrouw Clasien Mol of Serooskerke, Mnr. R. L. Helmut and Mnr. H. A. van Cranenburgh of Veere; and Mnr. H. A. J. Lobbe of the Olau Line, Flushing.

To Anthony J. Wensvoort of Middelburg, I owe a debt of gratitude not only for his vivid reminiscences of the German occupation of Walcheren and the Dutch Resistance Movement, but for his friendship, which I value greatly. Anthony Wensvoort is seventy years young. During the war he was a code officer in the Dutch Underground Army. He belonged to the famous Section 15 based in Middelburg and his code name was "Cornelius."

I am grateful to Captain J. Petshi, Royal Netherlands Navy (Retired), Mr. H. P. J. Heukensfeldt Johnsen, and Miss A. Stenfert-Krosse, former Cultural Attache, the Royal Netherlands Embassy, London.

Finally, I am indebted to my wife, who helped me to correct the numerous drafts of the book and to my entire family for their blind faith. A special thank you goes to my youngest son, Nicholas, my toughest critic, who more than once saved the day by giving me his honest opinion.

A. L.

Abbreviations and Definitions

LCG	*Landing Craft Gun*
LCI	*Landing Craft Infantry*
LCT	*Landing Craft Tank*
MOF	*Dutch slang for a German (Moffen, pl.)*
OBW	*Oberbefehlshaber West (Supreme Headquarters West)*
OKH	*Oberkommando des Heeren (Army High Command)*
OKW	*Oberkommando der Wehrmacht (Armed Forces High Command, Hitler's headquarters)*
SHAEF	*Supreme Headquarters, Allied Expeditionary Force, the force that fought in western Europe from the invasion of June 6, 1944, to the German surrender*
WEHRMACHT	*The German armed forces, literally "defense force"*

Dell Bestsellers

- [ ] **FEED YOUR KIDS RIGHT**
  by Lendon Smith, M.D. $3.50 (12706-8)
- [ ] **THE RING** by Danielle Steel $3.50 (17386-8)
- [ ] **INGRID BERGMAN: MY STORY**
  by Ingrid Bergman and Alan Burgess $3.95 (14085-4)
- [ ] **THE UNFORGIVEN**
  by Patricia J. MacDonald $3.50 (19123-8)
- [ ] **WHEN THE WIND BLOWS** by John Saul $3.50 (19857-7)
- [ ] **RANDOM WINDS** by Belva Plain $3.50 (17158-X)
- [ ] **SOLO** by Jack Higgins $2.95 (18165-8)
- [ ] **THE CRADLE WILL FALL**
  by Mary Higgins Clark $3.50 (11476-4)
- [ ] **LITTLE GLORIA ... HAPPY AT LAST**
  by Barbara Goldsmith $3.50 (15109-0)
- [ ] **THE HORN OF AFRICA** by Philip Caputo ... $3.95 (13675-X)
- [ ] **THE OWLSFANE HORROR** by Duffy Stein .. $3.50 (16781-7)
- [ ] **THE SOLID GOLD CIRCLE**
  by Sheila Schwartz $3.50 (18156-9)
- [ ] **THE CORNISH HEIRESS**
  by Roberta Gellis $3.50 (11515-9)
- [ ] **AMERICAN BEAUTY** by Mary Ellin Barret ... $3.50 (10172-7)
- [ ] **ORIANA** by Valerie Vayle $2.95 (16779-5)
- [ ] **EARLY AUTUMN** by Robert B. Parker $2.50 (12214-7)
- [ ] **LOVING** by Danielle Steel $3.50 (14657-7)
- [ ] **THE PROMISE** by Danielle Steel $3.50 (17079-6)

At your local bookstore or use this handy coupon for ordering:

Dell DELL BOOKS
P.O. BOX 1000, PINEBROOK, N.J. 07058

Please send me the books I have checked above. I am enclosing $ _____
(please add 75¢ per copy to cover postage and handling). Send check or money order—no cash or C.O.D.'s. Please allow up to 8 weeks for shipment.

Mr/Mrs/Miss _____

Address _____

City _____ State/Zip _____